LADY OF THE UNDERWORLD

OPERATION HADES BOOK TWO

SKYLER ANDRA

Lady of the Underworld (Operation Hades #1) © Copyright 2020 Skyler Andra
Cover art by Eerilyfair Design.

All rights reserved under the International and Pan-American Copyright Conventions. No part of this book may be reproduced or transmitted in any form or by any means, electronic or mechanical, including photocopying, recording, or by any information storage and retrieval system, without permission in writing from the publisher/author.

This is a work of fiction. Names, places, characters and incidents are either the product of the author's imagination or are used fictitiously, and any resemblance to any actual persons, living or dead, organizations, events or locales is entirely coincidental.

Warning: the unauthorized reproduction or distribution of this copyrighted work is illegal. Criminal copyright infringement, including infringement without monetary gain, is investigated by the FBI and is punishable by up to 5 years in prison and a fine of $250,000.

❀ Created with Vellum

INTRODUCTION

Welcome to my "Operation" series, featuring a world of godly avatars. **What's an avatar?** They're a human embodied with the essence and power of a god. An agent that works the will of the god on Earth.

Previously, I published Operation Cupid, featuring avatars of Eros, Hermes, Ares, and Athena. Hades features in books 2 and 3. You don't need to read the Operation Cupid series to understand this story, but it will help to familiarize yourself with the characters, especially since Cupid and her men return in *Lord of the Underworld*, Operation Hades 2. For your reference, *Lady of the Underworld* is set prior to the events in Operation Cupid Book 3. *Lord of the Underworld* and *Rulers of the Underworld* will be set after it.

'OPERATION' SERIES UNIVERSE

Operation Hades
    Lady of the Underworld
    Lord of the Underworld
    Rules of the Underworld - coming 2021

INTRODUCTION

Operation Cupid (completed)
    Battlefield Love
    Quicksilver Love
    Awakened Love
    Stupid Cupid (a short story not available in paperback)

CHAPTER 1

Autumn

Death. Afterlife. A dreary day for a funeral. I considered each dull prospect as Pearl, my boss, and I juggled the giant flower arrangement. Amid the fall drizzle, we carried it to the waiting van in the parking lot behind her shop.

"I'm too old for this," Pearl panted.

"You're never too old." I shifted my hands on the bottom of the display to try and take more of the weight.

Although potting mix bags were pretty heavy, nowhere in my education taught me that florists needed to be gold medal Olympians in weightlifting. But, I couldn't complain. I'd built up some decent muscles from all the lifting.

Florists brightened days with single roses enhanced with a sprig of baby's breath and a sprout of fern wrapped in green floral paper or stuffed into a vase. Our expertise lay in the delivery of floral arrangements that conveyed apologies, brightened foyers, scented homes, and sending off the dead with beauty rather than competitively creating and displaying awkwardly large arrangements. Classic lines on cards like, *I'm sorry for screwing your best friend.* Or *Honey, you're always right. Let's never argue again.* But every once in a while we'd get a strange order like this, and when a customer paid five hundred bucks for an arrangement, by all that was good and right in the land, we arranged. It paid my wage and kept me in a job.

Pearl grunted as she yanked open the van door, and we set the monster of an arrangement on the edge of the step. First deliveries were set closest to the door for easier access. I went around the back, opening the doors, shifting three arrangements to the rear, to accommodate the beast.

Nothing said *goodbye* like a giant foam baseball stuffed with red, white, and blue roses to match the deceased's favorite team. Not my first "special" request as a florist. But grieving people spared no expense to bid farewell to their departed loved ones. I only hoped the client liked it. It had taken me a good three hours to decorate the foam with just the right touch of white roses.

Pearl crawled in beside me to load the display into the back of the waiting van. For a woman in her early sixties, she was pretty fit, and carried around heavy boxes of cards, twine and ribbon, like a woman half her age.

She shook her head and frowned. "I swear, the arrangements get bigger and more ridiculous every year." I laughed, because in my six years of working for Pearl, I'd never made anything quite like it.

A flower pun sprang to mind and I threw it out for her. It was our little game we did every morning. "Hey, Pearl. What did the flower say after he told a joke?"

Pearl groaned and pressed her hand to cover her eyes. "Not again."

She said that, but secretly she loved it. So did all the

customers. It was what made Pearl's shop the most popular in town. That, and the fact that our flowers lasted the longest, sometimes up to months later. People came from three cities away just to buy Pearl's infamous flowers.

"Just pollen your leg." I nudged her. "Get it?"

She chuckled. "Oh, Autumn, I'm going to…"

"Going to what?" I inched deeper into the van to set everything into place and ensure it didn't move during transport.

Careful not to squash the flowers on the sides, I shifted the arrangement, nestling it next to the van's wall. Previous experience told me the roses would bruise if I did much more than touch them. Sure, the foam wasn't exactly heavy, but the ten pounds of flowers and sheer size of the display—twice as wide as me—made it tricky to negotiate.

The side of my hand brushed the edge of a rose, and it opened further. I blinked. Odd. Never seen a flower do that before. Curious, I touched another, and it unfurled, the tip of the petal tickling me. What the? I gasped and shuffled backward, hitting another arrangement, knocking it over. Shit. My hands shook and fumbled to set it straight again.

"God, I need a holiday." Pearl brushed the sprinkle of rain from her forehead. "I'm sick of this rain."

I glanced back at the two flowers. No. It was nothing. They just opened from the water and powder I sprinkled in them to keep them alive for longer.

"You keep talking about Florida." I grabbed two foam wedges from a box situated behind the seats. "Why don't you take some time off? You work too hard. I can cover the shop." Thanks to her diligent training, I was way past needing supervision.

I braced the flower arrangement with the foam rectangles to prevent it going for a roll in transit. Not that it could go far with all the other vases of blue, red, and white flowers to be placed around the coffin and viewing room.

Pearl scratched her forehead. "About that…"

An oily sensation swirled in my stomach.

She leaned against the van's frame, not meeting my eyes. "I'm closing the shop and moving to Florida."

Junipers!

I pressed a hand to my stomach. I had an apartment to pay for. Car payments to make. Plants to house. And I'd been working at minimum wage for too long to have much "rainy day" savings tucked away. For months, I'd been planning to go to night school to finally get my botany degree which would give myself more prospects than working in the flower industry for ever and earning a pittance.

Cautiously, I crawled to the van's step and Pearl moved to stand beside me and rubbed my back while I scrubbed my hands over my cheeks.

"Don't worry. I'll look after you." Her hand slipped into mine and squeezed. She'd looked after me ever since my mom died. So not only was I losing a job, I was losing a second mother and the grief hit me all over again. "I can give you a month's wages. Get you on your feet until you find another job."

After my mom's cancer, she didn't have much left, and I'd worked hard to keep us alive, missing school to work and pay the bills. I'd continued after she was gone. I released a shaky breath. This couldn't be happening. Not now. Not near the anniversary of my mom's passing. My back felt red and raw, like someone had ripped the Band-Aid off. Although instead of the pain fading, it intensified. Burned over every inch of my skin.

But I had to get going. I snapped to my feet. Autumn Rankin was no quitter. She was a look-on-the-bright-side kind of girl. I just had to find the silver lining to this news.

"I...I have to get going." Body numb, I jerked the side door of the van shut, and walked to the driver side. I closed my eyes and leaned my head against the door's cool metal before I got in.

One twist of the key in the ignition got the van started and I was glad I'd scored the *good* truck over the one that required a pair of pliers to turn the key. Well, it was something, anyway.

With a sigh, I wiped the drizzle from my forehead. A quick glance in the rearview mirror revealed frizzy green wisps surrounding my face, thanks to the rain. I smoothed them down in an attempt to look decent for Mr. Cotterly, the client. He was a fussy old fart who demanded his staff and contractors to look respectful for the dead.

With no time to think about the bomb Pearl had dropped on me, I switched on the radio. Lo and behold, a song with the chorus, "Everyone loves a funeral," jammed through the speakers.

Creepy. I turned it off. To get my mind off it, I hummed another song, Don't Stop Be-leafing... because I just loved flower puns.

When most people thought of flowers, they usually brought up images of wedding bouquets, prom corsages, the just-because bouquets, and the good old sorry-I-messed-up flowers. That last group always made my day. A certain joy came with listening to the dirt bag boyfriend or husband grovel out their card apologies to me when they ordered.

Yeah. My job provided a fascinating insight into relationships. And I wasn't just talking about romantic relationships, either. I observed all sorts of connections: friendships, work colleagues, acquaintances, family, and even group associations.

But our main stock in trade at Pearl's, as I mentioned, was funerals. Not everyone married, or went to prom, and not everyone had occasion to say sorry for sleeping with their significant other's sibling, but everyone died. That was one of Pearl's favorite bits of wisdom. And if anyone would know, it was Pearl. She'd been in flowers longer than I'd been alive.

Six years ago, at seventeen, I'd shown up at her shop with the hope of an after-school job. She said that I would do just fine as long as I was willing to spend the afternoon slightly soggy after unpacking the flowers for the front.

A tap on the window brought me back to the present, and I wound it down.

"Job well done, Autumn." Her grey eyes crinkled at the corners. "If he still had eyes to see with, the dead man would be weeping with joy at how nice that looks."

But I wasn't thinking about the dearly departed, his funeral, or relatives. I had to find a new job. A new adventure.

"Back soon," I replied with a smile.

"We can talk more then." Pearl patted me on the shoulder, then tucked her hands in the pocket of her apron and watched me pull onto the street, waving at me in the rearview.

The van chugged in the cold and overcast morning. Other people might have been staring at the grey drizzle, thinking it ruined their day, but I saw a bulb planting day that would allow me to leave the pots of the porch for a good watering. I only had the one delivery today and then I was finished. An afternoon off to run to the store to grab some ingredients for a big pot of soup and some serious me-time after working nine days straight.

And by me-time, I meant snuggling under a blanket on the couch, binge-watching the British TV shows *Monty Don's French Gardens* and *Love Your Garden*. My favorite was *The Big Flower Fight*, a reality show that I got a kick out, with designers thrown into designing and creating flower sculptures, while tearing their hair out, stressing over materials and expenses. God, if I could be a contestant on that show…

A fifteen-minute drive to the suburbs took me through the part of town with the massive estates, then past the mall and a couple of schools, which meant traffic. Crawling east along the main road, I approached *Freaky Florals*, one of our competitors. The owner used to work for Pearl way back. Sometimes she dropped in to borrow wrapping paper or salal—the greenery the balanced out a bunch—when she run out, but she always repaid the favor. Something twitched in my stomach, and I pulled into the curb out the front of her store, and hopped out of the van.

When I entered, Jo glanced up from the Snapdragon stems she was stripping. "Hey, hun. Pearl run out of sponge foam again?"

She knew Pearl too well. Floral sponge foams were a material we used as a base to secure the flowers in a vase. We let them sit in water to absorb it and feed the flowers for several days. But that wasn't why I dropped in.

I smoothed down the front of my uniform, a black cotton dress, fifties style with a full A-line skirt, a deep V in front and carnations decorating the fabric. "Uh…actually…"

Jo set the flowers on the bench and came around the front. "What is it, Autumn?"

I jammed my hands in the side pockets of my skirt. "Pearl's closing the shop, and I need a job."

"Oh, hun." Jo gave me a long hug and then pulled back. "I wish I could help. But things are tight at the moment. No one's buying flowers these days."

I smiled. True. Much as I hated to admit it, death really *was* the biggest business in town. "Okay."

She stepped back. "I just had to put off one of my girls last week."

Oh God. Business must be bad then.

"Thanks anyway, Jo." I backpedaled to the door. "See you round."

Well, damn. I walked back to the van. Not much call for a high school drop-out, even if she could navigate traffic. "Cheer up, buttercup." I twisted the ignition and waited for a truck to pass before I pulled back onto the road.

I glanced at the clock. "Junipers!"

The visit with Jo had cost me five valuable minutes and yielded no results.

I was going to be late for my drop off to Cotterly's Funeral Home. Worse than being unprofessional, Mr. Cotterly hated when I was late. There would be stern looks as I unloaded the van. Angry grumbling. Probably a report back to Pearl. Well, not this time, pal. Not on my shift. Jamming my foot down, I sped up, and the van groaned and shuddered.

Finally, I arrived at Cotterly's Funeral Home, a modest cream building with pleasant gardens. Deceptively designed to hide the fussy and particular, Mr. Cotterly who looked as if he'd stepped out of Central Casting for a Victorian undertaker. Definitely not my favorite client to work with, but as one of Pearl's best customers he was guaranteed top-quality service. But since she decided she'd grown *too old to deal with schmucks,* she made me go deal with him.

By the time I pulled up to the funeral home's loading dock, he was already waiting for me, tapping his wristwatch, wearing his usual scowl.

Impeccable in his black suit and twenty-four-carat glare, he said, "It's about time," when I hopped down from the van's raised seat.

Good morning. Dreary day, huh? Let me give you a hand with that. Things he'd never say. Come to think of it, he never engaged in small talk or even smiled that I could remember.

This was a man who'd either chosen a job to match his personality or adapted after he'd taken the position.

"Hey Mr. Cotterly." I disarmed him with a grin before throwing in one of my classic flower jokes as I walked around to open the side door. "How do two flowers greet each other?"

He fisted his lapels and shook his head.

I answered anyway. *"Hey bud, how's it growing?"* I laughed, reaching for the handle. Because nothing said *F you* to a grumpy, old man better than subtly teaching him a lesson on basic human interactions.

"We needed the delivery at nine," he said pointedly.

I'd checked the clock in the van before exiting. 9:02a.m. Two minutes and about twenty broken rules of the road later. Ran a red light, ignored speed and stop signs.

"Then I'm just on time." The key with Mr. Cotterly was to smile and keep moving. So long as I was actually doing a decent job he would walk on and attend to his own business. Besides, no one was paying me to fight with a senior citizen funeral director. Not that I wouldn't if someone wanted to put up the money. I was always pinching pennies while making about a buck better than minimum wage at Pearl's. For a couple dollars more an hour, I'd happily stand there and argue with him.

"In my day, being punctual meant arriving fifteen minutes early." Mr. Cotterly's jowls tightened.

"Mm-hmm." I smiled, collecting the arrangement. If only I'd left the thorns on the roses. Right now, I stood there considering whether or not I would actually poke out one of his eyes with a wayward stem, but no way could I justify giving him the pleasure of my wrath. That I reserved for my mailman, who delivered me crushed seeds and broken packets of water crystals. And with that, I lowered to my most serious tone, squinched my brow and wiped the smile from my face. My best Cotterly impression. "Viewing Room B?"

Mr. Cotterly blinked. Maybe he was impressed with my rendition of him "Yes. And remember you only have–"

"I know where I'm going. This isn't my first–" I realized that rodeo and goat-roping were comparisons that would only confuse and probably anger Mr. Cotterly, though Pearl would have cackled. "Don't worry about me."

To my surprise, he softened just a touch. "I usually don't. You've always done very well by us."

Wait for it… three, two, one.

"Now if you could only be a timelier…" There it was. He couldn't say a compliment without an insult.

"Of course, Mr. Cotterly." I feigned a smile and stormed forward, jostling the display as I entered the rear of the funeral parlor.

According to Pearl, today's decedent had once been a big deal—in his wife's eyes at least—and she wanted to make sure that everyone knew it. Two days ago, she sat in the consultation area at Pearl's, describing a vision of white, red, and blue flowers and hanging arrangements, as well as flowers scattered into every nook and cranny of free space.

Spare no expense, she'd said. Until I had totaled up the price for her. Then her husband had become less deserving, but still achieved an impressive display for what she could afford. Not that I was judging. My mom didn't have any flowers when she died. Neither did a lot of people. It wasn't like the dead could see them anyway.

In the viewing room, a big picture of Alan Parsons rested on an easel next to the raised coffin. Round-faced with a good smile and balding with wire-rimmed glasses and a Mr. Rogers cardigan over his tie, his image screamed 'middle school principal' to me. I smiled at the picture as I set up the floral sprays and the baseball display.

Looks like he was a nice guy.

A baseball fan at heart, I hoped he would have loved the flowers I'd spent the last two days putting together for him.

But... I also knew the truth. The flowers and everything that Mr. Cotterly and I did was for the living, not the dead. The dead didn't care, and to put it bluntly from the point of view of someone who lived in a studio apartment and ate rice and beans at least four times a week, they weren't paying the bills.

While I crouched, straightening out some stalks that bent during transport, the cold fingers of a chill trailed up my spine. Not fear. More a strange déjà vu, a moment of spooky recognition.

It was probably Mr. Cotterly glaring at me or Mrs. Parsons behind me. Maybe even one of the mourners. They weren't due to get there until 9:30, but time didn't always stop people. Gathering my wits, I turned to find out.

CHAPTER 2

Hades

SOMETHING WAS AMISS. I recognized it the moment I looked into the green flames of my fireplace. What should have reflected faces, souls in my realm, instead showed distorted figures. Horns sprouted from their foreheads, jagged edges stretched along their cheeks and jaws and mouths opened in silent screams. I ran my fingers through the fire, waving away the images, clearing it of the grotesque demons.

I touched a pillar in the hall, reaching into the Underworld for my daily activity report. Flashes from each of the four of regions played in my mind. Faded, patchy and blurry.

The echoes of tortured souls sounded across the Fields of Mourning. Denials and refusal to repent, and the red-hot flames, the heat, sweat, constant thirst, headaches, cramps and never-ending nausea of Tartarus. Forgiveness and redemptions in Asphodel Meadows, where souls bathed in the soothing waters of the River Lythe, the river of forgetfulness which stripped them of all sorrow and allowed those souls the peace to enter the ultimate paradise, the Elysian Fields. The images faded.

Almighty Olympus!

I yanked my hand away and curled my fingers into a fist as I stared at it. Something interrupted my magic, preventing me a clear picture of the afterlife.

Immediately, I departed for the temple at the River Styx, where Charon, my ferryman would deliver the four generals, one from each realm of the Underworld. I strode down halls of dark marble, flecked with gold and encrusted with jewels. Vines curled around the pillars and plants sprouted from vases. Servants drifted through the halls with a nod to me in passing.

When I arrived at the open temple next to the dock, the boisterous tune of my four generals carried on the water, celebrating their retirement for the evening as the hounds took up the night shift. Charon's ferry approached, an ancient thing almost as old as the sailor himself. I glanced from the water, shimmering with a rainbow of colors like the inside of a pearl, to the last of the violet light disappearing behind the mountains of Tartarus.

Late again.

In the Underworld, the sun set every evening right around the time dinner was served.

Nothing ever moved fast with my ferryman. He took his time, maybe because he had all the time in the world. It was probably why he only managed a single boatload of fresh souls per day when he could easily deliver three. What was he doing? Sight seeing?

"My Lord," the chorus of four generals greeted me as Charon maneuvered the craft to tie it to the dock.

My generals alighted the boat, their sandals clapping on the wood, the leather lappets of their Pteruges slapping their thighs. The noise wiped out the stony silence of my palace behind me.

Each evening, I waited for them at the dock, a kind of thank you for their service, and also because I had nothing to go home to.

"A fine day for redemption," Thaddeus, my general from The Fields of Mourning, advised with a bright smile for someone left in charge of the souls damned for minor transgressions. "Ten souls today."

"Excellent." I nodded. Ten was a respectable number unless one counted it along with the world's burgeoning population. But I didn't. "Anything else to report?"

He looked at me with an odd expression, a combination of confusion and disbelief. "No, my lord."

I turned to Cumaean, the dour general of the Asphodel Meadows.

"The forgotten do not complain," he claimed.

"All smiles in the Elysian Fields," Dotraxes declared.

A good result. But in their answers, I found no explanation for what I'd seen in the flames or the grainy images in my mind's eye. Perhaps Lucius, the general of Tartarus, might enlighten me.

"Our fires fade, my lord," he stated. "The furnaces are not hot enough for the torture chambers."

Not again. It was back. Winter had crept into my realm, and its iciness settled inside of me, dulling my connection to my realm.

Curse the goddess for leaving! But no wonder. She hadn't wanted to deal with winter.

Cumaean trudged away.

"General," I called out and he turned. "I have not dismissed you yet."

Cumaean scowled, tapping his feet, his fingers twitching. He just wanted to get home. Of my four generals, he was always the first to try and sneak away.

"Anything else, my lord?" Thaddeus cocked an eyebrow.

My shoulders curled. I had hoped he might ask a different question.

"Let's meet tomorrow morning." My voice came out choked. "For now, drink and be merry." I forced a smile even though it stung to utter the words.

Thaddeus blanched. He thought me blind to their visits to the tavern in the Elysian Fields. Probably because they'd never invited me to share in their ambrosia wine. No one wanted to socialize with the cold and hard Lord of the Dead. The one whose heart had died long ago with his wife.

Loneliness settled heavy beneath my breastbone. Each night, I subjected myself to the same torture. The wish to be included in their adventures, spend time in someone else's company but my own, if but for a single wine.

I nodded, dismissing them, and they stomped away.

Thaddeus glanced over his shoulder at me twice.

"How'd he know?" Dotraxes whispered as they retreated down another corridor. The hearing of a god allowed me to catch it.

"No idea," Cumaean muttered.

My throat burned as I swallowed the lump stuck there.

"Maybe we should invite him?" Thaddeus offered.

"You must be mad," Lucius added. "You want to drink with your lord commander?"

My chest ached and I laid a hand over it. They all had wives to go home to. A warm bed at night. Soft, silky flesh to lie beside and comfort them. An ear for comfort, a companion for liveliness and conversation. I'd lost my wife to the plague over two hundred years ago.

I wanted to leave too, return to my cold and empty palace, but I had one more to question.

"Late again." I reminded Charon as he climbed from his

boat, bones creaking. Why he chose to torture me with his grating limbs when he could float, I'd never know. But he'd served the gods and I well over the last few millennia, and I wasn't about to retire him. Maybe I could get him some olive oil to lubricate his skeleton.

"Apologies, my lord," Charon rasped, his bony knees protruding from his cape as he hobbled toward me. "The river has frozen again, making it harder to navigate."

I summoned my bident and squeezed. The tip of the two prongs on the long pole glimmered in the violet light. I thought we'd fixed this problem, but obviously this wasn't something that could be easily solved.

When the goddess left the Underworld to return to Olympus, a palace in the stars, she took her essence with her, instead of leaving it in her human avatar like the rest of the gods. An avatar like me... only I was different. The absence of the Lady of the Underworld had somehow affected the realm. I felt it deep inside of me, like a gaping hole, growing wider by the day, but I never knew how to fix it, and neither did the god within me. Three times the god had begged his wife to return, but each time she had refused him.

Avatars were infused with the essence of the gods, working their magic in the Land of the Living, doing their patron's bidding. I was not like the avatars before or after me. Some two hundred years ago, the god and I merged into one being because Hades preferred to remain in the Underworld than go to Olympus. I had long since forgotten my name and come to know myself as Hades, too.

My attention snapped to the water, lapping at the edge of the wall-less temple. "Show me." I boarded Charon's craft, standing at the helm.

"Yes, my lord." Charon climbed on after me, and jabbed his oar into the water, pushing the boat back. The ferry rocked from side to side, but I remained steady, thanks to years of sailing with my father, a merchant and trader.

While the other avatars received messages from their gods, I had mine permanently in my head along with the stark, painful and constant echo of the torment of losing my wife. Here we were; two lonely and sad old... what could I call us? Entwined souls? Whatever we were, we were forever weighted by heartache and loss.

The god and I tried to keep busy to forget. We judged the dead in the morning, led the worthy to drink from the River Lethe to have them forget the bad things they'd done in their lives before taking them to the Elysian Fields, . Delivered some torture after lunch to end the day on a high note. Spun Ixion on his wheel until he vomited, made Sisyphus push his rock up the hill until he ached and collapsed, and Paris, well, who didn't want that ladies' man to suffer for stealing Helen and instigating the downfall of Troy? A good old prodding with a red-hot iron did the trick. After dinner, I quite often settled in for a game of chess. But I still yearned for that missing piece of myself.

Warm air with a hint of a chill tugged at the silk of my dark toga. It ruffled the edges of Charon's frayed and holed rags, his hood peeling back enough to reveal his skeletal features and eyeless sockets.

Almighty Olympus.

He resembled one of the dead he brought to me daily. As Lord of the Underworld, I had to maintain a level of decorum in my realm. I clicked my fingers, and a green flame crawled over his rags, transforming into a new velvet robe. That was more like it.

Charon glanced down. "Thank you, my lord."

I nodded, then returned my attention back at the River Styx which bordered my palace and flowed to the gate of the Land of Living in the north and the Elysian fields to the east.

Souls ventured into the water, wispy apparitions, incorporeal bodies, floating heads with mist curling behind them. Some vanished when they saw me drift past, terrified. Others played, swam and bathed, even though they had no need. Some habits remained with the dead. Distorted faces in the water reflected the loneliness in my expression, haunting my palace, my empty bed, forcing me to look away.

The Underworld was a place of contemplation. Some souls took an eternity to come to terms with the abuses they committed. Neglect, betrayal, deception, dishonesty, jealousy, and revenge. But once they expressed remorse for the pain they inflicted, then they could find peace in the Elysian Fields.

"Rest now," I commanded the souls, and they retreated from the water, returning to their paradise, an endless field of full lakes, flowered fields, trees, gardens, paths, temples and green-flamed sconces. All the beauty of Olympus. Tall statues of all the gods in the Greek pantheon watched over the dead. My eyes and ears in my realm.

My ferryman carried me five miles into the river, where sheets of thin green ice floated on the surface.

"How far does it extend?" I asked.

Charon extended a bony finger. "All the way to the gate, my lord."

"Take me there," I ordered.

Charon's knuckles creaked as he navigated around the floating ice.

Even from this distance, I sensed the gate at the end of the river, where the Land of the Living and Dead met, a place guarded by Cerberus, my three headed dog. The pain of the living stirred within me, twisting my insides.

The side of the boat struck a piece of ice and rocked. I shouldered Charon, and we both fell.

"Almighty Olympus!" I climbed back to my feet. "I hope you are a lot steadier ferrying the dead to the Underworld."

"My humblest apologies, master," Charon rasped.

We hadn't sailed but another mile when I detected a flutter in the air, a pitch of wings, and I glanced up. When I recognized him, carrying some lost soul, I almost sent of bolt of green flame his way.

He landed in front of me, a tall and lean thing with golden, perfectly styled hair and high cheekbones. Winged sandals fluttered on his feet. Out of all the gods and avatars, only Hermes could cross into the Underworld.

I leaned forward. "What brings you to my realm, Avatar of Thieves?"

"That's Avatar of Messengers, Thieves, Liars, Travelers, Sports, and just about everything in the ancient Greek world." He straightened his collar. "I addressed you with your correct title. The least you could do is get mine right. Or address me by my human name. Mads." He smiled as if he'd suddenly become the imparter of information, since his title wasn't quite long enough yet.

The smart-mouth. Part of his "charm" to Hermes.

"What do you want?" I glanced at the soul he carried. A pretty young nurse only a year departed from her earthly existence. Confused. Lost. "Stealing a soul? Even for you, that's low."

"Take me back." She wrestled against his grip. "I have to feed my children."

I examined her. She didn't yet have the touch of the Underworld on her: a green stamp on her wrist. But there could be no doubt she belonged to me.

"I found this lost soul lingering in the Land of the Living." And Mads was smug. "Are you getting lazy in your old age? Not bothering to summon them anymore?"

Impossible. All the dead were carried to the Underworld

by my magic which made sure they didn't linger too long in the Land of the Living..

I glared at him. His smile and the crossed arms said he enjoyed taunting me. The fool. He wasn't a god and needed reminded never to pretend he was. Especially since he was no more than an avatar which made him mortal and subject to those things that killed mortals. Things I could summon and control with nothing more than a blink and a wave.

With a sneer, I warned, "Come back again, and you'll know a fate worse than an eternity in the Underworld." I clapped my hands to transport him through the gate, back to the Land of the Living.

"Is that all the thanks I get? Last time I tell you that the afterlife has a serious problem." He hobbled away, muttering under his breath about the nurse being the fifth soul he'd encountered in days.

I sucked in a long breath. Five souls. A trick. Hermes and his avatar were known for playing them. But when my gaze fell to the lost soul, I knew it was no sleight of hand or prank. Panic and set me chest ablaze. No soul had ever rejected the call of the underworld's magic.

I scraped a hand along my jaw. Three urgent problems requiring investigation had arisen today. The strange, distorted faces in the flames. Ice forming on the River Styx, blocking the navigational path of my ferryman of souls. Lastly, this lost soul who had not followed the call of the afterlife. Something was wrong in my realm, and only a trip to the dreaded overworld would uncover the mystery so I could fix it.

For now though, I had something else to deal with. A confused woman attempting to climb over the boat, shouting she'd swim back to them.

I took her by the arm as the details of her death, her name

and situation became clear in my mind. "Come with me, Mary."

"My babies!" Tears spilled down her cheeks as she reached a hand into the mist hanging over the water.

"Not your concern anymore." I pulled her toward me, folded her against my chest and gestured for Charon to turn the boat around. "Now come. Your judgment awaits."

CHAPTER 3

Autumn

I TURNED and gasped at the tall, pale man with black hair shined like patent leather, slicked back from a face that didn't have a single smile line or feature that would indicate it had ever known happiness. His suit alone said he didn't work for the funeral home. Black and crisp cashmere. It probably cost at least six months of my pay.

Mr. Cotterly and his staff all wore good black suits, but they were the soft and flexible. The kind that made working in them easy. This one was razor sharp lines and stiff angles. Cold.

This man, a mourner most likely, glanced around as if he didn't even see me. Confused. Irritated. A long-lost son or nephew. Maybe the black sheep of the family. Either way, not a good day to be him.

He struck me as someone who needed help, so I gave the

LADY OF THE UNDERWORLD

baseball display one last pat and dusted my hands along my dress to brush away any tiny stalks.

"Hi," I kept my voice soft and respectful as I walked toward him. "Is there something I can help you with?" I wasn't Cotterly staff but I didn't exactly need a roadmap to be able to tell him where he needed to go.

"What in the *world?*" He had a deep voice that rumbled pleasantly through me—his diction the kind to make me think of old movies. Stern or not, up close, there was something sweet about his mouth—sensual, almost beautiful—which contrasted with his strict expression.

I blinked, drawing back just at the way he glared at me. It wasn't an angry glare, but clearly, he didn't want my help. Probably resented having to deal with me at all. Well, that was what his frown said.

Made sense since grief came in so many forms. One time, a lady at the flower shop shouted at me for suggesting something as "old-fashioned and plain" as lilies for her sister's spray. Then she spent forty minutes apologizing and weeping when I told her my name was Autumn and not Molly. The poor thing ended up sitting in our consultation area until we closed, de-thorning roses under Pearl's watchful eye.

Then there were the stories the funeral home staff told—mourners having sex in closets, impromptu poetry sessions, fist fights. People got weird when it came to death, but I still didn't expect the guy in the nice suit to stare at me as if I'd crawled out of a crypt.

"I'm with Pearl's, the florist." My stammer was a direct result of his wide-eyed shock. Or maybe mine. "I'm just here to handle the sprays, but I can help you find what you're looking for."

His lips parted, and he gave me a thorough once-over, as if he'd only just noticed my presence. His examination sent a piercing thrill through me. Every so often, a guy would give me a whistle or a smile that said he'd noticed my bosom or my shapely legs, but no one had ever looked at me like this. Assessing. Calculating. Fascinated. Sexual.

"Who *are* you?" he demanded, his dark eyes narrowed. "*What* are you?"

I laughed. Along with the whistles and catcalls, I never got that question. "I'm Autumn. I work for the florist. You know, flowers, bouquets, *apologies to your wife*."

Okay, so I might have thrown that last one in there to fish for his marital status, since he wasn't wearing a wedding ring. Not that I practiced picking up men at funeral parlors. I mean, it had been a while, but *Autumn, please*… I had a wild-child inside of me that was inching toward asking this stranger if he wanted to try out the closet.

Oh, the shame. It amped when he didn't respond to my inner closet-monologue. "I'll just tell Mr. Cotterly that you're here and–"

"No!" He gripped my wrist in a pale hand. I yelped. He was fast. And pale. Did I mention pale? Well, his long fingers wrapped around my arm were. The kind of pale you'd expect from someone that hadn't seen the sun in ten years.

A pleasant electricity sparked beneath his palm into my bones, my soul. If he'd actually been trying to stop me from moving, I didn't want to. I wanted to stay in his grasp forever.

Reality snapped back, and I opened my mouth, ready to remind him about bad manners, when everything changed. A feeling, like sitting on the edge of a very nice dream when a body twitch yanked me back from it, hit. My head swam, and my stomach dropped before I dropped back to reality, but I couldn't be sure anymore if I was asleep, dreaming of the most delightful touch of a man or if I was awake actually experiencing it. Then another twitch and the world crashed in a hail of shattering glass and screams of metal. A rush of heat—the warmth of a cozy fire, the pleasure of being wrapped in a cocoon of safety—bloomed in my chest. Happiness spilled through me and my heart opened like a flower as though it was perfectly normal and appropriate to be open to him, and to let him be open to me.

Thank goodness you finally showed up a little voice inside me said. *Where have you been? I was waiting forever!*

This interaction was unusual even for me. Eager to know everything about him or not, I didn't get as far as I had by just letting anyone with a handsome face and a sharp suit into my heart like this.

I should've been racing toward the van, speeding out of the parking lot, running for my life. But he jerked back a step as if he'd come to the same realization. Dark eyes stared at me, long and hard, something behind them flashing, like a bolt of recognition.

"You. Are you…?" He stroked my hand with his thumb.

"What?" I brushed a hand through my hair when the door burst open and a bunch of people in baseball jerseys spilled into the room.

Mood killers. Texas Ranger fans charging in, talking about the number of guests, reception food, and the upcoming season (apparently, the Rangers were absolutely going to kill it). Certainly no one who looked like they would think to wear a suit that costed as much as a nice car.

The stranger dropped my wrist and retreated to the back of the room. My heart sighed as he left. A soft glow warmed my hand where he'd touched me, and I wanted it to grow in heat and intensity.

I wanted to follow and ask him to explain, but the matriarch of the Parsons clan bottlenecked me so she could explain the rapture of a good ball game and relate it to the design of her chosen floral display.

After a rundown of this season's starting pitchers, she cupped one of the roses from the display. "Oh, Autumn. This is lovely." Her eyes teared. "Alan would be so touched, God rest his soul, and he was always so sensitive, too. A man who loved his flowers, just like he loved his family. Did you want to meet some of them?"

I glanced around the room. This was the kind of funeral I liked best: a celebration of the deceased's life, their spirit, and the things they cherished. Of course, it was still sad, but it was always nice to see the impact a person had on a family.

"I'm sorry, I can't." There was a van to return before Pearl set off into a worrying tangent, a store full of groceries I needed to pick up, and a blanket to wrap around myself as I watched TV. "I have to get back to the shop."

"Of course, dear." She patted my hands.

I glanced around the room for tall, dark, and well-dressed. But if he was there, he was lost in sea of Rangers' jerseys. My stomach sank with disappointment. *Oh, well.*

I did a final check to make sure Mrs. Parsons got everything she paid for, then made my escape by sneaking out of the viewing room. As I strode down the hall, I wished for another second of that warmth I'd felt with the stranger.

When I passed the next viewing room, I found him seated on the ground at the platform with his head in his hands. Long-limbed and graceful. Also, sad.

I had a moment of doubt, but in for a penny…. I walked the aisle between the chairs and stopped a foot or so in front of him.

"You okay?" He didn't look okay.

He leapt to his feet, then stared down at me with impossibly black eyes. I'd never seen eyes so dark, and I fell back a pace.

"Why the hell are you able to see me?" He reached for me, but I took another step away.

LADY OF THE UNDERWORLD

A part of me had liked—no, scratch that, *more* than liked the way he touched me before. But I wasn't itching to become a part of some creepy funeral home drama with some guy who wanted to know *why I could see him.*

I held up my palms and chuckled because Mr. Cotterly, wherever he was, wasn't ready for my kind of hysteria. "Your invisibility shield must not be working today."

His brow furrowed and his lips pursed. "What *are* you?"

And that didn't answer my question or explain why he kept asking me that. Or account for my eloquence. "What?"

Maybe I'd happened upon someone seriously detached from reality. But then the lights around us flickered, dimming and then brightened, and a chill settled over me. A man stood by the light switches at the door. Something in my brain recognized him before I could put a name to the face. My body iced over, and a bucket of cold water on my head couldn't have had me more frozen. The picture on the easel…the man in the coffin…

"That's… that's Alan Parsons." My body shook like I'd just seen a ghost. Because I had just seen a ghost. The room dimmed again and this time it didn't have anything to do with the lights.

Mr. Parsons wandered out of the viewing room right through the wall. Through a solid wall.

I stumbled backward into the stranger. He righted me, brushed past me, then chased after the apparition.

Okay. There had to be an explanation. Maybe…or…. I hadn't taken any medicine or had anything to drink. This morning, I'd had three cups of coffee so I could be dehydrated and imagining things in a caffeine-induced haze. For the love of God, where were the Ghostbusters when I needed them?

Just as I'd convinced myself I needed a good day or so of sleep—I'd been working hard—the mystery man's husky voice shouted. "You need to come with me!" It came out like a command given by a master to his slave. "It is not right for the dead to walk the Earth, Alan Parsons!"

I pressed my hand to my forehead. "Oh, Autumn." I tapped my head a few times. Bonkers. I was going crazy.

As he departed, I caught a glimpse of his shadow, of a long, forked pole in his hands, of spikes protruding from his shoulders. My breath hitched and my legs bent. Junipers. I was having a breakdown. Exhaustion and job loss induced hallucinations. Because certainly there was no real reaper come to take Alan Parsons to the afterlife! But these events had caused a disconnect between body and brain. My body won and my legs carried me out after him. This horror show wouldn't be complete until I woke up screaming.

"Oh, Autumn, this is how people end up in unsolved podcast episodes." But I wanted to see this and no force of nature of ectoplasmic goo was going to stop me.

The handsome stranger in the suit was fast, but so was I and I followed him down the back stairs.

As we reached the refrigerated part of the funeral home—the area where they stored the dead bodies—it hit me like a sack of fertilizer. I was chasing a man who walked through a wall and the ghost of a man whose family had ordered and I'd spent days making a four foot baseball/rose display! Ghostbusters indeed.

I should have stayed put. Claimed fatigue and had Pearl deliver today. As the owner, certainly she should've been the one to deal with apparitions and…walking corpses that could float through walls and smelled like cinnamon and spice. A detail that hadn't occurred to me until this minute.

And still, I chased.

Usually downstairs wasn't such a creepy, dark place. Amelia, the makeup artist of the deceased, blared bubblegum pop while she worked, and Mr. Cotterly's niece kept everyone well-supplied with cheerful crayon drawings at their workstations.

Today was a different. The lights flickered as I caught the sound of footsteps, louder and more deliberate now, ahead of me. With the lights off for a few seconds, I groped for the wall, my breath wheezing in and out of my lungs.

Somehow, I knew where the ghost formerly known as Alan was. Ghost. Seriously. Junipers.

Chills rolled down my body, and I shook my head. This wasn't one of those situations where I could let myself lose focus. Because no telling where my mind would wander off to. I was in enough trouble with this incident.

Alan was directly below the viewing rooms where they had put him in an oak coffin for his final party. But maybe someone should've checked his pulse first, because if this wasn't a ghost—and I wasn't quite ready to buy into the theory yet—the man himself now walked along the hall in pitch darkness.

Finally, the lights came back on and it took a minute for my eyes to adjust, but when they did...the stranger and I paused in the door. I gripped his arms, looking around his broad shoulder. Alan stared at the refrigerators. His brow was drawn and his mouth turned down. Then he approached a single body laid out on a table.

Oh god. This had to be a dream. No way it was really happening.

It took me a few seconds for my mind to kickstart. Alan was searching for himself. When my mom was sick, I'd spent a lot of time in hospital, seen many patients reflecting on their death as it came for them.

"Oh, the poor guy," I whispered.

"That 'poor guy' has somehow managed to do something that hasn't been done in centuries." Tall, dark and handsome stranger's tone sent a deeper chill through me.

In the basement of a funeral home with a dead man circling another dead body and the lights flickering like crazy, the stranger made me want to run because I'd seen my fair share of scary movies and the perky florist wasn't ever the one who made it out alive. I held my breath, not sure of what was going to happen next. But before I could full-on panic, a question niggled at the back of my mind.

"What are we going to do?" I asked softly.

The stranger—did I mention gorgeous with dark hair that brushed the edge of his collar and those dark eyes— glanced down at me quickly, his brows tightly knitted and lips tight. Had a lot on his plate by the look of him. I got it. But I wasn't exactly sunbathing by the pool either.

"You need to go back where you came from." His order came with such assertive power that something deep inside of me responded to his directive. "The living and the dead should not mingle."

He said the last part like my great-aunt might have said that you couldn't wear white after Labor Day. Of course Great-Auntie Thelma wouldn't have touched my arm when she said it and that touch wouldn't have sent tingles from my brain stem straight south to where the east and west separated. The entire peculiarity of the situation along with my own thoughts inspired my snicker.

But before I could bring on the contrite apology or challenge him on the living vs. the dead comment, he entered the room with Mr. Parsons.

Alone, everything made sense. I must have slept in, missed the delivery, and this was all a dream. One of those good dreams with handsome strangers... and if I played the cards in my hand the right way, I'd be able to wrangle some alone time with tall, dark, and broody...of course I'd have to get rid of the ghost of Mr. Parsons first then hope I didn't forget all this when I woke up.

"Alan Parsons!" The suit's voice was firmer than it had been with me. "It is time to come with me."

Mr. Parsons turned to the stranger with a severe frown, full of heavy brows and narrow eyes. "I can't find my family. I need to find them. I thought they would be here."

And now my ghost talked. This wasn't a dream. Not a nightmare I'd wake up from and dispel with a cup of chamomile and honey tea. I was wide awake, seeing ghosts which made the hottie in Armani what I could only believe was a reaper.

Junipers!

"Your family is fine but not your concern." The stranger took another slow step forward. "You have a new journey to take."

Mr. Parsons scowled. Journey. Not his concern. Yep. This guy had reaper written all over him. And I was about three seconds from running away as I peed my pants.

"I'm not going anywhere until I've seen my family."

Gorgeous stranger man acted as if Mr. Parsons weren't even speaking. He simply reached for Parsons like he'd reached for me upstairs. "A place has been set aside for you, Alan Parsons, and now you must–"

The rest of his pompous pronouncement was cut off when Mr. Parsons wound up his arm and threw a haymaker straight to the pale man's jaw.

Whoa! I pressed a hand to my mouth.

Mr. Parsons might have looked more like Mr. Rogers than Muhammed Ali but that punch said he could have boxed middle-weight. The force of the blow spun the stranger on his back foot, but what I noticed was the wide-eyed shock on the reaper's face before he stumbled into the wall. I wondered if there was a punishment for punching a reaper. A jab from the prong I briefly spotted earlier? Extra doses of punishment in hell?

"I am not going anywhere *until I see my family!*" Parsons snarled, his voice so loud that car alarms on the street should've activated. I covered my ears as a greenish yellow light glowed in his eyes as if someone had scooped out his brain like a Halloween jack-o-lantern.

Oh, nice.

What I should have said was *don't punch a guy who could very well be a reaper unless you want to go straight to hell, you fool*. But instead I said, "Oh, Mr. Parsons, right?" more as a distraction than anything. Because really, I didn't know what else to say. "Your family's in Viewing Room B."

His head twisted toward me. Oh God. The phrase *overstayed my welcome* came to mind. I should have run away. Should have left the funeral parlor in a screech of burning rubber and smoky tires. But he inched forward, and I lost my breath.

CHAPTER 4

*A*utumn

AFTER A MOMENT, I figured out why the stranger wanted to keep me out of the room. Nothing inhabited Alan Parsons anymore but memory. All he wanted was to see his family and he couldn't understand why he couldn't, and his grief doubled since he also mourned himself.

"I want my family," he repeated. "I need to see them."

A tingling in my gut screamed for me to run down the hall shrieking like the heroine in a bad horror movie, and while if this was a horror movie, a funeral home was the perfect place for such idiocy, this was real life with real grief just up the stairs. Mr. Cotterly would lose his bananas. No thanks.

The man in the suit placed one hand to his cheek with a faintly bewildered expression. Apparently and quite unbelievably, no one had punched him like that before.

"I can take you to them," I offered before the stranger

interjected with another quietly spoken something that pissed off the deceased once again.

Mr. Parsons drifted toward me, a determined look on his face.

I took a step back and held up a finger. Time to impart some truth. Also, my arm was currently blocking any incoming blows that might come my way. "*But!*" My stomach tightened as his face hardened. "You have to promise you won't upset them, all right? They're having a hard day as is. No, um, talking to them or punching them."

Mr. Parsons blinked as if I'd insulted him. "I wouldn't punch them."

"Yeah. Well pardon me if I just want to clarify." I ignored the shaking in my voice because of I acted like it didn't exist, by God, it didn't.

"They likely won't be able to see you," the man muttered with a smidge of hesitation. I glanced at him and twisted my lips into a scowl because I thought we were on the same team —the keep Alan Parsons calm team.

Mr. Parsons glared and I didn't blame him. The suit wasn't playing nicely.

With a bubble in my tone, I clapped my shaking hands and said, "Excellent." Even though I was pretty sure this day was going to end with me either being sucked into a vortex of dark and evil posthumous energy or with me hopped up on psychotropic meds while a nurse fastened my straitjacket. "Now that we got that sorted, let's go."

Mr. Parson's harsh scowl softened. For a moment, I thought he might try to take a swing at me too by the harsh lines cutting across his face. The well-dressed wall walker behind me must have shared my sentiment because he stepped in front of me like he planned to provide some sort of supernatural protection. Would've been endearing but for the ghost. Ghoul maybe. Zombie not yet turned. I had no idea.

But Mr. Parsons only nodded with a melancholy that stole my breath. "It's only that I already miss them. I worry about them so much sometimes."

"Oh, I know how that is. Come on. This way." I curled my fingers into a fist. I wanted to pat his shoulder, offer some comfort, but if my hand floated through his skin, I was going to faint and then I would wake up in the basement of a mortuary and probably faint again. And no telling how long that would go on before I was rescued or stroked out.

And even though I'd seen both of them walk through a wall, I led my strange little procession up the stairs, my footsteps the only sound slicing through the silence.

"I'm Autumn, by the way," I said when we reached the top level of the parlor. "The florist."

Mr. Parsons gave me a weary smile.

I decided to try to lighten the tension. "Hey, Mr. Parsons. What do you call two flowers who are dating?"

"What?" His tone wasn't that of a man who cared about the answer. It was the tone of a man who couldn't believe I was standing in a funeral home during his funeral making jokes.

I gave him the punchline as if he cared, and only because I made jokes when nervous. "A budding romance." The stranger sighed. "Get it?"

"Not the time, maybe." Well-dressed and smug. Annoying combination.

Later on, when I had time to sit and think, I'd reflect on what an idiot I was for standing in a corridor, trying to make a dead man laugh. I was crazy to waste some of my best material on this guy.

God, I hoped my straitjacket wasn't too tight.

Thankfully, we arrived at the public area where more guests had arrived for his funeral. They all ignored me, and I had no idea if they could see my companions at all. On one hand, I hoped they couldn't. I'd never seen a stampede for the door at a funeral, but if my companions made their presence known, it could happen. On the other hand, if someone else besides me saw them, I couldn't be crazy. I just wanted to make sure Mr. Parsons got to Rest In Peace and Tall, dark, and Armani got to do whatever he'd come to do so I could go home and drown my memory of this day in a big bottle tequila with a vodka chaser.

Instead of heading to the main doors that led to the viewing room, I took Mr. Parsons through the service door close to the front of the building where we could watch without having people pass in and out all the time.

He stood, still as a statue for a long moment before he pointed to the woman who had come in for the flowers. "God, she's so pretty. I mean, I thought she was pretty when I married her. Then she got prettier every year we were together. Maddie, my daughter, is like that too you know. She doesn't see it, but someday..." His tone leaned toward the wistful. "She's smart, too, smarter than me or her mother."

"Aw, she sounds great." My heart pinched at both the pride and sorrow in his tone.

He pointed to an older man with a frown. "I loaned my brother Glenn my chainsaw last summer. Never returned it." He shook his head. "Won't do it now, either."

I hid a chuckle behind a cough, but the man in black scoffed. He either had a pressing engagement we were keeping him from or we were boring him. Not that I cared since this was my hallucination—probably inhaled too much pollen—and he was a guest in it.

"This is unnecessary and unseemly," he started, but I shushed him with a glare and whoosh wave reminiscent of my great-grandma Lucy. "He can talk as long as he likes. After this, he might not see them again. Have a heart."

The stranger frowned. Yeah. I talked back. To a ghost. Or the angel of death. Or the grim reaper. Grim definitely. The verdict on reaper wasn't in yet. But creepy was undeniable. And dark. Humorless. And gorgeous. Because I certainly wouldn't hallucinate an ugly reaper who scared me none whatsoever. Another point my shrink would undoubtedly find interesting after I woke up from my sedation. Fingers crossed the shrink would let me go and just tell me that I needed to get laid instead of hallucinating hot reaper fantasies.

I focused on Mr. Parsons, who pointed out his niece who always sent a card on his birthday and Christmas, the brother he never got on with, and the one he actually liked. A lifetime of connections and affections filled that room and with each explanation I sent up a wish for peace, not just for the mourners but for Mr. Parsons. And the pretty-boy jackass behind me scoffed at each of my thoughts as if he knew what was going on inside my head. The jerk. I was going to have to work on my fantasy men for my next hallucination.

"They're all so wonderful," Mr. Parsons said, every word sadder than the one before it. My heart wrenched for him again.

"They are. You have a lovely family." I smiled as he turned to me.

"Thank you," he said. "Such a kind young lady." And though he spoke to me, he scowled at suit guy.

Unaffected, Tall, Dark, and Broody tapped his foot, impatient. Rude. Petulant. "If you two are quite finished, I have other things to do today. Can we please get on with—"

He was cut off again when Mr. Parsons put his arms around me and held me against his shoulder. He was pretty solid for a guy who'd walked through a wall. Although I didn't hear a heartbeat when I pressed my ear against his chest. His chest didn't pump in any air either.

"And thank you too, dear," he whispered. "For the flowers. They are beautiful, just beautiful."

"Don't!" The man in the suit raised his voice, but we ignored him.

I hugged the deceased back, smiling. "You're very welcome, Mr. Parsons."

When I let him go, the stranger touched him lightly on the arm and Mr. Parsons faded away, leaving me with a taste of sugar on my tongue and a vague feeling of calm sadness and ease.

Junipers.

I stumbled backward into the wall, glad for it since my wobbly legs were about to give way.

I'd just had a whole conversation with a ghost. And a… something else. That I could stand up at all probably was a case for Ripley's Believe it or Not museum.

I glanced at one of the mourners; a man in a suit a few paces in front of me. Not a ghost. A man. Mourning his uncle. A normal blond haired man who probably couldn't walk through a wall.

What a weird day. Maybe I'd make an appointment with Dr. Halifax next week. No harm in making sure all my seeds were getting enough sunlight.

On my way out of the viewing room, I passed Glenn, who was seated on the end of a row of chairs. I leaned down to whisper in his ear.

"You should return the chainsaw." He turned to stare at me open-mouthed and wide-eyed.

After that, I snuck out of the funeral home and made my way back to the van.

It's gotta be exhaustion. Or a mental break down from finding out that I'd lost my job. I'd spent barely an hour at Cotterly's, but it felt like much more. I wasn't sure whether to reevaluate my entire worldview, register myself in a psych ward, or take a nap.

I swung myself up into the seat of Pearl's van and stuck the keys in the ignition then screamed at the flash of movement next to me. A scary movie scream worthy of Stephen King.

The good-looking guy in the expensive suit sat in the passenger's seat staring at me with those gorgeous, stern dark eyes of his. "We need to talk."

CHAPTER 5

Autumn

"Junipers!" I gasped, pressing a hand to my chest. When my breath returned, I added, "Anyone ever taught you not to sneak up on a person?

"No," he answered earnestly.

I glanced at the locked door. "How did you get into my car?"

He stared straight ahead. "I got in." Not surprisingly, not a straight answer. But I had seen him float through a wall…

"What do you want to talk about?" I snuck my can of mace out of my handbag beside me.

"Not here." He flicked his forefinger, acting like I was nothing more than his chauffeur.

"I feel like we've spent enough time together." I pointed the can of mace at him. "Get the hell out of my van."

He swiped the can and examined it as if he'd never seen one before. He shook it, holding it close to his ear, listening.

LADY OF THE UNDERWORLD

Then he sniffed it. His eyes widened and his lips smacked together as if he tasted it. The can disappeared.

Junipers. There went my only weapon. And my sanity. I curled my fingers around the door handle, ready to jump.

"I not here to hurt you. It isn't your time yet and yours will be painless and beautiful." His dark eyes landed on me.

Who the hell said that?

"I have a proposal for you." He paused and stared at me as if he'd just noticed that I had a face. "I could use someone with your talents with the dead."

I pinched myself until it hurt, then I chuckled. Too loud. Too long. Not panicked enough for the situation, certainly.

"Talents with the dead." I hoped he was talking about flower arranging because I'd had just enough time to convince myself I wasn't a whack job in need of shock therapy. "Thanks Joe Black, But I already have a job." Not true. Well, in a month's time at least. "Working for the grim reaper isn't on my bucket list."

Mr. Suit frowned again. "I'm no reaper." He turned to me with a sad, almost mournful smile. "Not death. Not a reaper for death."

I reached to touch him and…yep. Warm and real. "Not a hallucination. What exactly are you?" And why, oh why, was I talking to him when I should've been ass deep in tequila shooters and bad karaoke. And now, my head clouded again and I swayed in my seat. Toward him. Before I made contact, I righted myself.

He glanced at me. "Your blood sugar is low from fright. You need a goblet of nectar. Take me to the local tavern."

"Nectar?" Tavern, yes. Nectar, huh?

He snapped his fingers again. His manner, the coldness, the way he commanded me as if I was a chauffeur rather than… a delivery person, the magic he'd used back inside and in the van, told me he could have hurt me already if he intended to.

So, I started the engine, pulled the van out of the parking lot, and side-eyed him every two or three seconds, in case he had some sort of fold-up enchanted scythe in his breast pocket to kill me.

I took him to Mama Tickey's, a diner known in these parts for its cheap pancakes, endless eggs, and the policy that almost anything could be slathered in butter and fried on a griddle. They'd survived the big chains coming in, the competition that should've forced them out, by holding true to its artery clogging menu and the pride in it.

"I'll have the fried mozzarella sticks and a can of Fanta please," I told the waitress, breaking my vegan diet… part-time vegan diet. The mozzarella sticks were award winning, okay. No one, including this vegan with a weak will power for cheese, could resist the call of them.

"Coming right up." The waitress tucked her pen behind her ear and walked away.

Err… did she not see him? Come to think of it, no one in the funeral parlor had interacted with him either.

"Don't you want anything?" I asked tall, dark, and broody, prepared to order for him when the waitress returned.

He waved me away with his hand, obviously accustomed to telling people what to do.

"Rude. You could've just said you weren't hungry."

He stared at me with a combination of confusion and vague outrage. Maybe another flower pun would disarm him too. Or lighten the mood. They usually got a lot of laughs with my friends. Or maybe those were supportive laughs—you know the ones, laughing at me, not with me.

"So what do I call you, Joe Black?" I slid the menu between the salt and peppershakers.

"Who is Joe Black?" He quirked an eyebrow, frowned, and was still one of the most beautiful men I'd ever seen.

"Brad Pitt and Anthony Hopkins? Pitt plays Death." The more I spoke, the more vacant he went. "It's a movie. Never mind. I just...what do I call you?"

"By all rights, you shouldn't call me anything." His frown deepened. Still gorgeous.

I took a glance around the room. A couple people close by stared. Hard. Like a woman talking to a man in a restaurant was an oddity. Which led me to believe they couldn't see my supernatural companion. Nothing unusual there.

Or maybe it was because he was dressed like a *GQ* model in a place that catered more to *Road & Track* readers. He looked at least marginally aware of the fact he was out of place. But he didn't look like he was used to being, well, bothered.

I reclined against the leatherette booth. "Okay, but it's going to get awkward if all I can do is call you what I've been calling you in my head."

Curious, he leaned forward. "What's that?"

I tossed up whether to lead with *reaper* or *Tall, Dark, and Broody*. In the end, the latter won out, because he needed to lighten up, and a compliment never hurt.

"Oh, you know." I waved my hand. "Stranger, weird, Tall-Dark-Broody-and-Handsome." The last word popped out, and there was no calling it back.

He blinked at me, expression softening just a bit. "Handsome?"

Well, he was. My cheeks flushed with heat. "They don't have mirrors where you're from?"."

"Of course, they have mirrors where I'm from. Narcissus would shrivel and wither if she was unable to gaze upon her own loveliness." He spoke with just enough disdain to tell me he didn't agree with Narcissus... whoever that was. "I don't care how I look."

Sure, he didn't. Guys who didn't care always swore thousand-dollar suits and had eight-hundred-dollar haircuts.

"Still doesn't tell me what to call you." A name, for goodness sake. All I needed was a name. "I could pick one for you."

Ridiculous and flirty seemed to be my modus operandi of the moment. Maybe because ever since I met this guy, everything shifted. I wanted to touch him. Just the thought sent me into freefall. Spun me through space. Scary. Exhilarating. Exciting.

"I have a name of my own." He snapped the words as if I'd suggested naming him Fido.

Touchy. Okay. So he wasn't a flirter, but I didn't give up that easily. "Yes. And I'm just asking what it is."

He stared at the table as if he had several options to sort through and it only added to the mystery of his whole personae. And I loved a good mystery.

Finally, he shrugged. "Hades."

"Oh." Hades. A Greek God. I scrolled through my memory for any detail I could remember. He was a god of... something. "Well, it's nice to meet you... Hades."

The corner of his lips upturned. His dark eyes lightened. "It's Greek."

"Greek?" Oh, God. "Or Disney?"

He frowned. But why would someone who claimed to be —and definitely resembled—a Greek god have no knowledge of something so modern as Disney?

"Greek. I am Hades, Lord of the Underworld. Son of Titus Cronus and Rhea, brother to Zeus, Poseidon, Hera, Demeter and Hestia." He nodded and I guess I could believe he was godly. Mortal men didn't look so... sigh-worthy.

"Then shouldn't you be wearing a toga?" Because I would've liked to have seen this guy in a toga.

"No. I assure you I'm the Lord of the Underworld." He said it so flatly I burst into laughter.

"Sure. And I'm a mermaid. Fish out of water. My tail grows back in the bathtub, but only when I add sea salt." I rolled my eyes and sipped my lemon water.

"You know it to be true too." His words cut through my laughter, rendering me utterly silent, my breath catching, and my eyes widening.

The rational part of me didn't believe him. The part that watched those medium shows on TV and spotted the gambit they used before they finished the game, and the part who could spout the science to any idiot who didn't believe in climate change. But deeper, in a place I rarely let see sunlight, I did believe him. That part knew about monsters just beyond the fires, creatures that went bump in the night. Setting that part of myself free would've made it very scary to work so closely with mortuaries and funeral homes, so I kept it locked down like Fort Knox. If I let that part of myself see daylight, it would be today, over and over again.

I swallowed hard as he leaned across the table towards me, his eyes dark. For one single moment, I could've sworn I saw stars in them.

"You know who I am," he stated plainly, his voice quiet and commanding. "You know it in your heart, even if your mind doesn't want to recognize it." He brushed a finger over my arm and my world lit up with colored light. "Who am I?"

The words came from between my lips, from the memory of days spent in a classroom, learning. They came in my voice, but damned if I recognized them. "The Lord who rules under the Earth, King of All Wealth, Ruler of What Comes After, and Regnant Over the Dead." I gasped and clapped my hand over my mouth. "Wow."

Something opened up at his command like a blooming flower under the sunlight. And he'd made it happen. Of that, I had no doubt. And it scared the jeebs out of me.

He gently pried my tensed hand loose, and I gasped at the temperature of his skin. Ice. Monstrous cold threatening to seep into me. "Now tell me who you are."

CHAPTER 6

Autumn

HE WAS CUTE, yes, but he was also demanding and condescending and he had a lot to learn about how to speak to people. I yanked my hand back.

"No." I wasn't telling some freak show who claimed to be God of the Underworld and probably had as much access to Google as anyone else what my name was.

Hades frowned at me, but before he could respond, the waitress returned with my order. She gave me a curious look as she put down my basket of golden fried goodness.

"Going to a concert tonight?" she asked. "Your hair is wild."

"Oh no, we've just come from a funeral." I gestured back and forth between Hades and I.

She stared at me, then at the spot Hades occupied. Her brow furrowed and her lips parted. "Sorry for your loss," she muttered then moved away from the table, but she continued to watch me with the same uncertain look.

I winced. The rumor mill was going to have its own special field day with that one.

"Before, people were less fearful of death." Hades watched her, his eyes dark, his face drawn with lines.

I chewed a cheese stick. There wasn't a good answer to his observation. Nothing he shouldn't have known, but I said the words anyway. "Death's the end of everything we know. And the things we don't know are scary. It's like going to kindergarten. That first day is so… scary. First time away from Mom and Dad. And Kindergarten is just a day away. But death is… forever away from the people we love." I paused. "Plus the clouds and angels, flaming lakes and spinning wheels. Very scary business."

"That's not death. That a children's tale." Hades he shook his head, his face a mask. I didn't know what his problem was, but the darkness in his eyes scared me as much as the prospect of death. "Who are you and where did you get the amulet around your neck?"

Amulet? It was a necklace. "Um, what?"

He reached across the table but curled his fingers and inch or so before he managed to touch me.

He stiffened. I expected him to demand my name, rank, and serial number again, but the hard lines of his face eased, and there was something beautiful in the darkness.

More than beautiful.

He tapped his fingers on the table and smiled. "I have been rude." His eyes widened as if he expected an answer.

I nodded. "Yeah." I took another bite and watched him while trying to pretend I wasn't watching him. He glanced around as if he'd never seen a diner, never noticed the leather bench seats of the Formica tabletops, checkerboard floors and mini-jukeboxes on each table. Or the old-fashioned soda fountain and hand-dip ice-cream freezer.

He snorted. "Are you, by chance, the new Avatar of Hermes? Have I stumbled upon the good fortune of a replacement for that unsavory creature who last occupied the position?"

Hermes? Avatar? About the only words I understood in that mess was good fortune and replacement of which I knew nothing about and couldn't possible have. So, I smiled and very eloquently said, "Huh?"

Hades leaned across the table until his head hovered above my plate and his eyes focused on mine. After a moment, he sat back and shook his head.

"No. Not Hermes' avatar. Something else." He smiled again and I stopped chewing. "An intrigue I should figure out at my earliest opportunity," And suddenly he sounded as if he'd just stepped out of a Jane Eyre novel. "I beg your pardon, and I hope that you grant it."

He should've sounded ridiculous, but I had the ridiculous urge to close my eyes and savor every word. Heat blossomed in my cheeks and worked its way down my body. All the way down.

"Pardon... granted?" I didn't know the phrasing, but he smiled. And I would have granted anything else he asked so long as he kept staring at me like that.

He bowed his head and looked at me from beneath lashes I only just noticed were Beyoncé long. "Please, tell me who you are and why the touch of the dead didn't destroy you."

Touch of the dead. Destroy me. Well, okay then. "My name's Autumn Rankin." Oh god. I wasn't supposed to admit that. Oh well. "And I work at Pearl's flower shop." I probably didn't need to clarify, but the nerves induced babbling. Per my usual. "Today, for example, I delivered the baseball rose display to Mr. Parsons' funeral."

No use in telling him the rest when he knew what happened. And I didn't want anyone to overhear me admitting to socializing with and hugging a dead man. Even if said dead man appeared live and well to me.

Hades' face tightened and a muscle in his jaw ticked. "The dead are not meant to mingle with the living, which is why I needed to send him to his place in the afterlife. Had he touched someone not… prepared, one of his family, perhaps, the damage could have been…extraordinary, enough to throw off the balance between life and death."

"Balance?"

Hades nodded. "The dead don't understand, and one touch, one breath out of turn and–" He snapped his fingers and I expected Alan Parsons to materialize in front of us.

Okay. Even if I believed—which I wasn't admitting to just yet—that this guy was some powerful Greek god who decided life and death, he was getting bit intense. And if his story was true, then he didn't control anything. Fate did. The touch of the dead was out of his control. Or something. My head spun with the implications of it all until I looked at him. Then peace settled over me.

For a moment, I noticed how very strong Hades' hands looked. Pale and lined with veins on the back. I shifted in my seat wondering what they would feel like against my skin. Then, the sounds of the restaurant came back to me—the clink of silverware, running water, murmured conversations, a radio playing rock music in the kitchen. Last thing I wanted was the God of the Underworld getting handsy with me.

Better to concentrate on what happened today. "But Mr. Parsons hugged me."

"Yes. That's why I need to know what you are." His phrasing needed work. "I thought the daughters of the night sky were long dead. You're not a psychopomp, or at least, not one I recognize. You're also not a particularly clever revenant, though I had speculated."

Again, with the rude. "Do I look like a zombie to you?" And I had no idea what a psychopomp or Daughter of the Night Sky referred to. And since we were monitoring him for being rude, I wasn't inclined to pull out my cell and check Google.

"Quite the contrary. And might I say, I like the way you look." And I liked the way he spoke. Deep. Commanding. Confident. Certain his words conveyed the truth. "Since you're not any of those things—zombie included—I need to figure out what you are. Where did you come from? How did you come to be?"

"You're the Greek god. You tell me." I rolled my eyes when he firmed up his mouth and crossed his arms. "I don't know what to tell you."

But as I considered an answer, I chewed another bite of golden fried mozzarella.

"I was born here," I started on my life story. "Dad hightailed it to Australia when I was eight, and Mom died from breast cancer when I was seventeen. I work with flowers. I like to plant. Seeds. Bulbs. Sprouts. You name it, I'm sticking it in the dirt and using environmentally safe fertilizer to make it grow. You should see my apartment balcony." Okay. That was a lot of information. I didn't mind his impatient throat clearing. "I hike and mountain bike. And today was my first time seeing dead people."

Hades snorted at that. "First time." I couldn't stop watching his lips. On most people, eyes were the most expressive parts of their faces, but this guy had a mouth that told his every mood. Thoughtful meant pursing. Anger was a fine line that made his lips all but disappear. Confusion was a twist to one side. And curiosity—right now—was a brush of his tongue between them that made me think of soft kisses under a starry sky. He cleared his throat again. His own nervous tic maybe? "Obviously. I see no evidence that you've experienced the touch of the dead prior to when I saw it happen."

He narrowed his eyes, assessing me again with a sweeping gaze as if trying to take me apart to examine my components. *Sorry, pal. If twenty years of therapy couldn't make it happen, your pretty face and cashmere wool blend suit aren't gonna do it either.*

"I am *the* Lord of the Dead," he said finally. "I treat the souls as they should be treated. Fairly and with respect but I deliver justice in cases where justice is needed."

The cogs in my mind came to a shuddering and jolting stop. I probably should have just kept on stuffing fried cheese in my face. There were a million smarter things to do than mouthing off, especially to someone I was beginning to suspect was the real deal—the king of all the deadlands—Hades. But I did precisely none of them.

"I don't think they would say the same thing," I countered louder than I meant to be which earned me more than a few nervous looks from the other patrons.

Okay. Time to cut the crazy. I pulled out my phone and held it to my ear, pretending I was talking to someone. It was better than someone having me thrown into the looney bin for my somewhat erratic behavior, but considering that I was even thinking the mystery man in front of me was the Lord of the Underworld, that he might be invisible or that he was there at all, I might have been inclined to agree with them.

"What are you doing?" Hades flicked a finger my way.

"Just go with it," I hissed. Then, more carefree, I said into the phone, "Mr. Parsons was suffering."

Hades frowned at me, but obliged me. "Alan Parsons was a dead man." When his volume climbed no one so much as glanced our way. "He should not have wanted anything. The dead do not want. They no longer care about what happens on Earth. They're dead."

I stared at him—he who was so convinced that he was right, and suddenly remembered everyone who had ever told me that people on food stamps shouldn't get to buy candy or chips or anything that might make the grinding circumstances related to being on food stamps just a bit easier. I remembered them from when I'd had to use government assistance myself. But when things had gotten better, I'd started manning the line at my local food pantry.

"Are you *dead*?" I demanded, whispering the last word for fear of more crazy glances.

He settled back against the booth seat as he stared at me with his tongue wetting his lower lip.

"What kind of question…?"

"Answer the question!" Apparently no longer concerned about the impression I was making on other patrons, I jabbed a mozzarella stick at him. "You're pale, but more computer geek than dead man, so tell me. Are you dead?"

The couple opposite us slid out of their seats and hurried outside, leaving behind their half-eaten meals.

Oops!

Hades shook his head. "Neither. Yet this only means we have no idea, none at all, what the dead want. Because we're not dead. You can apparently hear them, and so can I."

I shoved my chair back and stood, glowering, my hands flat on the table. I was hyper aware of the glances and outright staring, and heat rolled up my neck to my cheeks before I slumped back into the booth. To console myself, I stuffed some more fried cheese sticks in my mouth, thinking it might have been better if I'd eaten my food and simply moved on.

He looked at me for what felt like a long time with a, thankfully, less harsh expression. Besides asking me what or who I was, the Lord of the Dead wasn't demanding anything from me—he wasn't telling me what I should want or what I needed to do.

One corner of his mouth lifted enough to give me stomach flutters.

"You go to funerals often, do you not?" He didn't do more than blink. "You commerce with the dead."

Err, no. "No. I have commerce with people who need flowers for funerals."

"Have you noticed anything strange? Anything out of the ordinary?" I delivered flowers and left. I didn't usually stick around to socialize with the deceased. That was new.

"Calhoun Family Funeral Home is on the verge of splitting up because Tommy Calhoun slept with his brother's wife. That's the weirdest thing going on in the local industry as far as I know." Although, it wasn't all that weird these days.

Hades looked slightly distracted at that. "Adultery isn't so odd. Tale as old as time."

"Unless the cheating brother is expected to become a priest."

"Ah."

I grinned and slid my platter to the middle of the table between us. If the Lord of the Underworld took one of these tempting delights, I wasn't crazy.

"There's an old saying." I didn't know if someone like this guy had grandparents, but I thought maybe he could use a bit of my Nana's wisdom. "Play dumb games, get dumb prizes." He cocked an eyebrow and slipped that tongue between his lips again. "If you stop fishing and tell me what I need to know, I'll be able to answer your questions more precisely."

His eyes blazed, and he shot me a slightly defensive look. "It has been a long time since I troubled myself with human agents. I had forgotten how focused on petty details you can be."

Ouch. Luckily, I didn't offend easily, always maintained a look-on-the-bright-side kind of attitude. I even felt a flower pun coming on.

"Damn the humans!" I rolled my eyes in reinforcement of my non-repentance. "Tell me what's happening. Then I'll tell you if I can help."

He scoffed. "You're human. I do not hold out hope you can even help yourself."

Again, ouch. "And yet, here you are. Sitting in my booth. Talking to me."

One more eye roll and I was going to have a permanent view of the inside of my skull. His tongue swiped that lower lip again, and my stomach fluttered. Again. He ought to stop that. Didn't he know how distractingly beautiful he was?

I jabbed my cheese stick at him. "I don't know why I'm here, in your booth, talking to you."

He narrowed his eyes and his mouth formed a tight line. "I think you care." He reached across the table as if he had some magical power of touch. And when he laid his hand over mine and used his thumb to stroke my palm, I couldn't very well disagree. "I think you care a lot."

Distracted, he picked up a mozzarella stick and ate it in two bites then picked up another. After popping them, he looked at me eyes wide, smiling if eyes were capable of such a thing.

"Good?" I hoped my life ended up being more, but I suspected that convincing a god to eat fried cheese at Mama Tickey's diner would go down in history as one of my greatest achievements.

"Yes. On occasion, I rather enjoy food." He stood up, offering me his hand. "Come."

"Where are we going?" Not that I didn't trust him, but come on. He claimed—never mind that I was starting to believe it—to be some sort of Greek god. Didn't matter that he looked like one. So did Brad Pitt twenty years ago. But I wouldn't have followed old Brad if I'd just met him and he demanded it either.

"The Underworld."

I made my eyes go wide. "The Underworld." Oh for the love of Pete. "A tempting offer, but… I'm going to have to decline." And babble apparently. "I mean how would I explain my absence? Oh hey, Autumn, where have you been?" I turned my head as if answering my imaginary friend. "Oh, nothing much, dropped in on the Underworld the other day."

Hades pointed his gaze at mine, hand still extended. "I need your help."

"Why me?" I leaned back in my chair and ate the last mozzarella stick just in case he teleported—wasn't that how all Greek gods traveled—us away and I missed out. But a new thought made my stomach knot before I even finished chewing. " Am I dead? Is this your way of trying to convince me to go to the afterlife?" The knot turned into a ball of agony and I would've doubled over had the table not stopped my forward progress.

"I assure you, you are very much alive. Now, come." Confident. Assured. Strong.

"Let me think about it." The answer was still going to be no, but I was out of food and tired of people staring. I stood up to leave.

"I'll reward you." Hades pulled a gold coin from his pocket with an imprint of a harp on one side and a double-pronged fork on the other. "Just call my name when you're ready to talk."

CHAPTER 7

Autumn

"Crazy, crazy day." I climbed in the van, cranking it to life and merging into the mid-morning traffic.

My mind whirred, and I struggled to concentrate on the drive back to Pearls. I sat through most of a green light before someone blew their horn and I raced through the intersection on a yellow. Almost ran over a man who stepped into the pedestrian crossing a second early. Then I drove over a wayward umbrella carried into the roadway by a gusty wind. Not my fault though. I blamed Hades. Or rather, the man calling himself that name.

Breathing hard, I slammed on the breaks. I pulled out the gold coin Hades had given me and stared at it. I couldn't stop thinking about him or his claims of the Underworld. When I calmed, I eased into traffic again. But my thoughts returned to the stranger once more. He'd offered to reward me for helping him. And who didn't like money?

Red and blue lights flashed behind me. Probably an ambulance. I flicked on my indicator and slowed to pull to the side of the road. But when I glanced in my rearview, a squad car had pulled up behind me.

Junipers!

That'd teach me to pay attention. I'd already had three warnings.

I tossed Hades coin in the center console, switched off the ignition, sighed, and leaned my forehead against the steering wheel. I really didn't need this on top of everything else.

At the knock on the driver's side window, I looked up at the officer, a middle age man with a moustache that would have made Sam Elliott jealous.

I wound down the window.

"License and registration, please," he said. "Nice and slow, ma'am."

I reached for my handbag, removed the requested ID, and handed them to him.

He pulled his head back and squinted, apparently overdue for reading glasses. "You were doing forty in a thirty zone."

Pearl got fined eighty bucks for a measly five miles an hour over the limit. For ten, I was bound to get a couple of hundred dollar fine for sure.

I wiped my sweaty palm on my dress. What I wanted to say was, "I just lost my job, sir. I wasn't concentrating." But it came out as "No, sir gafjdjdjdjd."

The officer recorded my details on a form, tore off a carbon copy and handed it back with my ID. "Next time, slow it down."

I looked at the ticket and banged my head against the headrest. A two hundred dollar fine I couldn't afford. Unless I wanted to eat every third day for the next two months. Maybe less since my impending loss of income made the math of fasting for dollars trickier. I knotted my fists, tempted to swear, but didn't. No point. He wouldn't take the ticket back anyway.

I glanced at the gold drachma Hades had given me. Now it seemed even more tempting. I was going to regret this, but with all the common sense God had given a fruit bat, I sighed. Wasn't going to be pretty. Probably nothing would happen anyway.

But... "All right, Hades. Let's talk."

He materialized beside me, and my pulse thrummed a can-can tempo. Oh, but for the power to summon a hot guy at will.

"Very well." A ghost of a smile traced his lips.

The ground shifted underneath me. It triggered my pure panic, and I screamed as the world warped. When everything stopped spinning, I groaned, my palms, cheek and front of my body flat against something icy and hard.

I waited a few moments for my vision to stop whirling. A long hall full of shiny black marble stretched out in front of me. The floor was cool under my cheek, and the thought of staying there for a while made my head stop aching.

Then I remembered what had happened at Mama Tickey's and shot up into a sitting position. Graceful columns held up the enormous arched ceilings, each one beautiful but cold, sparking a sense of incredible loneliness inside me. Green flames burned on the scones braced along the walls, providing light to the long hall. Tiles painted with blossoms trailed along the centerline of the walls. Rectangular mosaics patterns stretched along the floor, consisting of waves on the outside, then a row of straight lines that looked like a maze.

Needs a few plants, I thought aimlessly, admiring the ceiling. *That'd probably help... wait. Does he get any light here?* I glanced around, searching for windows, finding two at the other end of the hall. Arched structures with pediments on top, one a half circle, the other a sharp pattern that looked like angel wings.

Gold-leafed vines weaved around columns. Flowered patterns on the ceilings, twinkling in the green light, caught my attention. Closer inspection revealed them to be made from thousand of jewels: all the wealth of the Underworld. I gaped at the detail and intricacy of the place, which must have taken hundreds of years to construct.

I rubbed my forehead while turning around, climbing halfway to my feet, but wobbling from dizziness.

"I forgot that teleportation is not easy the first time," Hades said from behind me.

I closed my mouth as he stretched out his hand, helping me to rise. That sensation hit again—warmth, falling, and pleasure.

"Impressive digs you've got." I brushed myself of the fine coating of dust on my dress. I mean, I half expected wails of pain from tortured souls or something because of how strict Hades came across. And on that note, I mental noted every possible exit, just in case.

"The cleaning staff around here are terribly unreliable," Hades grumbled, clicking his fingers. A green flame crawled over me, and I gasped, whacking it. It removed any trace of dust and then went out.

Okay. Now I was really starting to believe this might be the Underworld.

I wanted to say thank you, but all trace of my voice had vanished along with his magical flame.

If I thought his magic was impressive, then I'd been blind. When my gaze glazed over Hades, my eyes widened and I swear I started to drool. Whatever he was the lord of, it was apparently the king of the quick change. Back in the world, he'd worn a suit too expensive to be anywhere near appropriate for a funeral. Here, wherever here was, there wasn't a need to pretend any longer, so he wore a long robe draped and clipped at one shoulder, the fabric pure white and edged with black. Pinned with a golden brooch studded with small red rubies, his outfit emphasized his muscular form. My eyes traced his bare arms, and the broadness of his hips and shoulders before I landed on his slightly smug expression.

Ugh.

Hades didn't need to be told he looked good. He knew it. And I wasn't going to give a prodigious ego another boost.

"Welcome." He inclined his head. "Come. We can speak in my study."

When he started to walk, I hung back. It had been ages since I studied and Greek mythology, but I still remembered a few things. But the mosaics on the walls reminded me of all its glory. Depictions of famous Greek heroes: Hercules fighting the Nemean lion, Achilles fighting in the Trojan War and Hector and the Golden Fleece. Then I came to an image of a Hades in his chariot, kidnapping Persephone and spiriting her to the Underworld and forcing her to marry him. This was followed by another impression of Hades offering the goddess a pomegranate.

"So, um, are you married?" I asked. "Is there going to be a super-pissed off goddess of the springtime who doesn't want me spending time with her husband?" Pure clarity. Nothing to do with anything that resembled interest. Or attraction. Or sexual... nope. Not going there.

Hades stopped but didn't turn around, as still as the statues of famous gods in the pantheon in the recesses of the walls.

Oh no, I said something to upset him.

Eventually, he turned his head toward me. I couldn't read much from his expression, but what I could make out was calm as a deep pond.

"I am not married." His short, sharp answer implied

deeper words like *vicious divorce*, or *she set my collection of Bon Jovi cds on fire before she left me for a Lithuanian bodybuilder*. Wait. A god like Hades wouldn't own a Bon Jovi CD. He'd probably listened to ancient music like Mozart of Burt Bacharach. Music aside, his answer, and the tone delivered, told me he wasn't happy with the outcome, but faulty relationship aside, I *probably* wasn't going to be smited (smote?) by some jealous goddess.

As such, I didn't need further clarification. For now. "All right."

This place was huge. Historical. Museum-worthy. Perfect architecture. Every statue in its niche, every artifact preserved. Classy for a place called the Underworld.

"Do you like it?" Hades asked as we walked through the halls, covered in unimaginable artworks, mirrors, vases and other decorations. A breeze ruffled the silky curtains hanging in the windows.

"You already know it's beautiful." All this ego stroking was beneath both of us.

"But do *you* like it?" An odd question. And if I said no was he going to rush out for new curtains? I was relatively sure hellfire and brimstone lurked somewhere, but if so he'd disguised it with a big dose of perfection.

I replied to his back, frowning. "It's fine."

"But?"

"I'm not an interior designer but…" I put my hands on my hips and looked around. "Okay, so maybe I want to get a sharpie and doodle some mustaches on those statues."

"Really? You don't like them?" His voice, instead of being shocked or horrified at the idea of vandalism, was amused or perhaps even indulgent.

I raised an eyebrow and cast my gaze over the hint of chest showing through his toga. "I'm not a prude or anything but did you people not have clothes?"

He chuckled at that.

I lifted my chin. "It's what happens when anyone sees anything that's too perfect. Sometimes, you just want to mess it up a little."

"Really?"

"You could stand to be messed up a bit," I muttered.

"What was that?"

"Nothing at all."

"You are terrible at lying," he said, causing me to make a coughing noise that I decided passed as an answer.

To my relief, we arrived at what appeared to be his study, which was as surprising as it was cozy, with a desk, shelves lined with books across all the walls, and an enormous window that opened up to a balcony that overlooked white fields. Not exactly the space I would have expected the Lord of the Underworld to have in his palace.

I gravitated to the balcony, placing my hands on the cold stone, looking down onto the field of white below. Flowers—tall, white, and gorgeous—and they covered the hills outside Hades' study as thickly as the fur on a cat's back. As a florist, I should have known, but I'd never seen anything like them before. They had a slight splotchy redness to them, and they waved lightly in the wind, incredibly beautiful and tempting to see up close.

Hades came up beside me.

"What are those?" I asked him.

"The old word for them is eberium," he said dismissively. "The happy dead, some of them at least, wander there."

I squinted, examining the field for spirits. "There are... dead people out there?"

"You can't see them, but they're there."

But I saw Mr. Parsons back at the funeral home... "Can you see them?"

"When they want to be seen. Humans have hurt them and it makes them wary."

I gripped the balustrade tighter, alarmed by the idea of invisible dead people wandering through the flower fields, but the matter-of-fact way Hades said the last line made my heart ache.

I checked again, and this time I caught wisps floating through the meadows. White apparitions, fading in and out of sight.

My gaze returned to the beautiful flowers. Mom had always loved white lilies. The thought made me wonder if my mother was down there somewhere. If she was, I wanted to go to her right away.

"This is my realm," Hades intoned, almost to himself. "I was… chosen a long time ago for this position. I rule it well, or at least I do no worse than those who came before me, and I like to think that the dead are satisfied. The ones who come here, at least."

"Don't they all come here?" I had questions. A lot of questions. Like why I'd found myself flat on my face in the halls of an expansive palace. Why we couldn't have our chat in my neighborhood instead of his. And why the ornate fireplace, carved with figures battling each other, suddenly had small green flames in it. Oh, and some more personal stuff I'd never have the courage to ask. But one question in particular burned with a kind of hope I felt was childish, but I didn't want to ask it. Heat burned in the apples of my cheeks as I bit my lip, and before I could embarrass myself, Hades shook his head.

"Some do," he said. "Others go to nearby lands belonging to a different pantheon that I do not rule. It depends on which pantheon they were born into. You were born into the Greek Pantheon." He paused then moved to stand beside me.

LADY OF THE UNDERWORLD

Our gaze met and his eyes lightened a fraction as if he pitied me.

If my mother was here, then I couldn't leave without visiting her. I had to see her. Just one last time.

"Your mother is not here if that's what you're wondering," Hades said.

My heart split in two at his words. He looked away as I stared out the window, composing myself while releasing the fabric of my dress that I'd bunched in my grasp.

"Where is she?" I asked. "Which afterlife did she go to?"

His eyes flared green. "She first incarnated in this world in the Ancient Egyptian pantheon. Therefore she belongs to Osiris' Underworld. Every ancient civilization has one from the Greeks, Romans, Norse, Celtic, Asian, Aztecs etc."

"Oh." I ran my finger along the balcony, trying not to cry. "Don't suppose you could hook me up with a meeting with Osiris then?"

"Perhaps something could be arranged," Hades said softly. "If you agree to help me."

That was a bargain I'd be more than willing to make.

"Let's talk then." I composed myself, wiped at my eye, sniffed, then returned back to his office.

"Are you cold?" he asked. "Let me warm the room for you." He clicked his fingers and the green flames in his fireplace roared. Heat blasted from the fireplace and chased away the chill that had settled in me from the news about my mother.

So hospitable. I smiled at Hades.

He sat down in the chair in front of his fireplace and gestured for me to do the same. I traced the faces carved into the wood of the chair before sitting.

"I've spent a long time doing this job," he began, "and now, a few souls, like Alan Parsons, who are meant to heed my call and come to me for judgment, are not arriving in my realm."

I had to bury any thought of my mother deep to concentrate. Then I remembered Mr. Parsons and his desperate desire to see his family. I knew how he felt, that desperate longing to see them one last time.

I swallowed hard. "You mean… like they're getting lost."

His eyes flicked up toward my face, his expression blank. It made my stomach plummet, and I almost stepped toward him before I remembered myself and stayed where I was.

"Something like that." His voice dropped. "It is hard to explain… to anyone, actually. I always know when a soul has passed because my magic carries them to my world. But these souls slid under my radar, so to speak. My realm aches in their absence." He paused to pace the length of the room. "I don't expect you to understand."

Oh, but I did. I felt the hollow ache in my chest beyond my mother's absence. Something far more greater reaching than my own loss. A chasm of darkness and endless loneliness. A jewel split down the middle that lost is other half and never stopped searching for it.

"No, I might," I said. "You're describing grief, you know."

Hades scowled at me more expressively than he had before. Maybe I should've been a more alarmed at having a death god stare at me with such intensity, but I was right, and I knew it.

"You miss them," I pressed. "I don't know how it works, and I don't know what it means or how it feels to you, but you miss them."

Hades crossed the space between us. For such a tall man, he moved quickly. One second, he was looking at me as if he couldn't believe what he saw, and the next, he was right on top of me, his fingers curled around my wrist. It didn't hurt, but it was clear I wouldn't be able to pull away without a struggle.

This close, I could smell him—earthy, like rolls of cinnamon bark, fresh loam for a potted plant, a hint of sweetness like jasmine blossoms, and a touch of spice. He held me so close that if I wanted to, I could reach out and press my lips against his bare bicep. Struggling was the last thing I wanted to do. I glanced up at him, swallowing hard.

His gaze dropped to the floor. "You know nothing about…"

I touched a nerve, one endless, and sizzling with resentment.

He gripped my wrist tighter. We both felt it then, I knew it. Less dramatic than the moment before, but still exceptional, we stared at each other. The only thing in the world I wanted was to be close with him, to find out what it would be like to touch him. God, he had a beautiful mouth. Not much I wouldn't have given up to kiss him. To taste him. To feel him sigh against my lips. My thoughts raced as I fought my desire…

Hades let go of me and I staggered as he returned to his seat. The way he turned away to gather his thoughts made him almost endearing.

I studied him quietly. "I know a lot about grief and missing my mom."

He stared at me, his face slack. "What are you talking about?"

He was bluffing. I smiled at how he concealed his emotions. But somehow, I had scratched away at his frostiness, revealing the pain I suspected he guarded below.

"But what do I know?" I replied. "I don't know anything about this world of yours."

I was still sure I was right but didn't push it, especially not when an unexpected rawness flashed in his eyes. If he was grieving, or doing whatever the immortal equivalent looked like, he didn't need me staring and poking at him like I thought it was funny.

After a few moments, he sighed and his face relaxed, while still managing to remain wary at the same time. Hades wasn't a man—or god, I supposed—who did anything without knowing why he was doing it. *Hah!* Little old me threw him for a loop and I liked it!

"We need speak no more of it," Hades declared, as if the matter were settled. "Anyway, I've brought you here for a reason."

"Because you need my help with your little problem?" I prompted, intrigued, because what I could possibly do to assist the Lord of the Dead.

"Yes." Hades sat down across from me. Cool. Neutral. But at the same time anxious. Maybe even desperate. This day couldn't have been anymore normal for him than it was for me so I let him have a moment to compose himself.

He took a deep breath. "First, no more games. What are you?" The question he never seemed to tire of asking. Same question for which I didn't have the answer.

"I'm a hippie at heart," I said, and he shook his head. "I like dressing vintage. Exhibit A." I held up a foot so he could see my 1950s sandals.

That didn't get a reaction. Normally my humor got a good laugh. Tough crowd. Extremely tough crowd.

"I love plants," I continued, "and own twelve rare species, which I keep in a makeshift greenhouse on my balcony. On my days off, I attend rallies to save forests from being bulldozed for development, and on the odd occasion, I have been known to chain myself to old trees to protect them. I may have an arrest on my record for it." I paused and waited for a reaction that after an entire minute didn't seem to be coming. "Hope that doesn't disqualify me from helping you, because I'm still interested."

He tilted his head as if to say, *"And?"*

Geez, what more did he want from me?

I threw my hands in the air. "I'm a plain, old human."

He leaned back in his chair with an air of impatience, tapping his fingers, mouth drawn and tight. "No, you are not. No human could have seen Alan Parsons. That means that you're something else."

"Beats me." I reclined beside him, minus the stiffness. "Psychics can see ghosts, you know. Maybe I'm one of them. But today was certainly a first."

The skin around Hades' eyes tightened. "No human can survive the touch of the dead."

I glanced at my shoulder where Mr. Parsons had touched me.

"Look, Mom was a human, and as far as I know, so was my Dad. Unless they were secretly aliens. So guess what that makes me?" My pulse tripped and a flush of heat flamed my neck. I was starting to feel irked. "You're the God. You tell me what I am."

"In the old days, before my time, the gods would come to Earth," Hades explained, almost to himself. "Some of them took human forms and lay with them."

I yelped. "My *mother* was a demigod?"

A thin smile stretched across his face that reminded me how very quaintly human I was. "It might have been your father. Athena was born from the head of Zeus, and I'm led to believe that was a messy, bloody business…"

Oh, Hell no! I could see Mom in the robes, sunning herself in the field of those white flowers outsides. Harder to picture Dad. "My Dad was no saint. Zeus was a bit of a douchebag wasn't he? Raped maidens and goddess? My dad is a jerk, nowhere near the caliber of Zeus, but he could be a son of his."

Hades cast his gaze downward. When he looked up again, I caught his soft smile before his face morphed back into its usual all business expression of semi-frown, narrowed eyes. "For now we shall set aside the truth regarding how you have your powers."

"Oh, we shall?" I muttered, but he continued, ignoring me.

"We'll simply test the ones you know you have."

I gulped. "What exactly are you testing?"

CHAPTER 8

*A*utumn

HADES LEANED over his desk and snapped his fingers. The tap of claws on the floor behind me forced me to turn and face a beast, staring me down. A three-headed dog about the size of a small pony, and easily two or three times as heavy as I was. Any of the various heads could bite one of my arms off.

"Son of a–" I gripped the arms of the chair, and my nails dug in. I pushed it backward away from the beast and the legs scraped on the marble.

The dog (dogs?) sniffed the air, and at a low whistle from Hades, stepped toward me. Before it could come very far, however, it dropped its heads as if looking for a specific scent... and then all three sets of eyes locked on me.

Junipers!

I pushed my seat back until it hit the fireplace, and I remembered the fire and didn't want to burn to death and end up in whatever Underworld I belonged to. It was certainly not my time just yet. Eyes glued to the dog, I reinstated the chair to its rightful position.

"He's not going to hurt you." His voice sounded far away, and God help me, there was a hint of amusement in it. If I turned around and found him laughing, he was going to see some seriously divine rage. But first, I had to deal with the *three-headed dog* creeping at me.

"Okay. Okay." I'd volunteered at an animal shelter as a teenager. I could handle this. My wobbling legs didn't think so, but I'd prove them wrong.

Hades gasped when I stood, presenting the dog with my side, and only glanced toward it. Non-threatening. Like they'd taught at the shelter.

"Hey, what's your dog's name?" My voice shook, and I cleared my throat, trying to get rid of that. Animals communicated through basic instincts like fear, and if I showed any, it might prompt this three-headed beast to view me as its prey. And I was no dog's dinner.

"Cerberus, the Hound of Hades." He nodded to the dog. "Guardian of the River Styx."

"What's with all the fancy titles?" I rolled my eyes.

The dogs gave a growl in protest.

Okay. Okay. Don't mock the names. Got it.

Hesitantly, I offered the back of my hand, curling my fingers to protect them from a bite. One head, the left, leaned forward for a curious sniff. That was good. Real good.

"Oh, you like the fancy titles, huh?" I said in a slightly singsong way.

Cerberus twisted its second head, the middle one, at me, and I sat still, unable to look any of them in the eye.

"Hey, Cerberus," I greeted.

All three heads lifted, their six ears springing up at the mention of its name.

LADY OF THE UNDERWORLD

I glanced at its body, not making eye contact. "Hi there, sweet boy."

Two of the heads made soft grunt-whines that I recognized as curiosity, presumably in response to my soft and encouraging voice. Good. Curious was better than nervous. The head on the far right had its ears back. When I turned to examine it, I found white caps across his pupils. Less good.

"Come here, sweet boy." I patted my leg. "I'm a pal, right? My name's autumn. Want to be my friend? I love dogs, and I want to meet you all so much."

Hades startled with a choked cough, but I was so intent on getting Cerberus to relax and come over and not eat me in the process.

I waited until the single tail wagged before I reached out again for the other heads to inspect. They accepted, fighting for space to take in my scent.

"Come on, baby," I cooed. "I have so many pats just for you, yeah? Come over. Your owner's being a weirdo. Don't leave me all alone with him."

Center woofed in agreement. That won a laugh from Hades. Before I knew it, three hundred pounds of dog romped up to me. I braced myself, but they stopped at my feet, eyes bright and two out of three mouths open in wide doggy smiles. Right still hung back—probably stiff and cold like his owner—but his ears rose and he'd lost that nervy look that meant he might tear into anyone who came too close.

"Aww, you're just a big puppy, aren't you?" I reached out my hand. "Aren't you just a big, sweet boy?"

Left and Center jostled for space under the petting hands. I chuckled. It reminded me of a lap full of puppies, only they were enormous. I cooed at them, digging my fingers into their scruffs and behind their ears. Hades approached. He reached a large pale hand to scratch Right under the jaw.

Immediately, Right lost that nervy look, its eyes going soft and mouth gaping open, suddenly acting like the softest puppy.

Hah! A sucker for his daddy. "Well, no wonder the poor baby is so nervous about strangers. You should–"

Hades' laughter, although soft, and maybe mocking, tickled my ears and buzzed through me. "What? And take him to a dog park? Get my many friends to come over and pet him? Get him used to friendly company?"

"This says way more about you than me." My turn to laugh now. But stopped after a quick moment. Best not to rub it in to a god that he was an irresponsible pet owner. Judging by the stale, god-awful dog breath, this poor bunch of dogs hadn't had a decent bone in a millennium. Well, I'd see what I could do about that.

"Likely. Here, you probably smell enough like the other ones now." He took my hand in his, sending that soft shiver through me again. Torrential. Powerful Wow. And we apparently made a silent pact to ignore it.

With my hand in his, Hades let Right sniff my palm, and then laid it on Right's head. The third, initially recalcitrant head whimpered with happiness as he nosed up underneath my hand. Soon, I had three happy dog heads vying for my attention.

"He just… needs more time," Hades suggested vaguely.

"Oh, he does?" I asked, wondering if the Lord of the Underworld was hinting at something.

"Yes."

Then suddenly, because someone was jealous their master had gotten all the attention, Center shoved his nose under my palm, whimpering ecstatically, making the entire body wiggle with happiness. It broke the tension, and I started to laugh, relieved, but regretful as well. While I was distracted with his dog, Hades took a step back.

Whatever was on his face before vanished, and his mouth pressed into a firm line. He stood up briskly, acting like he had come to a decision.

"I have one more test for you."

"What kind of test?" I asked.

"I have seen how you relate to the dead." So casual when he spoke. But for me, just the phrase *relate to the dead* was … odd, much less the fact I was doing it. Well, he dealt with death every day, so it wasn't unusual for him. "And the Guardian of the Underworld likes you, so that is a good start."

I failed to see how the Cerberus meet-and-greet related to my interactions with the dead souls, but anyway.

"I need to know how you handle them before I make my decision."

"Okay." I didn't know what else to say.

"It's time for the judgment of fresh souls."

CHAPTER 9

*H*ades

I summoned Charon, who waited atop his rocking ferry on the banks of the River Styx.

"Bring me the dead."

Souls huddled behind him, some stretching out their necks to see, others clutching the dead person next to them, while some stood alone, glowering.

Cerberus growled at one and they retreated from the edge of the boat. I kept my eye on that one. A young man of about twenty-eight. My guardian had a good nose for souls with a penance to pay in the afterlife.

If I were inclined, I could pry into his history and debate his actions, but I left that to my three demigods. Rhadamanthys, Minos, and Aiakos sat on golden chairs below my dais, each clasping a golden scepter of judgment.

I cared not for the fate of the dead or their ultimate resting places. I entrusted those decisions to my wise judges.

I ensured the realm's smooth operations so that the souls of good heart found peace and returned to the Land of the Living in a new life, and souls who had wreaked atrocity upon others sought forgiveness and spent time dwelling on the path of deliverance.

With a nod, Charon threw a rope over the pole stuck in the ground, securing his boat. "Late today, master?" he croaked.

Normally, the Underworld operated like clockwork. Judgment first thing in the morning, running until midday. Punishment in the afternoon. Relaxation in the evening. I hated to delay any of the servants of the afterlife. But after the alarming news from the avatar of Hermes, I had to investigate, thus throwing the day's proceedings off schedule. But we were here now for the judgment.

"And we have a guest." The ferryman's cloak twisted to the right in Autumn's direction on the throne of Persephone, Lady of the Underworld.

My eyes fell to the jewel-encrusted gold seat, equally as magnificent as my own, but decorated with fine vines wrapping around the crest of the back. For five hundred years, the chair had been stored in a locked room somewhere in the palace, because the god within me couldn't bear the *torture* of its cold and lonely gold by his side. Today, I ordered my servants retrieve it for Autumn. An honor for my guest. The god buried himself deep within me, unable to look upon the reminder of his absent wife.

She didn't hear Charon rasp because she was busy admiring the armor I had changed into. Her eyes caressed me from neck to knee. A vest, open at the chest, overlain with armor, made from leather and the strongest metals on the earth. She gazed at the prongs on my shoulders, at the patches of my chest between the lapels of the vest, down my arms to my gloves.

I tilted my head, lifting an eyebrow as her gaze travelled lower, at my apron, consisting of a series of leather lappets, ornamented with hand-carved metal. My judgment outfit. Conveyed my strength and power as master of this realm. Said the new souls must obey. When our eyes met, she sat straighter, cleared her throat, and turned her body to face the room.

"Who are we judging today?" She tilted her head side to side, raised her eyebrows, scanning the row of waiting souls. All an act to pretend I hadn't caught her studying... no... ogling me.

She certainly had a way about her. Stubborn and strong-willed. A lot like... *no... don't say her name.* I didn't want to think about her. *She* was gone. The god didn't need another knife to his heart. But having such a special human as lovely as Autumn with powers that complimented my own, filled me with a warmth I'd not encountered in centuries.

"Welcome, Great Lady." Charon bowed and then waved over his shoulder at the waiting souls to descend from his boat.

The dead trailed behind him, glancing with wonder at the tall ceilings, pillars, and golden statues of Zeus in one corner, Poseidon in another, and my own in a third. Other lesser gods posed against the fourth wall, silent and ever watchful. Through these statues, the gods, the elementals in the heavens above, could witness today's judgment.

My mind returned to why I had brought Autumn here. I had a theory about her identity, the reason the she could see the dead, and why they didn't harm her. The earlier encounter with Cerberus had fueled this theory. Only the Lord and Lady of the Underworld commanded the servants of this realm, like the hellhound.

Through this next task, I intended to test her instincts with the souls. Already she had demonstrated an innate ability to deal with the dead—a useful talent that could be of assistance to me if I were to venture again to the Land of the Living to retrieve more souls and bring them to their final resting place. I'd never had to perform such a task before, and this morning's events had demonstrated my lack of success at it. If Autumn proved to be who I thought her to be, then I needed her help.

Charon stopped at the foot of the dais and faced the souls. "Stand in line and await your judgment."

The fifty or so souls fell in single-file, each one huddling close together. Some shook, some stared, and some fidgeted with nerves. Only fifty. An easy day. We could finish in a couple of hours, leaving me free to make my proposal to Autumn, return her to the Land of the Living, and then retire to my chambers for an early night.

I noticed Alan Parsons in the middle of the line, and I glared at him, touching my jaw, remembering where he had hit me. On severe occasions, I could intervene against my judge's decisions, and assign a punishment I saw fit. Unfortunately, no soul had ever accosted the Lord of the Dead before, and no such rule existed to justify hanging Alan Parsons on the torture rack for such an offence. Maybe I could get him on some other heinous act committed in his lifetime. I'd await for his soul parchment.

Today had been eventful. I wasn't used to souls refusing my orders or punching me. Maybe I was losing my touch. Something I needed to rectify immediately. I couldn't have disorder in my realm, nor could I foster weakness regarding my reputation. Time to reassert my authority.

"Isaac Thornton," Aiakos announced, crossing his golden scepter over his chest. "You are hereby judged for your transgressions."

The green flames in the pit before the dais roared in response.

Rhadamanthys, my second arbitrator, lifted a golden scroll made of light. The soul's contract, listing the man's history of deeds both good and bad. My judges highlighted the important ones which they felt best represented the character of the soul.

"You cheated your brother out of his inheritance," Rhadamanthys began, reading from the list of offenses. "And ran over your neighbor's cat but did not tell them. You also owe seven hundred dollars in parking tickets."

Autumn gasped and I glanced at her.

This soul had insecurity and lack of virtue etched into the very fabric of his being. Any threat to his security, and he would cheat and lie to wriggle free. Stealing from his brother had been just the beginning. I wanted to see if she sensed these same qualities or sensed the soul's misdeeds. This would prove her identity beyond a shadow of doubt.

Minos, the third judge, tapped his scepter against his seat several times before delivering. "You shall spend the next hundred years in the Fields of Mourning."

"It is so." I stood, descending the steps to face Isaac. "We will assess your repentance in a century."

I reached out to touch him and send him to a resting place when Autumn interrupted. "Just like that? No attorney? No fair trial?"

All three judges stared at her. No one had dared question their decision before. To debate my appointed judges, whom I had trusted for millennia, equaled disrespect. Only the Lord or Lady of the Underworld could get away with such a challenge.

A smile curled on my lips as I brought my fingers together, waiting for her opinion.

"Don't you also judge him on the good things he did?" She leaned forward in her seat. Her eyes filled with that fire, that passion that had bewitched me.

"He was a good father to his three sons."

Autumn jerked her head backward and her eyes went round. She clearly didn't know how she knew the details about the soul or why she had leaked them. But I did. Now I knew who she represented. After a few seconds, she lifted her head, gazing at me with fiery and challenging eyes that reminded me of the goddess.

I smiled, knowing she had a lot to learn about who she was becoming. Whose powers she had inherited. The legacy she had to bear. There hadn't been an avatar like her in hundreds of years. The goddess had returned at last. Her husband rejoiced inside of me. They hadn't spoken in six hundred years. Far too long. I needed Autumn even more now to determine what was happening to the Underworld.

"That is not the essence of his soul," Minos argued with her.

"Only one good deed of few." Rhadamanthys held up the scroll with the long list of bad deeds beneath the three good deeds at the top (two of which were from his childhood and didn't count because they were outweighed by the number of bad).

"Fine. Carry on then." Autumn puffed out her cheeks and leaned back in her chair.

"My lord," Aiakos pleaded, his cheeks and neck redder.

I opened my mouth to speak when the soul shouted, "Wait! I want to bargain."

My jaw tensed, and I swiped my bident from the side of my throne to calm me. Clever little manipulator. He'd read up on me. Hades, Lord of the Underworld, was also a god of deals, and the souls of myth sometimes made bargains with him.

"Speak," I said, my voice strained. I didn't like bargaining with souls. They always asked for less penance or to see their family one last time.

My judges watched Isaac intently.

"I want my good deeds to be judged," Isaac, the soul undergoing judgment, proposed. "Like the lady says."

I squeezed my bident handle, and it creaked under my touch. "In return for what?"

"For a lesser sentence," Isaac cried.

Almighty Olympus!

I flicked my fingers, allowing it. Strict, but fair, but I glared at Autumn for giving the soul the idea.

For the next few moments, the judges weighed up Isaac's good deeds, lowering his sentence by one hundred years. Once the amendment was recorded on the golden scroll, I touched his shoulder, and he faded away, transferred to the fires of the Field of Mourning to reflect on his actions until he showed any remorse or shame for his wrong doings.

While the proceedings continued, I admired Autumn as she watched with intent interest in the judgment. This woman was no mere mortal. At first, I'd suspected she possessed clairvoyant gifts, able to see and communicate with the dead. But no. Only the Lady of the Underworld could read a soul. Or her avatar. The Lady of Spring, the goddess whose name I dared not speak, had chosen Autumn.

I grasped at the sudden sting in my chest. How would I tell Autumn of this crucial detail? I couldn't. To do so meant I had to speak the name I had banned in my realm for centuries. The name that had dried on my tongue, crumbled to ash, and blown away in the wind.

My head spun with a combination of mine and the god's emotions. Confusion. Heartache. Rejection. All the pain of the goddess' departure resurfaced in face of the discovery of her newest avatar. Perhaps, I should've returned Autumn to the Land of the Living and corralled souls alone. I could remain cold and frozen, hidden from the touch of pain, and trapped by the god's longing torture.

I didn't want to feel again. Not after my wife had been torn from me, leaving my heart bleeding and desiccating on the ground.

When Autumn touched me, her avatar magic had brought me to life again, like a flower in spring, basking in the warmth of the sun. And I wanted her. Wanted her because those emerald eyes burned a hole through me. Her green hair smelled of flowers. She made my heart flutter. And her voice, like the comforting patter of rain during the first of spring. They weren't the only reasons I craved her, however. The essence of the goddess inside her enchanted me once more, and I hungered for her touch. Fate in Greek mythology dictated the Lady and Lord were destined for each other. That complicated matters when it felt like I betrayed my wife's memory. Even after all this time I had not processed my grief or let her or my child go.

That wasn't my only issue. Every night when loneliness consumed me, I fought a losing battle against my heart. It was time the god and I forgot about the goddess. Accept that she wasn't coming back to him, and only restoring her essence to her avatars. We had to move on. I couldn't have Autumn by my side to collect the souls when she would remind me of what I'd also lost in my human life every passing minute—of what I missed and craved. No. I had to send her away. Forget about her.

"Continue the judgment without us," I ordered my three judges, climbing the stairs and gesturing for Autumn to come with me. "Send the souls where they need to go."

"My lord," Minos started, but I didn't bother looking at him. "You cannot leave the ceremony."

As I studied her face, Autumn bit her lip, her bewilderment evident.

"Back to the Land of the Living." I led her out of the chambers.

When we were a safe distance from the judgment hall, she asked, "Did I do something wrong?"

"No." I gripped her wrist to stop myself from pressing her against the walls and kissing her—and keeping her here forever. So I would never be alone again.

"Why are we going back?" she asked, rushing to keep up.

I growled. "Because I should never have brought you here in the first place."

Before she could say or do anything to convince me otherwise, I clicked my fingers, and we spiraled up through the earth and into the work truck she had left in the parking lot outside the diner.

She slumped against the steering wheel and groaned. "Warn me next time before you do that, okay?"

"Thank you," I whispered, touching her cheek with the back of my hand. She lifted her head to gaze at me. But I didn't want to see those eyes, shining like the finest emeralds. Bright green. More beautiful than any plant or jewel on this world. "Goodbye."

"Wait!" Her cry echoed in my mind as I transported myself elsewhere, following the call of another lost soul.

***

I STOOD IN THE DESERT, a war zone, untouched by the heat blazing down on the world. My body quivered and I hunched, unable to catch my breath. It felt like my heart had been ripped out all over again. I fell to my knees. Sand grazed my skin as I braced myself, staring at the tiny grains as if they held the answer. Each one had formed over millions of years and was as old as Hades.

I sucked in a painful breath. What had I done? I sent her

away. I didn't want to feel again. Didn't want to be hurt. Didn't want the misery.

Smoke burned my nose and glanced up from the ground.

An American military vehicle lay on its side. Dark fumes wafted off the half-exploded shell. Its rusted state implied the enemy must have struck it with a bomb six months ago or more. Now the locals had set it on fire in protest of how much they hated the western invaders. Among the wreckage, a soul leaned against the burning frame, cradling his weapon to his chest.

I crossed the distance to stand in front of him. "Come with me, Sergeant Jones," I ordered.

"Where's my squadron?" he asked, not bothering to look up.

"Long gone." I wasn't in the mood to argue. Lord of the Underworld. He who should have been obeyed. "Now come."

"No!" He flicked sand at me. "I won't leave my men."

I tuned my senses to focus on the men in his team. Two hundred miles from here. "They're safe on another mission to apprehend the men who did this to you."

"Did what?" The soldier glared at me, his brown eyes filled with contempt.

"Killed you."

"No... no. No!"

I leaned down to his level and touched him. The events of his death played in my mind. He and his team had crouched behind the vehicle for shelter as the enemy shot round after round at them. A missile ejected from a long projection device, screamed through the air, and hit the vehicle, slicing it in two. Sergeant Jones had been killed instantly. His men had been burned, shredded by shrapnel, but not enough for the touch of death to reach them. In the end, they were rescued by a helicopter that destroyed the enemy and carried away the wounded.

"The vehicle was cut open by an IED." As I explained the words, the military terms which I took from reading soul contract, the soldier shook his head. "The heat and force of it killed you."

"No." The sergeant's eyes were wild as he trained his weapon on me.

I pushed the muzzle aside. "That can't hurt me."

The gun clicked as the soldier tried to fire. He shook the gun and tried again with the same result. Enraged, his lips peeled back as he lifted the butt of the weapon to strike me.

I swiped it away with magic and rose to my feet. "This is the last time I'll ask. Come with me, soldier."

"I'm not dead!" he screamed.

"Yes, you are," I declared. "And I am The Lord of the Underworld, come to collect you and take you to the afterlife."

"No." The man started sobbing. "My wife. My baby."

"They're of no concern to you any longer," I said, holding out my hand and beckoning him.

"I can't!" he cried. "I can't leave them."

"You must."

He scrambled away from me.

Heat scaled my neck as my impatience intensified. Two souls had defied me today. Defied!

No more. I seized the soldier by the shoulder. I ruled with a firm hand, but never a vicious one. "You're coming with me."

Out of instinct, he shoved my arm in a defensive move he'd probably learned in his military training. But I was far stronger and resisted his blow. My magic carried him back to the Underworld.

When we appeared in the judgment room, my judges, along with the remaining souls waiting to be judged, stared at me.

"Deal with him immediately," I commanded my three judges.

"My lord," Aiakos began, "he must get in line."

I waved him away.

"Excuse me." I stormed out of the room, my breaths coming sharp and hard.

In the hall, I pressed my back to the wall and ran a hand through my hair then sucked in a deep breath to try to calm my raging pulse. My entire day had been out of the ordinary, starting with the intrusion by the Hermes avatar and ending with my rough handling of the soldier. Something wasn't right with my realm... with me. I never missed a soul. Never left one behind.

But what had shaken me the most was meeting Autumn, discovering her abilities, fighting the emotions she stirred in me. She'd not only charmed Alan Parsons into liking her, convincing him he had to leave the Land of the Living, but she had charmed me too. I needed her skills if I was going to fix the problem of the missing souls. Funny I'd never needed them before. As the Lord of the Dead, souls had always obeyed me. And my last efforts to retrieve two souls had gotten me almost nowhere except a punch in the face and a gun aimed at my chest!

I couldn't continue to let my authority slip away. I had to retain the Underworld through dignity and respect. Reclaim every last soul remaining on the Land of the Living. And, as much as I hated to admit it, I needed Autumn's help to do so.

CHAPTER 10

*A*utumn

"Oh, you're back," I said, downshifting to slow the flower truck. After everything that happened this morning, his sudden appearance didn't faze me much more than a couple extra blinks.

"I need your help." His eyes said he meant it. His voice said he didn't like it. Oh, what it must have cost him to return and admit it after he'd behaved so ridiculously back in the Underworld.

"Things in the Underworld not going your way?" I smiled because he was even beautiful when he frowned. As much as when he grinned.

He glared and I smiled again. And I waited for him to speak. Mostly because I wanted to hear his voice. .

"In light of… *everything*… I'm offering you a job."

Funny that. I needed a new job. But, instead of enquiring about the job, I pushed my luck. "Say you're sorry first. If I'm not mistaken, you threw me out of the Underworld." The goodbye at the end wasn't too bad, but he didn't need to how I felt about it. Yet. "I feel snubbed."

He sighed and rubbed his forehead. "You won't accept until I do?"

"Accept?" I jammed my foot on the brake, and he jerked forward. His forehead hit the sun visor. "You have a rather high opinion of yourself."

"I was wrong to have been so rude," he muttered.

"All right." I tempered my sass. "Tell me about this job."

"I'm attending to the issue of the missing souls across the Land of the Living," he began. "I could do with some help corralling the dead; and after what you demonstrated today, I'd like you to accompany me. You've been... helpful."

I had to laugh. Helpful.

"*Helpful* isn't what I would call it." God, I was going to bargain his ass.

He must have caught the slightly teasing tone in my voice. To my surprise, he eased up on all his Greek god stiffness enough to smile at me.

"Turns out I need a new job." He stared at me as I spoke and his gaze was the warm caress my skin needed. But thinking didn't work so well when I was so flustered. "I mean... I wasn't just... wandering around that funeral home for fun."

His eyebrow cocked with what was likely impatience.

"Well accept this one job." He shrugged as if he understood nothing about responsibility and good references.

"Uh-huh." I flicked on the indicator to turn left. We were two blocks away from Pearl's. "How about benefits? Retirement? Dental? Having a company pup, or three, is nice, but it doesn't really give me major medical."

Hades tented his fingers. "In return for your service, I'll

make sure you never have to work another day for the rest of your life."

Now he had my attention. I leaned forward, hunching over the steering wheel to glance at the sky. "Tell me more."

When I shot a cursory glance his way, he still stared at me, unblinking. "Two hundred drachma and whatever jewels you wish to take with you."

Drachma? Really? Couldn't pay Mrs. Minetti rent with drachma. Not without having to look for a new apartment. "What's the conversion rate for drachma these days?"

Hades glanced at the ceiling. "They are ancient coin. Worth a few million in your currency. Would you like a cost valuation?"

I gasped and almost crashed the damn van. A few million dollars! My hands trembled as I pulled the vehicle over to the curb. I left the engine running and wound down the window to hang my head out and breathe deep lungfuls of fresh air.

When I could talk, I mumbled, "Oh god."

"Yes?" He inched closer as if pressing me to agree.

"Well, I want everything in writing." I crossed my arms, hoping he might throw another hundred drachmae in as a bonus. "I need a binding contract and a valuation of the drachma. Then we can negotiate price, conditions, timeframe."

"Negotiate?" He said it with a haughtiness that suggested he'd never been turned down before.

But, I didn't throw my lot in with just anyone, and I certainly didn't make deals with the Lord of the Underworld every day. On the other hand, I could live with never having to work again. Or maybe I could buy Pearl out since she announced her retirement. I'd always wanted a shop of my own. But I was hiring someone to deal with Mr. Cotterly as a client.

I nodded at Hades. "This isn't going to be a forever job, is it? I don't want to lock myself out of any opportunities. I'll get bored with nothing to do but sweet-talk the dead. And if I have kids, that money isn't going to last long. Starts with diapers and rattles, then private school uniforms, ballet recitals or drum lessons, college, wedding, then grandkids. It never ends."

"Obviously." Hades fiddled with his fingers, looking up at me with a smirk.

God, I'd wanted him to smile again.

Stop it. Stop being a sucker for him because he's gorgeous when he smiles. Even more so with those deep brown eyes that drank me up...

"How long do you think this job will take?" Really, my question danced along the line of when could I buy Pearl out and get myself my own house with a garden?

He hesitated, glancing at me, and I realized how close to me he'd moved. He smelled of an intoxicating combination of the earthy scents of his realm, cinnamon, vanilla, and spices. The darkness in his eyes faded, revealing a softer brown similar to the shade of the soil I used to put my plants in.

He was looking at me like he felt my want and fear in equal measure. His lips were slightly parted, his breath light and shallow. His hands twitched as if he wanted to reach for me but didn't quite dare.

I didn't have any such reservations.

"Oh, beautiful," I murmured, my hand grazing over his hair, then falling to brush his cheek, my finger tracing the shell of his ear, or whatever he would let me touch...

"Tell them you'll be back in the spring." I shivered. The command. The firmness. "I'll have the contracts drawn and the proof of the drachma ready for you."

Ugh. Back to business. He pulled away as if to remain

professional even though I sensed he wanted to kiss me as much as I wanted to kiss him.

"All right." God. There went all my hard-thought negotiation! "But only because you said *sorry*."

***

THE OFFER CHECKED OUT, all right. More than checked out. Turned out that one ancient Greek drachma was worth fifteen thousand a piece. They were stamped with the image of Hades' bident on one side and a harp on the other and were made of pure gold. They had never been in circulation anywhere besides the Underworld. So, my payday was bumped to three and a half million for their rarity.

Of course, I made sure I added a bonus condition into my contract. For every soul retrieved, I got another fifty thousand in the bank. It wasn't like Hades couldn't afford it. He sat on a pile of gold. I, on the other hand, had to hide mine from the FBI through a series of cash-paid investments and safety deposit boxes, courtesy of the skills of an excellent accountant and lawyer.

Pearl was positively thrilled when I made the offer on her business. In cash no less. She stared at the sport's bag full of money, blinking for a moment, then she looked at me.

"Oh honey," she started, extending her hand to shake, and I did, sealing the deal. "I don't want to know which man you slept with to get this money, but I'm really happy for you." She hugged me so tight.

I hadn't dated in a while. And my secret garden could've used a good Spring Cleaning. Well, its first cleaning. I'd never gone *that far* with a guy. After my mom died, I'd been too scared to get serious with anyone, or to get too attached or get my heart crushed.

I blushed at her saying that. "Pearl! He's my business partner." Sort of true. Sort of a lie. But she didn't need to know the finer details. Call me a cheap floozy, but I wouldn't say no if he offered. He was a Greek God after all. A once in a lifetime opportunity.

Pearl pursed her lips and looked down at the counter. "Promise you'll come and visit me in Florida."

"You bet." I gave her a hug. No way I'd pass up an opportunity for some fun and some sun.

"Well, it's high time you were putting out." I coughed at her bluntness. Obviulsy this was how she would remember me. "How you ever expect to get anywhere with anyone without doing that is beyond me."

God, she made me laugh.

"Thank you again, Pearl." I smiled at her. "And thanks for looking after my plants."

I went back to my apartment that afternoon and checked my offshore bank account for the fifth time. Money from the sale of the drachma was already in, and… yeah, I just wanted to make sure it wasn't a dream. As long as this was real, I would be set up for a long time. And tonight, he'd scheduled my first collection.

Before he came to collect me, I watered my two dozen plants, making sure they'd survive a week without me. Then I took a nap. About an hour past sunset, I got a polite beep from my phone. Time to go.

As I made my way downstairs, backpack stuffed with clothes and toiletries, I wondered why he hadn't just magicked himself inside my apartment, like he had done in Pearl's van. Probably a good thing. It looked pretty shabby from the outside so I didn't blame him.

Hades waited for me in a sleek black Bentley that looked

like it ate lesser cars for dinner. Ohhh. Travelling in style. I liked it.

As I approached, he stepped out of the vehicle and came around to open the door for me. His dark crisp suit was back, which was just fine, but a part of me missed the robes and the teasing view they gave of his muscles and powerful chest. Sure, the suit made him look powerful and maybe just a bit predatory, but the toga and the armor… well… let's just say I had dreamed about it.

"What?" I said. "You mean you don't ride with the four horsemen of the apocalypse?"

"Not yet. Now, get in." His voice warmed me from earlobe to bootheel.

"No, seriously," I insisted. "You magicked me to the Underworld. Why do you need a car?"

"It's actually not a car." He clicked his fingers and I saw a flash of a black and gold chariot with two horses. Hades' chariot. I'd done a bit of homework in my spare time while I waited for Hades' payment to come through.

Rolling around in a gold chariot inlaid with jewels would probably raise some eyebrows. I liked the disguise. Pretty realistic. Too realistic if you ask me. I ran my hands along the shiny roof of the car. Cold and hard like metal.

I pointed my fingers to make the shape of a gun. "Gotcha."

"Besides, the teleportation made you ill." Aw. So thoughtful. I liked him even more. "Maybe when you can stomach it a bit more we can try again."

I ran my hands along the fine leather seats, then settled into the passenger one beside Hades. I could already tell I was going to enjoy traveling in style with him. "I think I like this for now."

He started up the car and pulled into traffic.

We drove on in silence until Hades cleared his throat. "There's a map in the glove compartment. Kindly pull it out and tell me which direction I need to go to get on the highway."

"But you've got a GPS." I pointed to unit combined with his stereo. How did a chariot even have a stereo… or leather seats come to think of it. But I shook aside those thoughts. Every else I'd encountered since meeting Hades had been unbelievable. This I just added to the pile.

He gave me a wry look with a twisted smirk. "This is a special map. One that shows the location of every soul belonging to the Greek pantheon. Alive or dead."

"Right." I found a map, a weighty piece of parchment rolled up in a leather sleeve. Small skull beads dangled from the cords that held it closed. "Oh, wow, this is a map…"

I unrolled it and whistled. Gorgeous, inscribed with all the roads—sparkling blue lines that represented the freeways, and green ones for the county roads. Names and designations were written in ink so sharp.

"Those black dots." I pointed to one in the next state. "I'm assuming they're the dead souls." There were so fewer of them across the country. About five in total compared to the red ones.

Hades nodded.

Then I pulled back my chin upon noticing something else.

"Your supernatural map has all the Waffle Houses listed." I glanced at Hades with my mouth open.

"In case you're hungry." He didn't look at me and his casual reply gave me the distinct impression he'd magically programmed this thing before we left.

Awww. How sweet. The stiff and stony god had an endearing side. Words I never thought I'd associate with a God of the Underworld.

"This is incredible," I said with a grin. "Thank you."

I wasn't joking. I liked Waffle House. A lot.

"Of course. Now, which way?" He gestured to the map. Always, back to business. "Press on the soul you'd like to retrieve and the map will do the rest."

Cool.

I scanned, checking for the closest black dot, and pressed my forefinger on it. Across the state, a tiny gold bead, glowing and pulsing gently appeared—our route to our destination. "West at the upcoming exit. Then follow that highway for three hundred miles. Where do you even get something like this? Did you make it yourself?"

"I…borrowed it…from Zeus."

I looked at him with narrowed eyes but paused to let him merge lanes before I spoke again. "That sounds an awful lot like you stole it from Zeus. Will I meet him, too?"

Wrong thing to say. Hades' lips thinned as he shook his head. "It's complicated."

"We've got time," I insisted, glancing back at the map and mentally calculating the approximate distance. "Looks like we're going to be on this stretch for, hmm… I would say about five hours?"

"You should get some sleep. I'll wake you when I need you again."

Touchy subject. Maybe one day he'd share the story. For now, I shrugged, rolled up the map and returned it to the glove compartment. I'd already taken a nap, but this florist was known to rise with the sun, and I was way up past my bedtime.

"You know, we could do this ten times faster if we teleported."

He glowered at me, and I honestly liked the way he did that. It tickled my insides. Damn. He wasn't going to budge.

"All right," I responded. "Wake me when you need me."

He made a soft acknowledging noise. As I settled back, I tucked my hands under my thighs, suppressing the urge to reach over and rest my hand on his thigh. I'd seen a friend do it when I rode with them to a concert, and right now, I wanted that kind of closeness. I didn't know why when I hadn't dated in three years. Wasn't interested. Didn't have the time. Hadn't met the right guy. But something about this man called to a deep and uncharted part of me. It made me want to do all sorts of new things with him. Get to know him better. Get closer. So much closer.

No, Autumn. That'd be kind of creepy to do it to my new boss. I was here to do a job, not get cozy with a God. Best to be professional.

I pushed the seat back and sank into the ridiculously soft leather. This seat was more comfortable than my bed.

"Poke me if I snore." He cut a sideways glance at me; it told me that no one had ever asked him that. Well, the last few days had been full of surprises for the Lord of the Dead. Undoubtedly, there would be more to come.

CHAPTER 11

Autumn

I FOUND myself walking through a forest dripping with hot steam, like a sauna or maybe the greenhouse Pearl sent me to sometimes to look over the stocks. The flowers around me bloomed with a lush exuberance and colors I'd never seen before. As I proceeded through the gorgeous greenery, I reached down to gently stroke the velvety petals and towering fronds, my fingertips coming away stained by golden grains of pollen. Stems and stalks brushed against my skirts as I went by.

Oh, very nice, very nice. It's so good to see everyone doing so well.

I hurried along the path as if I had someone to meet, and my bare feet dug into the dark earth. It had been such a long time since I was able to run anywhere without shoes. I lived in the city where outdoor barefoot running was just a silent way of asking for a foot full of glass; but here, there was no rubbish or litter or trash, just lush, healthy brown loam.

The forest opened up to a clearing, and a cool breeze dried the sweat on my skin.

Oh, that feels good. This is going to be so nice...

Up ahead, a void opened in the ground as if something enormous had been uprooted from the earth—a wound where there had once been something alive and growing. The violation, the sheer wrongness of its presence stabbed my heart, as my hands tried to piece the earth back together, to mend it.

"Shh, shh, I'll look after you," I murmured. "I'll take care of you."

Covered in dirt, my hands were warm, and I felt something wriggling inside of me that I couldn't understand. Soil. Millions upon millions of things traveled through it. Tunneling moles, ants bringing back food to their queen, burrowing earthworms, and all the little bacterial decomposers who worked hard to provide the nutrients the soil and plants needed. All of it to ensure the world didn't stop spinning. I knew how they felt. Knew how they moved. I was a part of them, and they of me. Whatever was beneath me was bigger, faster, and more frightening than any of them.

I should have pulled back, but I couldn't or wouldn't. Then it rose up, round and hard, and so cold under my fingers that I cried out in panic. It belonged to me, was coming back for me. I'd been wrong to bury it. Nothing stayed buried, nothing stayed inert. It wasn't the way of the world, and it wasn't the way of what had come back to me. In my hands I held something curved and white like bone... no, not *like*. It *was* bone—a skull. Oh, God, I was holding a skull in my hands, and someone had stuck marigolds in its eye sockets. Tangled with my horror was my helpless fury and offense.

A joke? Did they think that death was something cute and funny and beautiful?

In my fury, I dug my fingers into the skull, creating hairline cracks then crushing it like fragile clay. The moment I did so, however, I was consumed with horror and shame. I'd done something wrong. Unable to process my actions, I started to scream and cry, beating my breast with my fisted hand. My grief was powerful, intense. The only way I could dispel it was to scream, show the world how much it hurt, how unfair it was, and how brutal…

I woke up to my own wild cries, my shirt sticky with sweat. I was stuck in the moment with no past or future. I didn't know where I was. Didn't know what was going on. Why I was in a car pulled over to the side of the road with the blinkers clicking. Why someone's hands were around my shoulders. Through the haze, a man's dulcet voice whispered to me, telling me it would all be fine, even if I didn't fully understand the words he used.

Blinking hard, I cut off my own cries with a sudden surge of surprise. I looked into the deep pit of Hades' eyes, wide with alarm and worry.

"Darling, darling, it's all right." He repeated the words over and over again until finally, my brain registered.

When I stopped screaming, he cut himself off. He didn't let go of me, but I didn't want him to and I placed my hands over his. He swallowed, and I couldn't take my eyes off the movement of his Adam's apple. God, he was so buttoned-up. Literally. His tie looked as if it had been made of perfect geometric angles, and suddenly I couldn't stand it.

"You were so afraid." But that wasn't the reaction I wanted just then—not at all.

I reached for him, taking a handful of that perfectly pressed and starched shirt in my fingers. Somehow, I knew if he didn't want to move for me, he wouldn't. All that mattered was when I pulled, he came. One moment, he stared at me under the cast of the overhead light of the car, his hands on my shoulders, and the next he leaned in and kissed me as if his life depended on it. The searing intensity of it burned my lips, my throat, my entire body.

No sense of hesitation or nervousness existed. All my inhibitions disappeared. Only his mouth moving with mine mattered, the faint taste of something sweet—Underworld nectar wine perhaps—and his perfection. The kiss fired up the tension simmering between us ever since we first touched, reminded me of that roaring torrent of need. But this was nowhere close to enough to quench it.

His deep growl rumbled through me as he braced himself over me, pressing me back into the seat. In another world, I might have been nervous and startled. Despite everything that had passed between us so far, I really didn't know anything at all about him. All I knew right then was how incredible and hot this was.

His teeth grazed my lower lip, and I moaned. He slid his tongue between my lips, exploring me with a kind of need that made me weak. I reached for him, clinging to his broad shoulders and the strength in them, his need mirroring my own. There would never be any kind of guessing with Hades. Desire existed between us and we were drawn together, he felt it just as strongly as I did.

His hand brushed my hair from my face, trailing a sensual fire down my cheek before reaching my throat. Then, he lightly pressed my pulse with his thumb, and then he went lower, curling his fingers around the loose collar of my top.

Oh. Oh, wow. No. This is a bad idea.

Who said that? Certainly not me. It didn't even sound true. Wasn't true. The vast majority of me was shouting about what a very good idea it was and wondering why in the name of everything we should stop just when it was moving past good and into awesome, hopefully headed toward incredible.

"Hey," I said, my lips moving against his. "No. Stop."

Oh, God, why did I say that?

It might not have been the most coherent or decisive thought, but I felt the very moment he registered it. His hand slid to rest on the seat by my head, and he pulled back, his eyes wide and a little wild. His mouth was gorgeous, reddened by what we'd done, and in spite of what I said, I reached up to touch my fingertips to his lips, marveling at the color and the beauty there.

His tongue brushed gently at my fingers, but because I supposed he was the adult where we were concerned, he pulled back.

"You said *stop*," he confirmed.

There was no resentment in his voice. His entire body was cued to my response, and I sighed, knowing what it had to be.

God. I'd awoken, shaken from the dream, lost in confusion. And he'd held me, worked his magic with those damn hands of his. I was swept away by his kiss right up to the moment reality came crashing back.

"Yeah, I did." I unbuckled my seatbelt and pushed him back. He retreated easily and sighed.

I opened the door and swung my legs out of the car then stood to look out over the pure darkness of the stubbled cornfield. A real chill was coming on as fall pulled back to reveal the sting of winter. Shivering, I wrapped my arms around myself. I had a jacket on, but it was too light for the weather.

Hades moved behind me and I held my breath, waiting for him to say something potentially comforting or something with a bite so I could reorient myself. He did neither as I breathed in the cold air, letting it and his silence both ground and calm me.

"There's so much corn in this state." I cut through the quiet because I couldn't handle it anymore.

"Is there?" His voice was mild and non-committal.

"Yeah." Oh, God, I rambled. But I didn't know what else to say to break up the awkwardness. "It's the only reason this state runs in the black, industry-wise. It's not the type of corn people can eat, though."

"Explain."

"It's feed corn. They pick it and mill it up for livestock. No sugar is added, which is just as well for the cows and the pigs, but still way less good for any of us."

"Do you like... corn?"

I laughed at his politely confused question. Would he be polite even if... No. I wasn't opening that particular jar of snakes again—not right now, no matter how amazing it felt.

"I do. It's so easy to cook. Microwaved or in a boiling pot of water, but, man, is it good grilled. Just throw some butter on, salt and pepper. I like it with lime and chili, too, but I grew up eating it with butter, salt, and pepper."

God. Why was I babbling about corn? Maybe because even in the dark with my back to him, I could feel his gaze on my skin, smell that sweet and spicy scent of him.

"I would like to try that sometime," Hades replied, sounding more befuddled by the moment.

I sighed as I turned back to him. "Sorry. You don't need me to Rachel Roy your ear off about corn." He frowned at that reference. I forgot I was talking to an Underworld God with no concept of pop culture. I chuckled nervously. "We can get back in the car..."

He made no move toward the car, however. The empty road stretched in either direction. His car sat on the shoulder like a lone bastion of civilization.

"You sounded terrified." He frowned, then corrected himself. "No, heartbroken."

"Bad dream."

"Does it happen often?"

I quirked an eyebrow at him. "Sometimes. But I don't talk about it when they do."

His jaw tensed at that, expressing his discomfort with my mild reprimand. "I wouldn't like to think it happens to you often." Then more softly, he added, "I wouldn't like to think you were so unhappy on a regular basis."

I let out a long breath. We were just talking about dreams, passing time on the side of the road while I got my heebie-jeebies under control. Nothing weird at all.

I moved past him to the car door. "Well, I've officially thrown us all off schedule. Shall we get back on the road, boss?"

He gave me an incredulous stare but nodded, and opened the door for me.

"You shouldn't do that for me," I told him. "Otherwise, I'm going to get used to it and insist you do it every time we travel together."

Ah, finally a smile. An icebreaker. Finally, he was getting more comfortable with me.

I thought of our kiss again, and with a massive effort, I managed to avoid touching my lips, recalling it in incredibly vivid detail.

"I don't mind opening doors for you." He shut the door after I got in.

The sky, black tinged with blue, began to merge with the golden tip of dawn, telling me we had about an hour before sunrise, and we left the highway and twisted through county roads.

Long and snaking, they'd existed long before the highways. People still used them, but they had a forgotten quality, each one uneven and ill-maintained. So far, we were still on the paved roads. A mercy since we'd been driving for so long. More than a few were just dirt, heading off into the darkness of the cornfields.

With all the power Hades had at his fingertips, I still didn't understand why he couldn't just magic us to our destination. Surely, I'd get used to the teleporting more each time we did it. Although, maybe he didn't want to transport us quickly because he wanted the company.

"You know," I said. "This is a lot of trouble to go to just to dump me in the woods."

"Not funny," he chided, examining one side of the vast cornfields to the other. "Are you sure this is where we're meant to be?"

"Yup." I pointed to the red line that ended on the map. "Right down this road."

"There's nothing here." He slowed and glanced out the window.

"Not surprising. We're in the middle of nowhere."

He sped up again. "It's not nowhere, not to everyone that lives out here."

I was still figuring out what I wanted to say when he turned into a driveway.

"I think that's what we're looking for."

We weren't on one of those dirt roads I'd been eyeing so warily. Although Hades' car (chariot?) (chariot car?) moved as smoothly as silk, some potholes were deep enough to drown ducklings.

Fortunately, it looked like the house we were aiming at was just a mile further up the road, easily visible in the flat winter fields. The trees lining the driveway had lost their leaves in the cool of autumn. A few sheep nibbled on the grass in a paddock at the front of a house.

Unfortunately, as we got closer, I realized it was a horror

show. Tall arched roof beams. Pitch black in every window. Shadows cast by sharp and bare branches.

"Oh, come on." My complaint ended on a groan. "That place looks so cursed and haunted."

Hades shot me a slight smile as he steered the car toward haunting central. "Where did you think we were going when I asked you to help me corral the dead?"

"I don't know." I rolled the map and shoved it in the glove box. "More like what we did at the funeral home. You know, where it was full of life and people, not abandoned and creepy."

"Some would say those were strange notions to relate to a funeral home," Hades pointed out.

"Not if you're a florist," I objected. "But I was thinking more *that*, and less… this."

He eased the car into the end of the drive for the house, which looked no more promising up close. Tree branches raked against the house, producing all manners of alarming squeaks and groans.

"I need to go in." Hades shifted to face me. "If you want, you can…"

"No. No. I've got this." I raised my palms. "You are not paying me to sit in your car like a glorified navigator. I'm in. I'm a part of this."

"I see." He nodded.

"I'm also right behind you." I waved him forward. "So, you first."

That won me a real laugh, which sent a shiver of pleasure up my spine. He was always handsome, but when he laughed it was like the sun emerging after a long winter. It made me want to grab his sleeve and turn him around, to kiss that laugh right out of his mouth, but I stopped myself.

We got out of the car at the same time and approached the house slowly. Paint peeled from the wooden boards. A lopsided swing creaked in the night breeze. The front porch looked like it was about to collapse under our weight, and the steps cracked as we climbed them. At the door, a rusty old thing hanging off its hinges, Hades raised his hand. For a moment, I thought he was going to knock, but his magic simply pushed it open instead.

"Nice," I murmured.

"No doors shall stand against death." He looked at me with glowing green eyes, fitting the personification of death. That old familiar chill inched over my skin again.

Sometimes, when I looked at him, I saw a normal man. Maybe one with a real stick up his rear, but nonetheless, a normal man. Moments like this reminded me that he wasn't just any mortal man, and if I wasn't already treading water to keep up, I would be in way over my head.

I followed behind him as he stepped over the threshold, vaguely impressed by the fact he boldly walked inside like he had every right in the world to do so.

The moment I strode into the house, I felt as if I'd been dropped into a cold bath. One that my instincts told me to get out of right away. This place didn't feel right. The hairs on my arms and the back of my neck stood up as one thought came to mind: the spirit inside didn't want me here.

CHAPTER 12

Autumn

"Do you sense anything?" Hades stared at the photos in the foyer with a tilted head.

I squinted down the pitch-black hallway. "I sense we're in a house in the middle of nowhere that neither of us own."

Switching on the flashlight app on my phone, I shined a clear, strong white light over the entrance to the house. Somewhat to my surprise, it appeared normal. The entrance contained a standing coat hanger, shoe rack, and a table with a mirror and a bowl for keys.

I hadn't been expecting demon circles or the remnants of supernatural rituals scattered throughout, but I also hadn't anticipated a neat, normal little farmhouse, either. The couch, a mottled velvet job from the seventies, had doilies over the armrests. *So* grandma-ish. A shallow dish on the coffee table held a spray of old dried flowers. Overall, stiff, but well cared for.

"This place doesn't feel deserted," I noted, running a finger along the record player by the window.

"It wasn't until relatively recently that iy was." Hades peered out the lacey curtains, and that sent a chill up my spine as well. That meant that until recently, the inhabitant had been alive.

"So, who are we looking for?"

"I don't know."

"You're the God of Death, how do you not know? You knew Alan Parsons' name."

"God of the Underworld," he corrected. "Not the God of Death. That role is played by Thanatos."

"Oh." I really had to brush up on my Greek mythology.

"I only get a name and a description when I happen upon them," he elaborated, his voice fraying. "All I know, all I feel, is that there is a void. Someone is missing."

He'd been so calm this whole time and I hadn't stopped to think about what kind of stress he might be under. My hand reached out to take his, but then I curled my fingers and tucked them under my arm. We needed all arms for ghost-finding. And besides, holding hands during a breaking and entering would probably considered on the weird side of things.

We made our way to the kitchen, and I swung my beam of light over a clean counter, an ugly little cookie jar, and a neat stack of medication. Al the contents in the house were normal. Someone normal once lived here and ate their cookies and took their meds. We were the ones out of place.

I glanced at Hades, who outwardly looked very cool and calm. But beneath his exterior, I sensed his unease, his fear that if he didn't fix this, he'd fade away in his realm without any chance of hope. Everything about souls not showing up in the Underworld like they were supposed to was increasingly abnormal.

"I can't see anything," I complained, opening the fridge door, illuminating the kitchen with a dim light. Behind me, Hades grunted.

Hades shrugged apologetically.

The contents of the fridge were well stocked and organized by food groups. Fruit, vegetables, some leftovers, condiments, and a six pack of diet soda. What had I been expecting? A head? Some kind of horror? Silly.

Closing the fridge door, I turned to Hades, but just as the light went off, I caught a glimpse of something standing behind him—a slight figure just over his left shoulder. A solid someone. Not a ghostly mist. It had a face, and all I saw were teeth, teeth, teeth...

I let out a garbled, *"OhGodthere'ssomethingbehindyouohmyGod,"* and almost tore the cupboard door off its hinges.

The figure threw a door to one side and lunged through it. Hades ran just one pace behind, descending the stairs after it. Slower than both of them, I rushed straight to the open doorway but froze. Rather than leading into another room, wooden slat stairs led straight down into a black space, disappearing into the dark. A basement.

"Oh, come on." Too much horror movie, not enough getting the hell out of there.

At least I knew what I'd be yelling if I were watching myself from a television. I'd be saying, *"Get the heck out of there! Go wait on the lawn! Go wait for the sun to come up!"* And I might have done just that, but then I heard Hades' voice coming from the darkness.

I couldn't quite make out what he was saying or even his tone, but because of the thud that followed, and the fact his voice cut off for a moment, I took the stairs two at a time, shakily holding my phone up for light, and finding a light switch halfway down. I flipped it on, squinting at the brightness that followed, which preceded a crash. Yelping, I stumbled over the last step, which was two inches taller than the previous ones. Thankfully my adrenaline was going hard enough that I didn't do more than wince.

I was in a semi-finished basement, the walls lined with glass jars that held things I wasn't sure I wanted to look at. Hades stood in the center, tension straightening his body. Jars had smashed on the floor, their contents spilling all over the concrete. Obviously Hades had made a great first impression. What was it with the feisty and uncooperative souls?

"Are you all right?" Hades glanced at me then at a slightly ajar door at the opposite end of the cellar. His suit wasn't so crisp anymore but crumpled where someone—or something had grabbed him.

"I was going to ask you the same thing." I studied the vegetables amid the mess of glass. I was lucky I hadn't fallen closer to that mess. I would have been picking glass shards out of my skin for ages. "Are... are those pickles?"

"Root cellar, shh." Hades held up a hand.

The door at the end of the cellar pulled slightly, creaking, as if someone on the other side tried to tug it closed. Big and heavy, and the rust on the hinges and the uneven floor wasn't going to let it happen.

"Come out here at once!" Hades snapped. "You're dead. You can't stay here."

I flinched at the sternness in his voice. Dead or alive, I wouldn't want anyone talking to me like that.

The sound from inside the room made all the hairs on my body curl with fright. The hiss of a cat combined with the growl of a dog. The person making the noise obviously hated the idea of leaving its home.

Hades gave the spilled pickles a wide birth, stalking toward the door.

"I'm not telling you again. Come out."

Charmer. No wonder the souls didn't want to go to the Underworld.

He grabbed the handle with one hand and reached inside the room with the other. His arm flexed as though he'd gotten a hold of whoever hid from us. Before he could pull, he cried out a half-muffled scream. When he stumbled back, straight through the pickle puddle, his sleeve was in tatters.

"What the hell?" I shouted.

He stared mouth open at the door. "She doesn't even look human anymore."

"I wouldn't be very friendly either if the roles were reversed, and you came in uninvited," I retorted.

Hades looked down at me. "You have an idea?"

"I might." I examined the ripped fabric. A small amount of blood ran slowly from the shallow scratches lining the skin from his elbow to his wrist. They weren't bad, but they also weren't pleasant. I didn't think Gods could bleed.

He shook his arm. "No. If she could do this to me… I was wrong to bring you here. Go wait in the car, and I'll–"

But I was already moving to the storage shelves where jars were lined up as neat as soldiers. I'd been afraid of eyeballs and body parts when really, they stored asparagus spears, tomatoes, baby carrots, and corn. The neatly printed labels recorded canning dates and ingredients, and in the bottom left corner, a cute little old woman held a banner that read "Fresh From Mae's kitchen!"

"What are you doing?" Hades hovered behind me.

"Seems pretty obvious to me." I selected one of the jars. "Ms. Mae?"

Silence fell over the basement. Even though whatever was here acted like it wanted us dead, the sense of the urgency seemed to have died away.

I took that as a good sign. "Ms. Mae, I'm sorry, but we broke some pickle jars out here."

"She broke the jars," Hades muttered. "Threw them at me. And yesterday a man punched me. Does no one respect the Lord of the Dead?"

I glared at him, remembering the neat and tidy house upstairs. Judging by the spidery script on the jar in my hands, I'd bet a month's salary at Pearls' that Ms. Mae was house-proud. She'd hate the idea of vinegar and sugar soaking into the cement cracks.

"I am so sorry." I continued talking to Ms. Mae in my most contrite voice. "Do you have a mop and a bucket somewhere? We're going to clean this mess right up."

The rusty hinges creaked as the door opened a fraction, revealing something just past the threshold. Shorter and far thinner than I was, standing hunched over, eyes glowing.

Aw, man, I should have just waited outside.

Of course, I hadn't because I was getting paid for this. I swallowed hard and took a step closer, aware Hades was behind me the whole time. I was glad he had my back in case everything went wrong.

"What are you *doing*?" He grabbed my shoulder.

"Being nice," I muttered back. "You should try it."

He went to argue with me, but I cut him off with a wave of my hand.

"Once again," I said, "I'm so sorry, Ms. Mae. It won't happen again."

The door swung open wide this time, and I braced myself as Ms. Mae came out. The light of my phone gleamed off the lenses of her spectacles, and her mouth was pressed in a firm line.

She examined the mess on the floor. "Look at all this. Won't be able to walk barefoot down here."

"Just show me to the mop, and I'll get it," I promised her.

Her eyes dropped to what I had in my hands. She stepped

closer, revealing strong hands with sharp-looking fingers despite her age. I stood my ground.

"Well! That's my prize-winning asparagus." She reached for it, and I let her take it. I was curious to see if the dead could hold corporeal objects after they lost their form. Spoiler alert: they could. "I took second at the state fair with that one just a few years ago."

"Ooh, neat," I said. "I love asparagus. Do you do all your own canning?"

She nodded, her face beaming with pride. "Oh, yes. I have since I started living here. Every summer it was work-work-work to get the crops in, and every fall, work-work-work again to make sure that we could eat through the winter. So many good years in these jars." She stroked the glass lovingly.

I followed her around the basement as she pointed at her jars, showing us the tomatoes that she was working on perfecting for the ideal midwinter pasta sauce, the rosewater jam with strawberries suspended inside, the raspberry compote that was *just wonderful in anything*.

Hades stared at us, his jaw slack, his eyes lighter. Smiling. I'd done my job.

She paused close to the stairs. "I wonder who's going to eat these now."

Hades froze behind me.

I swallowed hard. "Um. You know you're—"

"Oh, of course." She smiled, glancing at the ceiling, probably recalling her dead body lying in her bed, her passing peaceful in her sleep. How I knew that, I didn't know. I just did. "So undignified. I don't relish being found like that."

"So…" I risked a quick glance at Hades, who inspected Ms. Mae as if she were a weird bug he had found. Not helpful at all, so I hurried on. "So why hide from us?"

Her eyes moistened and she swiped at her eyes, the gesture more absent than anything else. "Oh, I don't know.

Because there's all this food down here and my kids won't eat it. That's sad, isn't it? And it's such good food."

All the effort she'd gone to—planting the vegetables, harvesting them, sterilizing the jars, and preserving the food.

I hesitated. "Um. We can take it if that would help you?"

She gave us a hard look, a special glare for Hades. Given how he had scolded her, I couldn't disagree with her.

"And you're not just saying that to get me to go where you want me to go?"

I took a breath. "You can't stay here."

"Why?" she asked.

To my surprise, Hades spoke, his voice as gentle as I'd ever heard it. "Because this is over now. It is time to move on. The longer you stay here, the harder it will be for you to leave. I wouldn't like anyone to suffer that kind of pain."

His compassionate words brought a lump to my throat, but Ms. Mae only looked more thoughtful.

"You're likely not wrong," she agreed reluctantly. "Party's over. Time to go home, I guess. But you will take the jars and eat the food? It's all good, I promise."

"Yes," I said, accepting the jar she handed me. "We have an enormous trunk. We can take it all."

She smiled, looking years younger. "Well then, no time like the present, I suppose. How do we do this?" She glanced at us both.

"This way." Hades led her up the stairs.

I followed behind although I couldn't quite see what happened. She got darker, or she got lighter, but the air in front of me shimmered—strange and unearthly—and by the time we got to the top, there were tears in my eyes, and Ms. Mae was gone.

"What happened?" I croaked.

"It is fine now," Hades assured, his face solemn. "She is gone on. Are you all right?"

I rubbed the tears out of my eyes with my knuckles. No point to crying? I'd known her for just a short while. She wasn't a part of my family or anything like that.

"Yeah," I said, gruffly. "Just give me a second."

Hades set his hand on my shoulder. A light touch, not without the heat that always sprung up between us, but more, comfortable and kind.

"It is still a loss," he said. "She was here, and now she is gone."

I sighed, smiled, and patted his hand for a moment before pushing it away. "Time to get on with things."

I felt Hades' stare follow me as I went to the narrow closet off the kitchen. As I suspected, in there was a mop and a bucket as well, which I filled at the sink before giving it a few squirts of dish soap.

"What are you *doing*?" Why did he keep asking me that?

"I promised a dead woman we'd clean her cellar," I said. "Doesn't that mean anything to you?"

Hades hesitated, and this time it was my turn to stare at him.

"You were just going to leave?" I asked.

"Technically, *you* promised her, not me…"

I scowled at him. "No. No. If I'm doing this with you, this is a ground rule. Whatever we promise the person in question, we have to do, all right? That's… that's just basic."

After a few moments, he nodded. "I agree."

I half-expected him to argue, to claim the Lord of the Underworld was above mopping up pickles and brushing up glass.

"You made Ms. Mae's transition much easier, so we'll clean the damn cellar together." He said it with such resignation I giggled, and it sounded higher than I meant, maybe even shrill.

"Okay, I'm going to get to work. You should, um, look

after your arm. And then come down and help me because there're a lot of jars to load into the car."

"My car?" he groaned.

I pointed plainly toward his shredded sleeve. The blood had clotted, but was still a mess.

A number of emotions spread across Hades' face, too fast for me to see, but then he nodded. "Very well."

He was as good as his word. Once I was done mopping, he brushed the glass into a dustpan with a broom. Then we hauled up the jars upstairs and filled his trunk. By the time we finished, the light of dawn began to break, painting the air with a kind of rosy light that would soon turn to gold. I yawned, exhausted. What we'd done was so beautiful I wanted to sit down and cry.

Then I remembered Mae's concern, and turned back toward the house.

"What now?" Hades asked with an exaggerated note of resignation.

"Will you come help me? She... she didn't want to be found like that."

"Oh!" A blush spread across his cheeks. "I've never taken such care of one of his subjects before. But, yes. Of course."

We made our way up the stairs to her bedroom where we found her body lying still under the rumpled covers. My heartbeat quickened, my mouth went dry as cotton, and no matter what I told myself about having seen tons of dead bodies before at funeral parlors which did business with Pearl's... this was going to be different. In the end, I froze just inside the door. Hades smoothed the covers over her. Afterwards, he escorted me downstairs, tactfully letting me tear up on the porch while he locked up.

"That was... um." I pressed my fingertips to my lips.

"If this is too much for you, you can stop," he reassured.

I peered at him. He looked tired too, and if possible, less

like an underworld god than a man who had been driving all night. His gaze remained fixed on the fields around the house, and he exuded a dependable kind of silent strength.

I ran my thumb over my lips. "I doubt you're known for letting people out of their contracts."

"I am not." He smiled. "But there are always exceptions. You could be mine. If you cannot do this or will not–"

Be his exception? Promising thought, but I shook my head. "No. A deal's a deal. You need this done, and there's no one else, right?"

His lip's pressed into a grim line. "Afraid not."

"Then I guess you're stuck with me and all the jars in your trunk," I said with a faint smile. "Might as well get used to it for however long we're together."

The thought of this trip with Hades ending, me left with just my payment, and The Lord of the Underworld returning to his realm filled me with a dreadful sorrow for some reason. I didn't understand it, didn't know where it sprang from, only that a part of my soul didn't want this to give this up. Ever.

"Might as well," he agreed.

"Hope you like pickles." I started down the porch steps.

Hades caught my hand, stopping me halfway. When I looked up at him, my heart beat double time. I didn't have a second to think about it; I didn't have time to do anything but notice how good this felt or how much he cared and how just looking at him made me want to put my lips against his.

Flashing lights pulled my attention away, however. Red and blue. A dark car drove up Mae's driveway.

"Hades." I jabbed at the cop car pulling up in front of Mae's house.

CHAPTER 13

*A*utumn

NOT GOING TO LIE, having a dead body upstairs and a trunk full of our ill-gotten gains looked bad.

The cop got out of his car, walked to the porch, all the while glaring at us.

"You two don't live here, do you?" he inquired, taking in Hades' suit and car. "Mind telling me what you're doing?"

For a moment, I had a vision of Hades telling the truth. And then not only would we be two city weirdos on some nice old lady's porch, we'd be two crazy weirdos on a dead old lady's porch, and I just couldn't see that going well for either of us, ever.

Hades took charge. "What's the problem, officer?"

The cop's eyes narrowed. "You tripped an alarm."

Junipers!

"My aunt, Mae," I blurted. "We're passing through, and

she said to stop and pick up some preserves to take home with us, sir."

The cop examined me with narrowed eyes, the cool air in front of him steaming up with every exhale as if he were a dragon. "Un-huh. That true?" He looked at Hades.

Hades shrugged. "I say that my wife has the right of it. We're driving through, headed home."

I winced at his odd diction. I'd started to get used to it, like it even, but he sounded odd and maybe foreign. Not a winning combination for a cop when lying through one's perfect teeth to the police.

"Right." The cop turned back to me. "And your aunt, where's she now?"

Moved on to her reward? Dead upstairs? Oh, God.

"On a visit in the east," Hades supplied easily. "She left us a key."

"And where are you from?" The cop gestured with a finger. "Let's see some ID."

Trying not to panic, I went to Hades' car, accompanied by the cop, freaking because I just knew the officer wasn't buying this concocted story. He was gonna discover the body. Blame us because who else? And I was going to end up serving fifteen to life in a backwoods prison eating slop three times a day. Because I couldn't exactly use the excuse that I was helping out the Lord of the Dead. Straight to the looney bin for me.

The cop had his hand on the butt of his gun still in the holster as he stood beside me while I rooted around in my backpack. "Nice and slow." He lifted his head as I inched my wallet out of the bag. I didn't take another breath until he moved his hand away from the gun to take my license.

Oh, God!

I swallowed the lump in my throat. My ID wouldn't have

the same address as Hades, and the cop would realize we were full of it. Oh, God. Oh, God. Oh, God.

Okay, if you really are an underworld god, now would be a really good time to, like, open a portal and get us the hell out of here Or maybe... I don't know, turn into a demon or something and scare this guy into running for the hills.

Instead, Hades reached for a wallet I didn't even know he had and pulled out what looked like a very normal driver's license he handed to the cop.

"Stay right there." The cop went back to his car to run the licenses.

I grabbed Hades by the arm and squeezed. "What's he going to find when he checks those?" I was still thinking of the *dead body* he had left so politely arranged in the bedroom.

"A happily married couple," Hades said calmly in a lightly amused way. "I mean, it is not all sunlight and roses, of course. I have a few speeding citations."

"You... do?" I glanced at the officer's car, squinting through the flashing lights.

"It's a problem." Hades pretended to be remorseful. "You've spoken to me about it a few times. It has put some stress on our marriage. I've resolved to do better."

"Have you? Do I believe you?" My voice had taken on a calmer lilt.

"I hope you do. I really do mean to do better." His was voice perfectly sincere. "I know that winning back your trust will be a process, however."

I was stifling a giggle when the cop came back.

"All right." The officer reluctantly handed back our licenses, "looks like it all checks out." He scowled at Hades. "We take speeding very seriously in these parts." He couldn't have been more country in overalls with a chaw of tobacco in his cheek. "So, you be careful now, you hear?" The threat was implied.

"Perfectly." Hades smiled, and I almost buckled with relief when the cop got back in his car and reversed out the drive.

"Ugh, I'm shaking." I held up my hands as I approached the car.

Hades glanced curiously at me over the roof. "Why? I would have protected you."

"From a cop? After we've committed a breaking and entering and then stolen about twelve dozen canning jars and their goodies from a dead woman's house?" We both got in his car. "And um, no offense, but you're not any better with live people than you are with the dead."

He chuckled. "Do you think I need to be?"

He started the car and drove off the property.

"Well… I guess you're a lot more about what comes after you don't need the bedside manner anymore, huh?"

"Something like that. I guess I'm not known for my pleasant conversation."

Despite a flaming curiosity about the whole process and the world he lived in—were there other gods? Was Hermes in charge of high-speed internet? Did Hephaestus watch out for ironworkers? I didn't want to get too much into what that particular world was like.

"How's your arm?" I asked instead.

He looked at me quickly, then looked away again. His sleeve had been rolled up to hide the tattered edge, and the long scratches were livid against his pale skin but looking far better.

"Just fine. It doesn't hurt anymore."

He didn't look at me as he spoke, and I wondered if he was feeling awkward about being fought like that. It must have been a bit of a comedown for the Lord of the Dead to be scraped up by a nice old farmer.

Maybe I can teach him a bit about taking things easier. They're dead, not children. I bet he would be a lot more popular if he just remembered that one little thing.

I told myself I was being an idiot. Hades was a literal *god*. That meant he probably knew his business pretty well. He'd done it for thousands of years. But the dead stopped showing up in the Underworld. I, on the other hand, hadn't even gone to college. So, what did I know?

We drove in silence and I yawned as the adrenaline of our encounter with Ms. Mae began to fade, leaving me simultaneously exhausted and restless. I shifted, unable to get comfortable. Mid-morning light stabbed my eyes. I toughed it out for almost an hour until Hades pulled off the highway into a hotel lot on the edge of a town.

"We're stopping?" I wondered if the god needed rest because he seemed to go, go, go all the time.

"You look tired," he said, not looking at me. "You're going to get a crick in your... *everything* if you keep twisting around like that."

A faint tremor shook his hand as he parked the car. The way he clenched his jaw—hard with a muscle ticking in his cheek—told me I wasn't the only one who was tired, but it probably wasn't smart to point that out to a god right now.

"Thank you," I replied. "But the motel we passed on the way in was really more my speed."

He switched off the engine. "I'm not sleeping at an establishment with a flickering sign and a vending machine for toiletries in the front."

I grinned. "Like I said, more my speed."

No matter what I could afford on my own, the truth of the matter was that I was impressed with the bed and breakfast townhouse Hades chose. Five-star, a cabana, private pool, kitchen, and dining room. The room was bigger than my entire apartment. Of course, I lived in a shoebox. I gaped at the room overlooking the gardens.

At that point, I was more than a little shaky with exhaustion, so I dumped my bags at the foot of the bed. The only bed in the room. Hades and I were going to have to share. Not sure how I felt about that yet, especially after our little roadside make-out session. But a shiver of delight ran through me at the thought of sleeping beside him.

"Mind if I shower?" I asked Hades and he shook his head.

I was in and out fast, back to admire the view for a bleary moment and then crash into what felt like endless miles of white linens.

As my eyes drifted shut, Hades chuckled and sat next to me on the bed. It was too intimate for a boss and employee relationship, but it felt terribly right. The same went for the gentle hand he put on my lower back. The warmth of his skin soaked through the place the ancient fabric of my favorite T-shirt met my shorts.

"Delicate thing," he murmured. "You should have told me you were so worn out."

"I'm not delicate," I grumbled. "I *regularly* heft forty-pound bags of fertilizer."

His soft laugh sent a sweet thrill down my spine. I liked his laugh. It broke up his hardness. Who knew what else I might have heard in his voice had I not been so heavy with fatigue.

"I stand corrected," he said. "You've always been so tough, haven't you?"

"Darn straight."

"You can say *damn*, you know. You're an adult."

"And as an adult, I chose not to swear. Very mature of me."

"I'm sure." He leaned down, smoothing my hair out of the way to place a soft kiss on the back of my neck.

If I had been firing on all cylinders, I probably would have thought him out of line, but relaxed, on the softest bed I had ever been in, all I could think was that it felt good.

He was saying something else, but right then nothing kept me from falling into a deep, dark sleep.

***

THIS TIME IT WAS SPRING. Not just calendar spring, but the real deal—that first day it was perfect to step out of the house after winter finally surrenders. I glanced at my bare arms, and I didn't even care because the trees were misted with fresh green buds, the soil black as coffee, and I was out of the house.

I walked through an open wrought-iron gate into a public park and followed a path. The park was empty except for the birds that perched on the branches, chirping their springtide song. In the back of my mind, I knew it was wrong—their bodies the wrong shapes, their song melodies off key and flat. But it didn't matter because I'd finally escaped a deep winter.

I searched. For someone. So, I hurried along the path. My heart beat fast, and I couldn't stop smiling as I sped along. I came to a duck pond. A silly interpretation for a body of silvery water where I couldn't see the opposite shore. Still, I wandered along the edge, letting the wavelets tease my sandals. I'd been in such a hurry to get there, but now that I reached it, anticipation made me squirm with pleasure. I kept my eyes on the water because I knew he wouldn't appear to me from that direction.

One moment, I was alone with the water and the faraway quacks of ducks, and the next, a whisper of fabric brushed my arm. A burst of heat went straight to my core, along with the sense of sheer joy.

"Well," he said quietly.

I leaned back, and he wrapped his arms around me. There was no need to turn around; he would tell me if he wanted me to. The extent of his strength was communicated to me when I pressed into him. His immediate response, firm and ready, pushed into my lower back, and I ground myself against it.

His hands came down to wrap around my wrists. The feeling, slightly claustrophobic and enthralling, made me lean into him more firmly.

He put his mouth right next to my ear, so close that when he talked, it sent another shiver of pleasure and need through me. "Did you forget so easily?"

I whimpered at memories that weren't only my own. I saw myself through his eyes, tied to his bed, spread open. Oh God. So sensual. So… exciting.

He laughed, searing a soft kiss on my ear. "Then I suppose I'll have to remind you." My heart leaped at the low and determined growl in his throat.

He grew firmer harder against me, his body holding a new tension. I could never decide what I liked best when I was with him—his reactions to me, mine to him, or the strange and wonderful alchemy of what we were when we were together.

As he turned me around, I jarred awake, staring at the ceiling, my entire body fevered and restless, aware that my breathing came in short, fast puffs.

Wow. Talk about bailing out of the best part of a dream. The dream had left me aroused and in need of an outlet.

The memory of where I was and what I was doing came back to me. The room was dark except for a crack in the curtains that exposed a bar of sunlight. Low and gold. Late afternoon, maybe evening.

My thoughts trailed off. I wasn't alone on the enormous

mattress. Hades slept next to me, sprawled out with his head tilted to one side.

A half dozen things went through my head about appropriate boss and employee relationships, but they all vanished when I started examining him the way I'd wanted to since we met and never quite had the nerve to do.

With his face relaxed and his lips slightly parted, he looked younger. He had surprisingly long eyelashes—long enough I almost wanted to run a fingertip over them. His elegant fingers spread out next to his face, nails trimmed neat and short, and I had to pull myself back from kissing his palm. The need to do so was so intense that I shook with it and gripped the sheets tightly.

Come on, Autumn, what the heck? What are you doing?

Before I could figure myself out, Hades snapped awake and stared at me with a dark, smolder in his eyes that made me want to whimper. I yelped and almost rolled off the bed. Burning with the heat of embarrassment and arousal, I opened my mouth to apologize, or maybe to make a smart remark about staring at him like a creepy stalker while he slept. But I never got the chance because his hand curled around the back of my neck, and he drew me down for a long and drugging kiss.

Oh, God, I needed him.

CHAPTER 14

Autumn

IN THIS KISS he was in charge, commanding and sure, and because he was so certain, I was sure as well. He explored my mouth with a lingering urgency. I let him do as he liked, leaning forward on my elbows to explore him as well. God, he tasted good, so perfect, his kiss with an edge of dominance to it as well. He nipped at my lower lip, eliciting a whole-body shiver. He grinned against my mouth.

"You like teeth, little darling?" he whispered.

"Ye-yes, I do." Apparently, I did when I was with him. Everything was different with him. Fresh, raw, and new, yet like the most amazing homecoming at the same time.

"Precious little thing," he rasped.

With a strength I had only begun to guess he had, he hauled me onto his body and I yelped with surprise. He chuckled. He'd stripped down to a pair of black silk boxers. Perfect for the Lord of the Dead. I straddled his thighs, my body hot against his. The edges of my sight blurred when I felt the enormity of his erection pressed against my thigh.

His eyes were dark with desire. "I want to feel you, every part of you…" Soft but commanding. Intoxicating.

I did as he said, whimpering when he reached down to run his hands up my bare thighs.

New. Exciting. Shocking. Sensual. Intimate. I could only think in single words.

His hands curled back around my thighs, fingers digging in. Not hard enough to hurt, but enough to make me gasp and pull back to look at him. Strong fingers kneaded my flesh, and I groaned, letting him know how good it felt—God, he was strong. I couldn't ignore the way he hardened under my belly as I quivered above him.

He tugged me down to kiss me again. No matter who was on top, he was the one in charge. One hand cupped my face. The other explored my body with leisurely intensity. He was learning about me—what I liked, what I felt like, and it felt incredible.

"Eager little thing…" His voice was thick, his eyes dark.

At some point, I'd started squirming on top of him, rocking against his hips. My straddle widened, and I tried to stabilize, pushing my knees deep into the mattress. I opened my mouth to retort that I didn't have much choice, but then deliberately, he thrust against the center of my need.

"Oh!" My eyes closed as he did it again and again, rolling up against me like waves crashing against the shore.

A pleasurable tension rose up in me, and my thighs trembled. Then quaked until he pushed me off him.

"Hey!" I protested.

"Sit up and lean back," he ordered, his voice hoarse.

I shifted to lean back on my hands. Thank you, yoga! He reached forward and tore my flimsy shorts from my body with a rough purring sound as they gave way. The casual way he did it took my breath away.

"There you are," Hades murmured. "That's what I wanted."

The only thing remaining between us was my T-shirt. I swallowed hard, a blush warming my cheeks. I'd never been quite so open to someone before.

Using both hands, Hades pushed my legs farther apart, and I squeezed my eyes shut. He touched me with a gentleness that still hinted at the urgency I knew existed within him. Long maddening strokes brushed over my sensitive flesh. No hurry. No need for rushing. Only the sense that he was doing as he pleased, and he would take all the time in the world if necessary. I whimpered as my body responded to his touch. Soon, my voice turned to desperate whines when he hit that perfect spot at the apex of my slit.

"That's right, darling, tell me what you like," he crooned.

"I… I can't," I panted, my cheeks flushing. I didn't have words. Didn't have nerve.

I was afraid it might make him stop, but he only he murmured in a low voice, "That's all right. You're telling me just fine."

I moaned. At his quiet confidence. At the reality of the moment. At his fingers in the exact spot I needed him to touch. I let the pleasure mount. I could hear his fingers sliding across me, smell and almost taste my own arousal. He stroked my clit, his fingers firmer, not speeding up even as my hips rocked. When he carefully pushed a finger inside me, I cried out with need. Soon enough it changed, grew more tense, more taut. There was a shiver then an ache. I swallowed, fighting the urge to hold my breath, and I curled my fingers into the mattress, clutching the sheet in my fist.

"Oh… oh please," I whimpered, hoarse and needy.

His hands quickened, applying more pressure, sending

more delicious sensations spiraling through me, and I was close, so close when he stopped.

"Oh, please, please," I groaned, twisting onto my back to face him. How could he make me feel that good and pull away?

Then, answering my silent prayers and my louder begging, he was on top of me, kissing me hard. Finally he settled between my legs, hips against mine, his arousal brushing my clit.

Shaky and impatient, he pulled my T-shirt over my head before reaching to shove his boxers away. Now there was absolutely nothing between us at all, and yes, this was what I'd been waiting all my life to feel. What I needed…

"Wait." I pressed a hand to his chest. "What about a condom?"

"I cannot impregnate you," he said.

"Oh."

He kissed me with more fervor and hunger, and I arched against him.

"Please!" I begged, and he reached down, angled himself and pushed into me as I clung to him.

Blinding pain twisted into a strange pleasure. I moaned, and he gripped me tighter. His mouth fell open, and I laced my fingers together behind his neck, dragging him down to kiss me again. Into it I injected all of my need for him, using my mouth and tongue to let him know how much I wanted him.

"Don't…" I murmured softly. "Please don't… don't stop…"

He groaned against my lips, and then there was no question of us stopping—not when we both wanted it so very much.

Rocking into me, he took his time with each thrust. The pleasure receded and surged, making me moan each time. He thrust harder, his elbows on either side of me. We slid against each other, every stroke flaming the heat inside me

He pumped into me, striking every part of me just right. I shook beneath him, my throat dry from crying out. Every single nerve lit up like fireworks. I chanted his name as my blood roared in my ears. He called my name, setting off a climax that tore into me like a fire throwing sparks high into the midsummer sky. I dug my nails hard into his arms.

I was only starting to drop back into the world when he pressed into me a final time, filling me so I gasped with renewed pleasure. I held him as we both shook, and he pressed his forehead against mine.

In the shivering aftermath, we kissed. The darkness of the room took on a sacred air, so perfect it felt as though a lost piece of me had been found.

This is what I've always been missing.

Hades and I rested in each other's arms. At some point we'd have to get up, shower, get some food, and engage with the world again. But later rather than sooner. Better in my opinion.

Hades didn't agree, obviously. While my eyes remained half-shut, he rocked the bed by propping himself on his elbow to look down at me for a very long moment.

"You're staring," I said, my voice low and hoarse with the afterglow of sex.

"Why shouldn't I?" he argued. "You're beautiful."

I cracked open an eye to look at him. "You don't sound happy about that. That's not normal."

"You were also a virgin." The layers in his voice told me I wouldn't get away with just drifting in this warm and lovely sea of sensation any longer.

I sat up, wincing , and he pressed me back down to the sheets.

"Did I hurt you?"

"No, I promise. Look…" One way or the other—whether I admitted it or not—he was going to make a big deal about this, so I sighed. "Would you order us…" I almost said *pizza*, and then I remembered that he was likely a picky underworld god. "Get us some room service, please?"

He blinked at me.

"I'm hungry." The last thing I wanted to talk about was my virginity.

Hades stared at me, then his mouth curved into a smile that made my heart flutter. *Handsome* only began to describe him. But when he smiled, he could just about tear my heart out.

"What do you want?" he asked.

It came to me that I could ask him for just about anything. The intensity in his eyes made me shiver. Too much power wasn't good for anyone. God or not.

"I like breakfast for dinner," I said. "Anything breakfast-like."

He nodded, his face relaxed as if having a task calmed him. With him distracted, I snuck to the bathroom to take a quick shower. The tiny bit of pain from being stretched by his cock, was more sensual than painful, and I rinsed away the bit of blood I'd shed without regret.

Afterwards, I stared into the mirror, appreciating the way my green hair rumpled and how my mouth was red as if I were wearing lipstick. The whole look made it clear what I had been doing and that I'd enjoyed it.

Back in the bedroom, Hades pulled me onto the mattress the moment I reappeared, curling around me in a way that could only be described as protective, one arm slung over my waist.

"Did I hurt you?" he asked.

"If I had told you before I hadn't done this particular activity before, would you have stopped?"

"Not unless you told me to," he said, reluctantly, and I laughed.

"I'm not going to go off into fits of horror over ruining my bride price, okay?"

He snorted. "Where I'm from, bride price had nothing to do with virginity. It had more to do with beauty and promise. Family connections. Political allegiances. The feeling you got from looking at the woman you chose." Hades pulled his chin back as if surprised at what had come out of his mouth. He shook his head. "Never mind."

Words were fine, but we had more than words to work with. I leaned over and kissed him, sliding my hand over his jaw gently. It reminded me of something wild, and I felt like the first woman to reach out to a wolf.

He relaxed, and when I pulled back, a softness was evident in his eyes.

"You are a strange and wonderful thing," he said, and I laughed.

"That," I said, "is probably one of the nicest things you can say after something like that."

He might have responded, but a knock indicated the food had arrived, and I was starving. From the way he stared at the food trays, he was, too. As soon as he tipped the guy, I sat down on the bed with my plate and dug into the most delicious omelet I'd ever tasted. Hades took a bite of steak and chewed with a scrunched look on his face.

"I'd forgotten how good this was," he murmured, chewing.

"Don't gods eat?"

"We can. But we don't need to."

I nodded and kept eating.

After we devoured our food, I stood up. "Do we need to hit the road again, boss?" I liked that particular word on my tongue, and the craziness that came with sleeping with my employer. "

He frowned, sharper than I preferred. I wouldn't be able to squirm out of "where-to-from-here-" for much longer. With a nod, we packed our things and carried them to the car.

Inside the vehicle, I pulled magic map from the glove compartment again, checking the route he'd mentioned. A shorter drive north, but straight into the cold front that had blown in. At least the car was climate controlled. It was good we had a bit of a drive ahead of us because it let me sort out some of my feelings for him... and the strange ache of fear in my chest about what was brewing between us and where it might leave us once the job was done.

CHAPTER 15

Autumn

It wasn't the sex getting to me. Or the fact I'd crossed the line with my new employer. Contrary to what *Mr. Bride Price* might have said about things, I wasn't an innocent, and everything we'd done together was beyond good. Like a part of myself had come home, like things were falling into place in a way I'd wanted them to for my entire life.

After my mom died, I fought hard for everything I had. It wasn't always easy, and it was not always fun, but it was mine. I wasn't the type to wait around for a missing part of myself either. Except… maybe I was?

Sometimes when I drifted to sleep or when I woke in the morning, I had an ache in my chest that suggested something was missing with a grief that took my breath away. And I wasn't talking about my mom, either. When I woke up like that, I usually wrote off the day, did the bare minimum, and went back home to crawl into bed as soon as I could. But the

LADY OF THE UNDERWORLD

deep and dark feeling shadowed me wherever I'd go, and most of the time I could ignore it. Now it was gone, and I wondered if it had anything to do with Hades. Because if it did, I had to find out what it meant and figure out how to stop it from coming back again.

I snuck a glance at him, watching the amber streetlights flicker across his features, which stole my breath away. But there was more to it than that.

"I like you," I blurted.

We both blinked. I hadn't expected to say those words, and by the way he flinched, he obviously hadn't expected to hear them.

"I hope you wouldn't have done what we did if you didn't." I liked how old-fashioned he was. There was something old-school romantic and gentlemanly about it.

"I wouldn't have." I took a deep breath, swallowed, and forced out the rest of it because I wanted to know how he felt. "So... what do you think of me?"

"What?" His forehead pinched.

"Wow," I muttered with a wince.

Anger or humiliation or rage burned in my cheeks because I wasn't sure what I expected, but it certainly wasn't the sharpness on his face. He was my boss, after all and he shouldn't be encouraging further interactions. He probably didn't want anything getting in the way of restoring order to the Underworld.

I shifted to stare out the window, but Hades pulled the car into a shoulder off the road. He threw the brake on and reached for me, lightly grasping my chin to turn my head toward him.

Oh, God, here comes the talk. He'd say this was a mistake, that we shouldn't have done this—let's just keep it professional.

"No, that's not what I meant," he said. "Why would

you…" I wasn't sure how to read the look of dawning horror in his wide eyes.

"So, *you've* done this before, right?" I asked.

From the look of it, the Hades stared down, eyes flicking from one side to another, he ran through different explanations in his mind, discarding them one after the other.

The words startled him, and he looked oddly uncertain. "Autumn…"

He pulled me into a kiss as if he couldn't find the words. It shouldn't have worked at all, but it did. I hated the kiss-someone-to-shut-them-up trope in movies, I got it now. The kiss said words he couldn't. Or wouldn't. It burned with a degree of longing and need I could hardly stand. He pulled back first, his hand cupping my cheek.

"I just… didn't want you to think for another second that I didn't care for you," he murmured, licking his lips.

I put my hand over his mouth, shaking my head.

"That's all I wanted," I said firmly. "I don't need anything else. We've known each other for, like, three days at most. That's all it can be."

Hades took my hand from his face, kissing my palm. "That's what you want?" His voice deepened.

That was one hell of a question. *Yes,* was the right answer. When he asked me what I wanted, I recalled the feeling from the first time we touched—flooded with all kinds of possibilities and needs. Some of my thoughts were natural for a healthy young heterosexual woman who had just had her first and very satisfying sexual encounter with a good-looking guy.

No, I told myself sternly. *Don't be one of those people who thinks sex means that you have to move in with them. No.*

"It's what I want," I told him instead.

For a moment, his eyes went dark and if they had the power to frown, they did. But then, his expression cleared to its usual blankness. He traced a gentle fingertip from my temple to my cheek before curling under my chin. And took my breath away. I had to swallow hard or I would have leaned into his hand.

He retreated then pulled the car back onto the highway. "Pull out that map," Hades instructed. "I want to make sure we're going in the right direction."

"Sir, yes, sir," I muttered, wondering if he sat up straighter at that.

Probably just my imagination.

***

WE CROSSED the state line minutes shy of two in the morning, and I was just waking up from my nap when Hades exited the highway. This road, if anything, was worse than the road to Ms. Mae's house. I had to hang onto the door, gritting my teeth to keep them from clacking together.

"You take me to all the best kinds of places," I told him flatly.

I thought he would ignore me, but he smiled, not taking his eyes off of the road. "Oh? I suppose you only drive on paved, flat roads?" He grinned. "Amateur."

"So far we've been to a haunted house. Just saying you could take me some place really warm," I said wistfully. "Maybe some place where I can lie out in the sun and watch the ocean. I don't suppose there's anything like that in the offering?"

"Not for now, unfortunately," he mused. "But I will keep it in mind."

"What might you be keeping it in mind for?" I asked suggestively.

I didn't get an answer because he turned the car off the road into a deserted parking lot. An office off to our right, with boarded up windows, peeling paint and a do not enter sign, suggested it had seen little use in the past few decades. A rusty fence stopped us from driving farther.

"Seriously, the best places," I muttered as I got out of the car.

Driving north is bringing us closer to winter. The wind cut into my face. Hades didn't look bothered. Gods probably didn't feel the cold. I could have asked, but he was busy checking the map and walking along the fence blocking a long road beyond it. The moon provided enough light for me to see the white gravel road. A whisper of magic rose beyond the dark trees swaying in the wind. "It should be just up ahead."

I nodded, following along behind him with my hands shoved deep into my pockets.

I wondered what poor dead person had found their way to this desolate place.

We'd only walked for a few minutes when something tugged at the back of my coat. Only there was no branch poking out or no wire fence nearby. I yelped and spun to examine the trail behind us.

Hades turned to me, alert and scanning the terrain. "What is it?"

I shook my head. "Something grabbed the back of my coat." I put a hand to my head. "Like, grabbed a handful and pulled me back."

Hades peered into the darkness with a curled lip. "I do not see anything."

"Well, it really happened." I rubbed my arms.

"I know it did," he assured, cutting me off with a slice of his hand. "I just can't see it."

See what? The dead person? Were they hiding from him?

LADY OF THE UNDERWORLD

I frowned, but at this point, there was nothing to do but to keep walking behind him. I wasn't sticking around here to be yanked around by a ghost.

We walked a couple hundred more steps before he suddenly spun, reaching only to come back with a handful of air. He glared at the empty path behind us as if he could command whatever it was to come up again just by staring it into submission.

"You felt it too?" I stuck to his side, terrified that whatever had grabbed me might do so again. I was more than weirded out by now.

"Yes." He glowered, turning his head from left to right and back again. "I didn't think you imagined it, but now I know for sure."

His grimace deepened, so I let it go.

In the twenty minutes it took us to walk to the edge of a quarry, something tugged my coat again then my hand. Oh, *God*. A small and soft hand, wrapped around mine and give an urgent little pull before letting go. When I turned to ask what the soul thought it was doing, Hades tapped me on the shoulder.

I glanced over a thin ledge that dropped down into a great depression in the earth. Limestone was the big industry in this part of the world, and the crater left behind by the mining glowed white in the night light, giving the air around it an iridescent gleam. Gorgeous, but peculiar.

"If we're going down there, I hope you've got some magical way of getting us back out," I muttered to Hades. "I'm not built for climbing."

"I hope we won't have to," he replied. "Ah, there they are."

At first, I had no idea who or what he meant, but my eyes adjusted. A form sat on the rim of the quarry, so small it might have been just another shadow, if it wasn't sniffling.

"Aw, no. Not a little kid." I cupped my temples, heartbroken that I'd have to convince him to go to the Underworld.

"Mostly, yes." The uneven tone of Hades' voice told me he found the entire thing just as unpleasant.

Well, there was work here to be done.

"Should I take point on this?" I asked, to which he nodded reluctantly.

"You do seem to have… a talent for this that I lack."

"Years and years of customer service," I said with a slight smile. "Okay. But be ready to back me up?"

He nodded. "Always."

Warmth spread through me at the low timbre of his voice. That might not have been the most appropriate thing I could be feeling right before I went to the edge of a sharp drop-off to deal with this poor child.

I took a deep breath. "Hey!" I stepped up behind the little shadow.

It flinched, huddled in on itself, but closer now, I could make out long, lank, dark hair, a buttoned shirt, pants and britches. Whoever it was, they were all rolled up in a bundle of misery.

"Go away," a quietly wretched little voice replied. "I don't want to talk to anyone. Go away."

"I'm sorry, I can't," I said. "Can I come sit next to you?"

A shiver pulsated through the shadowy form. He momentarily hunched into a smaller ball, then straightened back up.

"I don't care!" came the ungracious answer, but this was progress.

I gingerly sat down on the lip of the quarry, letting my legs dangle over the edge. Hades lurked behind me. The tight expression on his face made it clear he didn't like this situation very much, and honestly, I wasn't too thrilled, either. I didn't hate heights, but the drop was a very long way down.

"Thanks. I was getting tired of standing," I said lighter. "How are you holding up?"

"How do you *think* I'm holding up?" The boy couldn't have been much older than fourteen. Small, clearly underfed, and red around the eyes.

"Badly," I admitted. "Sorry. Dumb question."

He threw a rock over the edge. "I just wanted to get out of the house for a while! Mom and Dad kept fighting, they never stopped, and I got so tired of it, and... and..."

"And you came here."

He nodded. "It was an accident. They said it wasn't, but it was. I didn't want to leave. I don't want to leave. I don't want to be alone..."

My heart wrenched at his heartbroken words. "I'm sorry, hon. Come here."

He leaned into me, his small frame tucked under my arm as I hugged him as tightly as I could. God, he was young. He clung to me, his face buried between my shoulder and neck. When I looked down at him, he gave me a crooked grin as hollow as I felt when realizing what had happened to him.

"But I'm not gonna be alone anymore," he declared, and then he threw us both over the edge.

In a brilliant moment of clarity, I realized where I screwed up—thinking about how it was going to feel to get splattered across the rocks and to be sorry for everything I wouldn't get to do. I screamed, long, loud, anguished. But we'd stopped, suspended in the air with Hades' hands gripping my arm as the dead boy still clung to my side, squawking. The Lord of the Dead cursed under his breath as he hauled me back over the edge with a growl.

"You hung on to him!" Hades chided, because of course I had.

"He still needs to go, right?" I asked shakily.

The boy made an escape attempt, but I wasn't letting him

go anywhere, maintaining a serious death grip on his arm. I dragged him upright, resisted the urge to punt him right over the edge of the cliff, and glared.

"Come on, kid," I said, vexed. "Work with me. We're trying to help you."

He started crying again, and although he might have been faking it, I didn't think so.

"I was all alone!" he cried. "I've been alone for forty years! No one comes here anymore! No one cares!"

His shouts rang in my ears. *Forty years*. How could Hades not have known this kid was missing from the Underworld for so long? I glanced at him, the question in my gaze, and his eyes were deeply troubled in response. He was hiding something. Things were a lot worse than he had let on.

I pushed that aside to discuss later. For now, the boy needed me, and I understood his pain. At first, the kid's mourners probably came to the quarry, leaving flowers, memorials, prayers—things that would have kept him company. And then… the years went by. People forgot. People healed. And he never could. They'd left him all alone.

"I'm sorry." I sighed. "But the attempted homicide of someone who was trying to help you, aside, you need to go."

"I do?" he asked with a note of surprise in his voice.

"Yep." I patted him on the shoulders. "Time for the next thing, and this man is going to show you the way."

The boy looked at Hades nervously, eyes wide, jaw trembling, and I didn't blame him. Hades' eyes had never looked darker, never more terrifying.

"Randall Willard," he intoned in a deep, booming voice that reminded me of a powerful wizard, "you will come with me."

A skull superimposed on his face as he spoke. Or did it? I shook off the thought, putting it down to a vision prompted by the adrenaline of almost dying.

The boy paled, but he glanced at me.

"It's all right," I encouraged. "It will be."

"You promise?"

"I promise. Go on."

He took the hand that Hades offered. Poor kid quaked with fear—probably

that the Lord of the Dead would bite it off. He'd been telling the truth about being stuck on that ledge for so very long. No one who didn't desperately want out would have gone anywhere near Hades when he glared like that.

I had a moment, like the one with Ms. Mae where the world went soft and fuzzy. I knew by now it was something to do with the spirits crossing over to the Underworld and moving on, and it comforted me.

Wherever Randall went next, at least it wouldn't be a sad, cold quarry in the middle of nowhere. He wouldn't be alone anymore. When he vanished, the wind whistled over the craggy rocks, rustling the trees around us.

"Wow," I said to Hades, "I hope he…"

He crossed the space between us, grabbed my wrist and dragged me close to him. I yelped even though there was no pain in it. But I'd never seen his eyes so dark, darker than the night around us; his white, sharp teeth bared.

"What are you doing?" I cried.

"What in the name of the gods were you doing?" he growled. "That was a dead spirit, forty years gone! What you did was dangerous, incredibly dangerous!"

"Did you know that he was dead for forty years?" I demanded.

He scowled at me. "Of course not. If I had known…"

I wanted to understand why the Lord of the Dead hadn't been aware of that crucial fact. It seemed like something he should have been aware of. But now didn't seem the right time to ask for clarification.

"And sure, I know now to be careful! I was just doing what worked before. You were happy to let me do it then!"

"And I was wrong!" Hades snapped.

He didn't let go of my wrist as he started walking back to the car, pulling me along with him. I trotted to keep up.

"I was wrong," he growled, almost to himself. "This is no place for you, no place at all."

Great. He was freaking out again. I expected an immediate teleport back to my apartment.

"Hey!" I butt in. "I thought I was doing a pretty good job. Two out of three isn't bad!" Unless the one I missed had a penchant for homicide.

"When that one might have heaved you into a quarry to join its haunting? Yes, it is bad!"

"I'll be more careful next time," I swore. "All right? We'll figure things out before we visit the next soul."

He let go of my wrist and pushed me flat against a tree. "You were so damned reckless, and all I can think of right now is teaching you a lesson so that maybe, just maybe, you'll be less careless in the future."

Maybe I should have been terrified, but I wasn't. I shook him off, striding back toward the car. I couldn't think when he was so close to me, and I desperately needed to be able to figure it out.

I'd taken about ten steps when something—someone— yanked me backward.

"Let me go!" I yelled at whatever clung to me.

The temperature dropped a few degrees, and I shivered, taking an icy breath. I turned around. A young girl with long and tangled hair, her head bowed, her body shaking stood between me and Hades. She was dressed in an old-fashioned dress, long skirt to the ground, an apron, suggesting she might be someone's maid.

"I'm sorry, mistress," she apologized with a strange

accent. "I didn't mean to, but yon boy has been festering for many a year."

"Oh." I stepped forward, my hands held outward to show her I wasn't mad. "And you were trying to keep me from…"

She nodded, her gaze still trained on the ground. "I am very sorry."

"Hey, it's fine." I took another slow step. "I'm probably too stubborn to listen anyway."

Hades muttered *probably*, but I ignored him, still focused on the girl.

"What's your name, honey?" I asked.

"Tillie, mistress," she replied in her childlike voice. "And I am so very sorry, but I must ask you. Please, may I go too?"

"Oh, Tillie, of c–"

"No!" Hades snapped.

I looked at his adamant head shaking.

"She's not one of mine," he said. "She's meant for someone else, some other afterworld."

How many other underworlds existed? Tillie's cries made my heart ache.

"I was the last one," she whimpered. "Everyone's gone, all gone, and it's been so long. I'm so tired of being here alone, too. Please, please don't leave me here. I don't want to turn into that wretched boy."

I reached for Hades' hand. "You can't just leave her. You wouldn't, would you?"

His face turned cold and hard. "She was never called to me…"

"She's calling now," I pointed out. "Will it end the world?"

"No." And God he was such a stubborn ass. So bound in his own traditions and ideas. But I needed an outside the box moment. A bigger than a god act.

"Will it throw things out of balance if you take her?"

He didn't answer that one.

But then, God help me, I did. Hades was a man of deals. He made them, traded them, ensured they were honored.

"Take her," I urged. "I'll give you whatever you want."

He drew a quick breath, and his gaze sharpened. I shook. Trembled. Tremored. Earthquaked. But dang it. This was important. I lifted my chin.

"Please."

"Means that much to you?"

"Yeah. Yeah, she is."

He considered this for a moment. "I'll expect you to honor your word then." He spoke as if the words were a threat.

I likely should have taken it as such, but my mouth dried out, and all I could do was nod. I'd promised an underworld god a future debt. Not my finest hour.

He brushed past me to talk to Tillie. They spoke together in what must have been her native tongue. At the first few words, she lit up. It must have been a long time since she'd heard the familiar cadence of her own language. They talked for so long that I ended up sitting at the base of the tree, watching them through half-lidded eyes. God, I was tired and so cold. I rubbed at my arms. All this night work was killing me. What was with dead souls and nighttime?

I must have dozed, because the next thing I was aware of was Tillie starting to glow. She laughed, a bright and crystal-clear sound, and then, with a burst of light, she vanished.

I blinked, letting Hades' help me to my feet.

"So that's it? She's gone?"

"We have come to an agreement," he said, his voice thoughtful. "It'll work for the time being. She and I can revisit the idea, find another solution if need be."

"You're a softie, after all," I razzed with a slight smile that died away when he met my eyes.

"I'm really not," he said softly.

CHAPTER 16

Autumn

AFTER WE GOT BACK into the car, Hades paused to watch me. I fought sleepiness but should have been genuinely disquieted if someone else stared at me with such intensity, but with him, it was different and filled me with a pleasant warmth.

"I like it when you look at me like that," I muttered.

When he blinked, I gulped.

Junipers, Autumn, shut up now.

This happened when I was sleepy—the blurting of random truths that often resulted in trouble for me.

"You promised me anything I wanted." His reminder stirred trepidation within me and I shivered.

I nodded. I trusted him not to abuse the vow, but there was a long way between 'okay' and 'abuse.'

"What's your price?" I asked.

"I want twenty-four hours of your time," he stated. "A full

day and a night. You'll obey me in every way. I won't cause you any lasting hurt or real harm. But–" He paused, and I swallowed hard. It was likely the least objective thing to do at this point, but I couldn't stop myself from reaching out to him, from laying my hand over his. "But I want you."

I shivered at the desire that made his voice thicker, his eyes darker. I could have pointed out that I was ready, willing, and able to repeat what we had done the night before. This was something different, and right now there was absolutely no caution from me, not when it came to him.

"I'm yours." The moment I said it, everything went dark.

***

When I opened my eyes, I was on the floor in his lap in the broad marble halls of his palace in the Underworld. He brushed my hair over and over, and I moaned.

"You were right. It was probably best we rode in the car," I rasped, feeling woozy from the teleportation.

"Yes." He lifted me to my feet.

He'd already changed into his robe that suited him so well. I couldn't decide how I liked him best. Robes or suits. But before I could contemplate such an important issue, he pulled me into his arms and kissed me, deep, longing and perfect.

Oh. His immediate arousal poked through the loose fabric. *The robes have a certain appeal...*

The kiss took from me without offering anything in return. It couldn't have been clearer he was kissing me for his own pleasure, and mine, intense as it was, was purely incidental. The truth of it turned me on more. I clung to him, trying to deepen the kiss, but he threaded his fingers into my hair, holding me still as he continued. While I liked being man-handled, to be his to do as he wanted also, it overwhelmed me, and I sank into the wonder of it. Someone else might have felt used, but a surge of power and heat burst through me. This was how much he wanted me. How much he needed me—what he was willing to bargain for.

He broke the kiss long enough to look into my eyes. "Last chance. Do you wish to go back on our bargain?"

I bristled at the idea that he thought me weak. I wasn't surrendering because of a bargain. Tonight, I wanted to belong to him completely.

"You don't scare me." That honestly might have been just about the dumbest thing I could have said to a god. A god that wanted to devour me.

He leaned forward and sucked my lower lip between his teeth, nipping the sensitive flesh. I cried out. Then his mouth was on mine again, drinking down my cry and he slid his tongue past my lips.

All that mattered was touching him, reaching for him, letting him make me feel as if there were nothing else in the world but him. I was starved for him in a way that I barely understood, and I scratched his skin as I clung to him, but I didn't care.

Hades pulled back, taking my hand to lead me down the hall. I suspected to a bedroom, but he opened the door to a marble, claw-foot bathtub big enough for three people.

"Ooh." And a hearty Wow.

He grinned. "So glad you're impressed." His gaze burned from my toes to my throat. "Clothes off." He spoke the words so guttural, deep, desperate, as if he had every right to tell me to get out of my clothing, and for the next twenty-four hours, he did.

"Do you need help?" His question contained menace, and I wanted his hands all over me, to stretch the tension out.

"As you command." My own voice sounded shaky to my ears.

I might have made a bargain with him, but I intended to enjoy my part of it too. So I stripped slowly, removing the strap of my dress, showing the skin on my shoulder. He smiled like a wolf that happened upon a rabbit. But I was no mere rabbit. I peeled off the other, pulling my dress down to expose my bra. His eyes told me that he wanted to tear it off me, but I made him wait. I shimmied the dress down my waist, over my thighs and down my legs, finally kicking it off.

Down to my underwear, I wanted him to do the rest. "Looks like I need some help after all."

With a smile, he closed the distance between us and tore my bra and my panties away from me with two quick motions. In my haze, I was dimly aware of my things dropping to the ground, and then being wrapped in his arms as he kissed my face with an intense sweetness. I sank into him with a mix of need and desire.

While he stopped to run the bath water, I rested with my head against his shoulder until he pulled away from me to help me into the tub. I whimpered at the heat of the water but adjusted after a moment, sighing and leaning back against the marble side. I expected Hades to come in with me, but he took a seat next to the tub and started to wash me.

Every stroke of his hand along my skin felt incredible. My eyes fluttered shut, my limbs languid and relaxed. I lost the words to describe it. I'd washed myself before, but this was something different. He took his time, ensuring every inch of me glowed as he scrubbed me with a washcloth that felt like cashmere. I wasn't sure what he used in my hair as he, massaged it in with firm motions. By the end, some timeless space later, I was utterly boneless, letting his fingers turn me to nothing but pleasure and need.

A now-familiar heat rose between us, this time with absolutely no urgency. I'd been put into a place where the timing of release was going to be on Hades' schedule.

"Up on your hands and knees now, darling," he ordered me.

I purred. *Darling*. I moved into the position he'd commanded. The water only came up to my chin in this position, and I shivered as he gently blew on my back.

"Cold!" I panted.

"Of course." He pressed the warm washcloth up between my legs.

"Oh, you can't." His laugh—low, soft, and utterly without mercy—made me moan.

"Of course, I can." His absolute authority had me letting go of everything but the arousal building from the strokes between my legs. "Stop thinking. Just feel."

I sank into his touch and the pleasure. Only his caress mattered, and I chased the bright sparks of need flying through me at the speed of light.

How can anything in the world feel this good?

I didn't know, but Hades did, and he was using that answer to make me see stars. All I needed to do was shake and whimper. He used the same slow rhythm, as if he had no concept of time, no need to be doing anything else.

Tension spiraled through me until I rocked in the water, and ripples danced across the surface. Just when the heat became unbearable, when I was sure I would spill straight over... he stopped.

"Hey!" He rewarded my protest with a brisk slap to the thigh. I cried out again, but my tone was entirely different from simply being startled.

"You're on my time right now," he murmured as he started touching me again. I didn't have the wit or the will to protest.

I only wanted what he offered, and lots of it. In another time, I might have been shocked at my own wanton greed, but as Hades had said, I was on his time right now.

The coiled tension scaled faster and more powerfully this time. I braced myself, afraid he might pull away as he had last time, leaving me gasping and wanting. In my delirium, I didn't know if I could bear it a second time.

That train of thought was derailed and then subsequently set on fire as I realized that Hades wasn't stopping. In seconds, my climax swept over me, consuming me, my uncontrollable cries echoing off the marble walls. Shame and decorum were out the door as his hand stilled and I rode out the pleasure. By the end, I was trembling and panting, almost shocked by how good it felt—having that washcloth pressed against my clit, having him hold me open so he could reach the parts he wanted.

"Wow, that was–"

I was cut off by my own sharp gasp when his fingers started moving again over my sensitive spot.

"What was it, dearest?" Hades inquired softly. "You were saying something."

"You're… you're touching me." I shuddered when he inserted one finger inside me, exploring, giving my more sensitive flesh some time to recover, but still arousing me as intensely.

"Yes?"

"Why?"

"I should think it would be obvious," he said, and another finger joined the first. I felt none of the pain from the last time we'd done something like this, no shock and disruption. Only a sweet and smooth slide of pleasure, something so good that my eyes closed, and my mouth fell open once more.

"You're beautiful," he began slowly, "you're mine, and I want you utterly exhausted with pleasure..."

He continued talking, and I did my best to listen, but it was difficult because my body tensed again, spiraling and plunging toward a shiver with an indistinguishable need. When I went over the edge a second time, it was with a wavering cry and a full body twitch that sloshed water all over Hades and the floor. But he obviously didn't care because *he didn't stop.*

"I... I can't..." I cried.

He paused, and I peeked up to meet his dark eyes. Something about his look shook me. One of complete and utter possession, but with so much depth to it that I thought I could have drowned in it. The palace could have burned down around us, but his gaze still would have penetrated to the heart of me.

"Does it hurt?" he asked.

"What?" I could barely get a word out.

A smack to the rear this time made me groan indulgently.

"Does it hurt?" he repeated with more force.

"No... no." I recalled my dream, and the memory of him tying me up, and what he'd done to me... in another lifetime. I didn't know why I was remembering these things or who I was in them.

"Tell me if it does."

And that was all. It sent a delicious lassitude through my limbs.

Things got fuzzy after that. I got lost in what he did to me, my climaxes lighter and shallower, but repeatedly coming. Rolling over me, exhausting me until finally I had to reach back, shaking my head.

"No... no more."

"Does it hurt?"

"It's starting to."

Hades pulled away, stood up, and retreated. For a moment, I worried that I'd pissed him off somehow. Before I could do or say anything, he was at the edge of the bathtub again with an enormous fluffy towel. Lifting me, wrapping it around my body. The pure luxurious delight of the cotton and his embrace as he scooped me up in his arms calmed me more than anything in the world could have. I pressed my head against his shoulder as he carried me out of the bathroom.

I murmured with pleasure as he gently kissed my forehead. I couldn't remember a time when I had ever felt this good. Hadn't even known it was possible. A strange and rare treat to be so exhausted . But still, I wasn't quite satisfied yet.

When he laid me down on a bed outfitted with black silk sheets, I clung to a fold of his robe, refusing to let him leave.

"Not done yet," I said, aware that my voice was hoarse from crying out.

In the dim light, he raised an eyebrow. "No?"

"I want…" I gestured in the air with my hands. "You. Want you."

He leaned back, tall and proud, which told me my request hadn't been in the plans. He probably intended to let me sleep for a bit, because yeah, I was worn out.

But I wasn't done yet—at least, not until he was—so I propped myself up on my elbow, looking at him. "Please?"

Hades swore, I wondered when he had learned Russian, or something that sounded a great deal like it.

"Look at you." He stripped off his robe. "You can barely move."

"So, move me." The way he threw his shoulders back made my stomach clench with renewed desire.

"At a future time, you are going to pay for changing our deal," he warned, crawling over me.

"Not now?" I teased, wishing for him to tie me up like he

had in the memory in my dream, or spank me again. That way he could have his way with me, and I didn't have to do a thing.

He answered by pulling a few pillows from the head of the bed and throwing them at the center. Then he picked me up and threw me over them with the same strength. I whimpered, and then he was on me, spreading my legs, his weight draping over me like something I'd been wanting for years.

"Most precious," he murmured, "and mine."

On the final word, he thrust deep, slowly but with no hesitation. I moaned, moving against him with all the strength I had. His body responded, pushing deeper with a need that left me moaning.

He kept whispering in my ear, some things I understood, some I didn't. When he finally came inside me, I cried out with him, clenching my legs around his hips as if it were the only thing in the world I cared about. Another climax of my own hovered near, but I pushed it back because I wanted more—wanted him inside me and hungry for what I could give him. The moment simultaneously stretched out forever and was over almost too soon at the same time.

Finally, he rolled off me, dragging me with him in his arms.

"*Now* we can rest." I almost purred with infinite satisfaction, startling a laugh out of him.

"You aren't afraid of me at all, are you?" he asked with a kind of wonder in his voice.

"If I were, I never would have agreed to let you have me for a day and a night." I yawned, curling closer.

Now that the heat of passion had dissipated somewhat, I was aware of a chill in the air. His soft laugh and the way he stroked my still-damp hair warmed me, and I smiled, already nodding off.

CHAPTER 17

Hades

I STAYED after Autumn drifted off, watching the rise of her chest, her soft exhales, and the peaceful expression on her face. Her nose was long and thin, and her lips full and luscious. So beautiful. So full of power. So unaware. I brushed away the emerald hair falling over her face and stopped. No. I didn't deserve her. Not when I hid secrets from her.

As a child, I had learned the hard way to keep things to myself. To avoid punishment from my spiteful and cruel mother, who would punish me if she discovered what I had been doing. I always had to fight for the last scrap of bread, which she'd reserve for her older children, denying me. Each night, I'd cling to my body warmth on the cold of the floor, which she forced me to sleep on even though my brothers and sisters received soft, cozy beds.

I had to fight to earn my father's attention, especially

when he worked long hours and oftentimes ventured on lengthy visits for business. And whenever he was home, mother played the dutiful wife, pretending to care for me. All for show, of course, out of fear of being struck or worse.

Although I had been born into a wealthy Russian family, I'd been the accidental child, my mother already in her forties when she delivered me. The product of rape, she never wanted me and had tried several times to kill me… or so Hades had informed me. My face, she used to tell me, reminded me of what my father had done to her.

After her initial attempts had failed, she continued her efforts to let me die, and I suffered every day of my life. She forbade the servants from feeding me or changing my soiled garments, and they, fearful of losing their income to support their own families, abandoned me.

Were it not for my oldest sister, seventeen at the time, I would have never survived. While mother was busy entertaining guests, or sleeping with one of her various lovers, my sister would sneak to my side to care for me, to feed me, to play with me. Those had been the happiest times of my life. None of my other siblings had given me a second glance, each one poisoned by my mother's cruel claims that I was a devil.

I had lost my sister when I was six, and she twenty-two, to some horrible chest infection. My life had returned to the hell by which it had started. But since I'd been older, I'd also grown wiser, using the tricks my beloved sister had taught me to survive.

When I turned eighteen, my father had employed me in his business, where I met the love of my life. A year later, we were married and moved into the marital home my father had purchased for us. My heart stung at the painful reminder of losing her.

I did not like keeping secrets, but it had been a way of life for me. Stealing some cheese here, a blanket there, or a goblet of water out of thirst—life had not been kind to me and secrets kept me alive.

My ability to keep them had led me straight to Hades, for the dead told plenty of them. They entrusted me with confessions of sins and regrets, which I stored away for their judgment, rehabilitation, and ultimate return to the Land of the Living in a new incarnation, once they lived out their penance or time of contemplation.

My gaze fell on Autumn and guilt choked me. She deserved to know what she was becoming. What she could do. Why she'd been chosen. But I couldn't bring myself to tell her. Whenever I'd spoken the truth as a child I'd been punished, and I feared, *dreaded* Autumn punishing me in some form too. Or leaving me like my sister had. Leaving me to the mercy of my mother like my father had. Leaving me to the all-consuming grief like my wife and child had after they died from infection.

I climbed out of the bed and paced along the long bed until the pain in my chest threatened to tear open, and I had to leave the room.

The goddess had chosen another human to represent her. Autumn. During her long period of slumber, she had only diffused small amounts of her essence into an avatar as dictated by decree from Zeus.

Yet, Autumn was different. Her powers extended well beyond those of previous avatars imbued with the magic of the springtime goddess. Every part of me ached to tell Autumn, but I didn't know how. I didn't want her to leave. Not when I needed her help collecting souls. When I needed her by my side after being lonely for so long.

I walked through the silent halls of my palace. Servants coasted about, conducting their duties—preparing my breakfast, fussing over the emerald dress I asked they make my guest, and maintaining order and precision in the palace, just as I liked it.

Eventually, I found myself in the garden I had made for the springtime goddess. Beds of narcissus flowers had been laid out in the geometrical pattern of the goddess in the stars above. There was no coincidence that the formation of the garden is the same as Autumn's necklace, also the symbol which depicts how the goddess had selected her. Gifted to her as a small child, it represented the springtime qualities throughout her human life.

I sat on the stone chair in the middle of the garden, running my fingertips over the top of the blossoms. Gold like the goddess' hair, as well every color of the rainbow. My chest contracted. I hadn't visited this place in centuries. It reminded me too much of her absence. But now, it seemed to be the only place that could bring me solace when so many thoughts crashed in my mind.

None of the other avatars chosen by the goddess could speak to the dead, or even see them. Something had changed. I wondered if the goddess decided to awaken and imbue more of her essence into her new avatar.

The God half of me brightened at the prospect of the Lady of the Spring, his companion, returning. But my human component, which made up the blend of human and god, blanched. I'd never loved the goddess. For so long, my heart belonged to the wife and child I lost to the plague. After three lonely and haunted centuries, I finally discovered another who warmed my stony heart. The woman lying in my bed.

A conundrum indeed. If the goddess were to return, that would present a difficult challenge and the strong possibility of the god unmerging with me to reunite with her. Olympus knew we needed that solution to fix the problems in the realm, the lost souls, and the winter plaguing the afterlife. But what did that mean for me? Would I return to being an empty avatar? I should have departed this world some three hundred years ago, but thanks to the god, I acquired immortality, advanced healing, and the power of the dead. Without that, I'd age and possibly wither away, ending up in the Underworld too. At least my soul could rest with my wife and child. But part of me was not ready to go just yet. I still had goals to achieve.

"Sorry to bother you, master." A dainty voice interrupted my thoughts. Melody, my servant.

I tensed and admired the grey and stormy skies instead of looking at her. Long ago the darkness had replaced the violet haze previously painting my realm.

"Yes?" I replied, my voice hoarse, tight from the decisions ahead of me.

"You've been summoned to the Fields of Mourning." She delivered a message from my general, the Underworldling I put in charge of managing a specific district within our realm.

"What for?" I turned to glare for the intrusion. "I'm busy. I have a guest."

Truth be told, I wanted a break from dealing with the afterlife when I had so many of my own troubles to ponder. Yet, I had to address these issues before anything got out of hand. The Underworld required smooth operation to prevent chaos. I wouldn't have my realm dissolve into the disorder that Zeus ruled Olympus with.

"Yes, I know." Melody lifted her gaze a fraction and smiled. "It's wonderful to see you happy again."

Happy. The word echoed in my mind. I hadn't been in such a long time. The combination of the god's and my own heartache and sorrow weighed on me. I missed the family and friends I left behind so many lifetimes ago.

Since Autumn came into my life, I hardly had any time to

think on the past. She kept me on my toes. Challenged me in ways I hadn't encountered in hundreds of years, and it excited and tested me.

"I tried holding off as long as I could while you entertained the mistress," Melody informed. "But it's urgent."

Entertained. It had been centuries since I'd brought or invited a guest to the palace. Just recently I had made a deal with Charon to play chess to distract myself from long and isolated nights. Before that, I only had Melody to fuss over me as my closest servant.

"It better be urgent to call me away," I acquiesced, swiping a flower and tucking it under the brooch on my toga to remind me of the woman lying in my bed.

"Yes, master." Melody retreated, nodding.

As I walked out, small, soft footsteps padded behind me.

"Master," she called out after me. "The mistress is… not going to leave again, is she?"

Leave. The word hit me like a boulder to the chest. Our greatest fear. Both god and man haunted by the same event where the ones we loved left us—mine in tragedy, the god's out of necessity. Neither of us wanted to be alone. We craved companionship, intimacy, and loyalty. But Autumn seemed a free spirit, content with her freedom, her own company. She was also burdened by the loss of her mother, which manifested in intimacy issues. I gathered that she shied away from relationships. Why else would a woman like her still be a virgin?

This information set a clock ticking in my mind. One that counted down the days and hours and minutes until she would leave. I just couldn't see the numbers yet.

Eventually she would discover who she was through expressions of her power. Each person took the news of their powers differently. Previous avatars had fled, worried the god would take over their entire beings and irreparably change them.

In my case, I'd vanished into the woods for days after Hades first visited me. It took time to process the news I'd been chosen, to overcome the denial. Of all the gods, the one responsible for overseeing the Underworld had picked me. What a warped proposal, coming on the heels of the death of my newborn and my wife. At first, I confused the proposal as a twisted joke. Oh, how I had raged, hacking at trees with my sword, cutting down anything that got in my way. But after exhausting myself, I calmed, and processed the meeting.

But my fears had been in vain. If anything, the power of the god enhanced avatars, made us better and stronger. Well, for some at least, excluding that annoying agent of Hermes. Mads. Such a disrespectful tool.

I lifted my hands and snapped my fingers to transport myself across the realm to The Crag, a district where I housed souls guilty of singular murder, rape, perjury, corruption, theft, vandalism, and persecution. Icy winds whistled off the barren rocks encasing the horrors within. Over the peak, a wasteland absent of scenery, of just pure stone, all grey, dull, and lifeless, awaited.

I glanced at the next district, miles to the east. Tartarus, where eternal pits of fire raged, was reserved for the absolutely foul, abominable, and despicable souls. Warmongers guilty of mass genocide; psychopaths so devoid of remorse they stole from the poor, murdered or raped; and those who had polluted drinking water, infected food with poisons, or loaded medicines with toxins that made the sick more ill and dependent on additional drugs.

I climbed the steps overlooking The Crag and glanced at the scene within. Souls writhed on the cold stone, wailing for release. But that wasn't the point of this district. Each sector been set up sort of like a prison, this one equivalent to medium security, with patrols and hellhounds like Cerberus to guard it.

"Thank you for coming, my lord." Thaddeus, my general for The Crag, greeted me with a solemn nod. "Sorry to drag you away from your business."

I examined the weary lines on his forehead, the keen grey of his eyes, and the silver in his hair. He was an old soul who had served the god faithfully for two thousand years, with honor and integrity. One of my top generals, whom I trusted implicitly.

"What's the problem?" I straightened, my back creaking with the weight of the Underworld's problems I carried.

"A breach, my lord," Thaddeus explained.

"What?" Unheard of. Not once in all my years had this ever happened. No one had ever escaped from any of my realms. The prospect scratched at the back of my neck.

"Come," he said, turning to leave. "I'll show you."

The stress amplified, and I hunched. Imbalance festered in my realm from the six hundred year absence of the goddess. She was meant to dwell in the Underworld during the winter and return to the Land of the Living in spring.

Over the past few days, I'd suspected this was the reason I hadn't realized souls were missing from the Underworld. As part of this realm, I too was subject to the imbalance causing the slowly consuming winter that dulled my powers and senses. I pushed aside that thought to focus on the task at hand, however.

We walked a few hundred meters to a fissure in the rock, as if split by the effect of an earthquake. Impossible. The Underworld existed in another realm separate from the physical and did not suffer the movements of the Earth.

I ran a shaky finger along the jagged edge just wide enough for a human body of medium size to squeeze through. "How did this happen?"

My gaze pinged between my general and the crack. I wanted answers. I wanted a solution. I wanted order and balance.

"We don't know, my lord," he replied, his voice hesitant and wary.

Long ago, the god had a temper. Right after the springtime goddess had left, he'd blamed himself and had taken his self-loathing out on everyone. What a horrible century that had been. I tried to bury it, but my faithful servants never forgot, even if I was a later date avatar.

"Did any souls escape?" I turned back to my general, whose thinned lips were all the answer I needed.

Thaddeus bowed his head. "Eight so far, my lord."

Almighty Olympus.

A vein in my forehead pulsed. It would take days or maybe even weeks to track each one down and bring them back to the Underworld. Days I didn't have when I still had to retrieve the souls who hadn't arrived in the afterlife. My mind spun with conflicting problems, each one a priority, each one pressing me to be solved. I didn't know which one to tackle first. An ache formed in my forehead, and I rubbed it, drawing in a slow and steady breath to calm myself.

Think, Hades, think.

First order: collect the stray souls who had failed to turn up in the Underworld. After all, I'd gone to the trouble of hiring Autumn to help me, and I couldn't leave her to find the souls herself. Too dangerous, especially after the boy had tried to kill her and take her with him. No. We would continue on that mission together until every last soul was accounted for. That way, I could ensure her safety.

As for the escaped souls, I refused to assign any of my generals to the needed searches at the risk of the districts falling into further disarray. I needed an alternative, someone to track down the escapees and alert me to their whereabouts so I could gather them myself. Oh, how I would punish those souls for fleeing. Their insolence and audacity. Straight to the Tartarus with them!

I stared deep and hard into Thaddeus' eyes, and he winced at my flinty gaze.

"Send the hellhounds to find the dead," I ordered with a careful and controlled tone. "Don't let the beasts return without accounting for every last one of the escaped souls. Tell the hounds to send word when they have tracked the prisoners. I want to personally collect them."

"Yes, my lord." Thaddeus nodded and retreated deeper into The Crag, drifting straight through the rocky face into the depths below, where we stored the hellhounds.

Tonight, I would unleash my deadly beasts on the wretched souls who had fled my realm.

CHAPTER 18

*A*utumn

NOTHING CHANGED. One day a virgin. Next day not. Screwing a god who screwed like he was a god should've made a difference. But again, nothing changed. Still needed sleep. Still needed food. Still had to pee.

I woke up to an empty room with a lunch laid out and a soft dress draped over the chair. The food, a platter of cheeses, olives, meats, dried fruits, and vegetables, delighted my tongue. The dress, a deep spring green, fit and hugged my curves in all the right places.

Alone in the room, I didn't like being left in a strange place. I missed Hades and didn't know what to make of it. I longed to hear his deep voice and went looking for him. I found him in the garden below. From the balcony, I observed him for a few moments. He sat on a bench, contemplative and tense, running his hands over the colored daffodils as he glanced at his gardens.

He lingered near beds laid out with geometrical precision, each surrounding tall, marble statues. I gasped at the medley of hues. I hadn't even known some colors were possible.

Then I noticed the shape of the garden beds, two back-to-back crescent moons on each side of a cross—the symbol depicted on my necklace. I touched the pendant as I moved away from the balcony, heading for the garden.

The Lord of the Underworld sat in the back, in his toga, without a hair out of place.

"Hi." I draped my arms over his shoulder so I could kiss the top of his head. He gripped my wrists and brought my hands up to kiss my palms.

"Who made this garden?" I asked.

"I did," he replied with a sting in his voice.

A sensitive topic, but I had to understand the connection with my necklace. "For Persephone?"

He tensed. "Yes."

I didn't understand, so I pulled away, unclasping my necklace as I walked around to sit beside him. I put the jewelry in his hand. "What does this symbol mean?"

His face hardened, and he stared at the pendant. "It is the Transpluto symbol, representing death and rebirth."

"Where is the spring goddess?" I leaned down to smell one of the daffodils. "Is this a memorial garden for her?"

"The garden was a gift," he answered, his voice tight. He closed his hand over the pendant. "No. She is not dead. Just gone."

"Where?" He jumped up when I asked.

"She left," was all he said, his back to me.

He was hiding something, some important detail I needed to know.

"A lady at a fair gave me this necklace," I offered, not

wanting to give up just yet. "She called me the Lady of Spring. Wasn't that what they called Persephone?"

He spun to drop the necklace in my lap. "We don't say *that name* here!" The snarl in his voice, more than the words, poke loudly and in detail. But I needed answers. He obviously still harbored feelings for her.

"So, is this a god thing?" I asked.

He looked at me, startled, red and flustered. "Is what a god thing?"

"All of this." I circled my finger. "We do what we did last night, then get back to work in the morning."

God. I was babbling. His fault for not opening up to me.

He stared at me like he was going to say then snapped his mouth shut. "I am employing you to help me solve an issue I cannot solve on my own."

"Oh." I had to blink back the sudden tears that sprang to my eyes. He'd really only wanted me for one night and day, nothing more. I guessed being in his garden had reminded him of who he really loved. My stomach clenched. "Um, I…"

In a moment, I was in his arms, holding him just as tight, running my hand along his back. "That wasn't…" he trailed off, his voice low.

"Did you mean that it's more important that we focus on the job?" I squeezed him, not wanting him to let me go.

"I did, but that's not all." He leaned his chin on the top of my head. "There's a job ahead of us that we must do." Urgency laced his tone, which stirred a lump in my throat. "The dead are… they need us. You know that, don't you?"

I nodded. The dead whom I had met so far had shared a common denominator of misery and helplessness. They needed both of us, and even if he was meant to be my boss, I couldn't deny the tug of duty any more than he could.

"We have to take care of that first." He stroked my back. "After that… everything else will fall into place."

Fall into place. What the bag of fertilizer fell into place mean? Junipers! Dark thought. Self-doubt. Ugh.

"You know." I tried to find my happy place. "I've found that that almost never happens in real life—things just falling into place."

Hades pulled back and cradled the side of my face in his hand. A stray tear escaped, and he thumbed it from my cheek with a gesture so tender I trembled. It was a strange contrast to look at how kind he was now while remembering what he had done to me just a few short hours ago. All the same man, yet different, and that enthralled me.

"I like to think of myself as an optimist," he explained.

I did a double take. "You know that dressing all in black doesn't really shout that?"

He laughed.

"I'm a man of faith, how about that? Is that better?"

"Faith…" I had never been much for faith. I didn't have a relationship with it, and it had never come to intersect with my life all that much. But Hades wasn't talking about some higher power. In his narrow scope, he *was* the higher power. No, he was talking about something else, and his eyes warmed me in places I wasn't even aware had been cold.

Me, I thought. *He has faith in me.*

"All right." I stepped back from him.

He looked disappointed with my answer, but the truth was if I kept on letting him look at me like that, because maybe if I kept letting him touch me, we would never leave the palace.

"All right?" he echoed.

"Yeah." I took his hand and tugged. "Let's take care of business. And then we'll figure *us* out, all right?"

Something made him smile, and to my surprise, he leaned in to kiss me on the cheek. It was lighter, sweeter, more playful than the kisses we'd shared before. No one just looking at Hades for the first time would have said that he was a sweet man.

"Good," he affirmed.

"Cool. Well, boss, let's get on the road. We have people to help."

***

After a brief spell of teleportation dizziness and nausea, I felt pretty darned in control when we hit the road that night, headed back across the state to a place not far from my hometown.

I only realized our destination when we rolled up to Allwin Medical Center, one of the biggest hospitals in the state. Trembles I'd long since buried reemerged. I pressed one hand to my stomach, cradling it with the other. This was where my mom had come for her treatment.

The doctors had given her a fifty percent chance of surviving, but no matter how hard she fought the sleepless nights, the pain, and the toxins leaching strength from her already frail body, she never gave up. Not until the last night when death came for her.

Hades had said that my mom didn't belong in his afterlife. Which one had she gone to? I wondered if I was destined for the same underworld as her. My choices—staying with Hades in the Underworld, or being with my mother in her afterlife—made me stomach roll. One with joy the other with pain. Not that I planned on leaving any time soon when I had a whole lifetime ahead of me.

The Lord of the Dead parked at the bright and bustling entrance reserved for emergency drop-offs. I almost thought he planned on magicking the car invisible or something, but when nothing happened, I shook my head and put my hand over his.

"No, don't you dare," I ordered, my voice tight. "Parking lot's to the right. You're a god; you can afford to pay the parking fees."

He gave me a quick and sharp glare, but he silently drove into the enormous garage and parked.

When I opened the door, I nearly threw up. Same acrid smell of exhaust and gasoline. Cold and subterranean. Years ago, I'd read that scent is one of the biggest triggers for our memories, and this scent spilled a whole box of memories in my head that I had marked *"Please do not touch ever."*

At Hades' curious gaze, I shook my head.

"Let's get this show on the road, all right?" I insisted, determined to get in and out fast so that I didn't have linger where all my pain resided.

"Is everything–?"

I hopped out of the car and crossed the parking garage to the elevators.

He had to follow me.

The parking lot had changed sometime in the last five years. Before, they'd been beige but now they were painted with bright cartoon characters, likely to reminders for specific floors of the garage. We were on Green Bear, and I imprinted that into my brain with a grimness that it didn't deserve. Traveling down in the elevator dredged up the old horrid sinking feeling of losing my mom and being unable to do a thing about it.

When we walked in, I stopped at the desk to sign us in and nearly threw up again, but the nurse didn't look at me.

"Excuse me." I swallowed my bile. "Can I get a pen?"

The nurse kept typing on her computer.

I waved a hand in front of her face. Nothing. Then I

looked at Hades. He hid—poorly—the fact that he had been examining me.

"She cannot see you," he advised. "I made you invisible so we could get past the desk."

"Oh."

He reached for me. "I can imagine what you're thinking."

But I made a cutting motion with my hand. "And I can assure you I doubt that."

He smoothed his jacket over his broad chest.

"You paid me to do a job, and it's a job I'll do, okay?" I brushed my hair with my fingers and took a deep breath. "Soonest begun is soonest done, right? Come on. Where are we headed?"

For a moment, I thought he might tell me *no*—that I wasn't up for it. Then he'd have had a real fight on his hands. It was a fight he'd win hands down given the fact he was an actual god. But I was stubborn, so I'd still put up a good fight.

Instead of arguing, Hades nodded. "That way."

I let him start walking before falling into step behind him.

My stomach twisted as memories played in my mind. The pillows propping my mother up, her sunken, sallow cheeks and deadened eyes, the smile she'd put on for me when I knew it killed her inside for me to see her like that. Her hands, weakened by the treatment, squeezing mine with all her might. God, how long had it been? Five years. Time had done nothing to erode the rawness curling in my stomach or the ache in my chest.

I concentrated on Hades' back rather than glancing at patients, nurses, or family members. I couldn't bear the memories. His figure looked like nothing else at the hospital, and I didn't remember anyone like him from the long months I had spent here.

During the evening, the hospital hallway traffic was reduced to its night shift, the nurses and custodians who kept the hospital ticking along until dawn. Behind every door we passed lurked a story, some kind of pain, and someone having what might be the very worst night of their life or the very last. I forced myself to take a deep breath, and then another.

Since her death, I dreaded visiting hospitals. After I started at Pearl's, I only did hospital deliveries for a short while, until I'd burst into tears one day after a traumatic flashback. No one wanted to make runs to the funeral homes, so I traded up. Weird, considering I'd technically traded the dying for death, but somehow it was easier once they were gone—the peace of passing on radiating through me.

I jumped when Hades took my hand, gentle and protective. I glanced up, but he wasn't looking at me. He charged forward with the same kind of single-minded intent that I was used to, except now he was doing so while holding my hand.

That's something about him, I thought suddenly. *He might look cold, hard, and unreachable. But beneath that layer's a kindness he doesn't want anyone to know.* And it made me wonder why he had shut himself away. Why he'd locked himself in his cage of indifference.

We didn't have to talk about the careful way he held my fingers like he was afraid he might crush them. Together, we made our way through the hospital until we found the person we were looking for. I expected us to end up in oncology, my stomach churning. But we arrived at neonatal, instead, which was almost worse. The tightness in my chest intensified.

Outside one of the private rooms, a tall man dressed in a rumpled suit was slumped in an uncomfortable chair with his legs tucked under to make sure he wouldn't trip anyone. He was maybe ten years older than I was, or maybe it was only his weariness and the silver stubble on his jaw that made him look that way. I could see the frame of the chair straight through his body.

Hades and I exchanged a look. Although what had happened at the quarry was still fresh on my mind, he gave me a small, nearly imperceptible nod and stood back. He still stood close enough, though, to jump in if I needed him.

"Wait just a second." I trotted back to the turn of the hall where there was a coffee machine.

Hospital coffee was never good, but it didn't have to be. It had to be hot, sour, and enough to keep you awake, and that was about it. I took a few packets of sugar and cup of creamer too, then went back. The man looked up, and the moment he saw I wasn't a nurse or a doctor, he looked away.

"Hi," I began. "What do you take with your coffee?"

He raised his eyebrows but sat straighter, glancing at Hades for a moment before returning his gaze to me.

"Um, cream and a sugar," he replied. "Thank you."

"Sure thing." I took my time mixing everything up because I didn't think he would be able to hold the cup, not with how transparent his hands were.

Soon I got him talking about who he was and why he was here. Barnard Ross had had everything going for him until he didn't, and one night at Allwin Medical had taken it all away from him. As he talked, his voice fractured while skipping back and forth over the night he had lost his wife and newborn daughter at once. The picture came together, and I knew that if I went looking, I'd find the death announcements for Lynne and Lucy Ross, followed shortly after by his as well, although separately caused by a car accident just two days after. Again, I didn't know how I knew. I just did. It was less important than telling me about the nursery they'd painted for Lucy, about their good-natured arguments about schooling, and the less-good natured ones about her parents and his. Each one had been promised lives they'd never get to live.

I glanced at Hades and noticed his eyes moistening. Had this soul softened him?

Barnard continued talking, until finally, he gazed at me and then at Hades. "I'm... I'm not supposed to be here anymore, am I?"

It was all I could do not to reach over and give him a hug. But I had learned my lesson, even if there were no cliffs to chuck me over. Instead, I gave him my hand, the one not holding the cooling coffee, and let him squeeze it.

"No," I told Barnard. "But this man can get you where you need to go."

He nodded, standing up and turning to Hades. Both of them looked as if they had the weight of the world on their shoulders, with their sagged shoulders and curled backs. But Barnard straightened his back as if finally ready to go.

"All right," he consented.

I gave him a grim smile before turning away, heading for the sink around the corner. As I dumped the coffee, a glimmer of the afterglow of his soul departing tickled me but didn't cheer me.

Hades took longer than normal to catch up with me. I'd mostly stopped shaking, and I hadn't thrown up. I deserved a pat on the back for that.

"Autumn?" Hades' voice was low and croaky for someone normally so stoic and strong.

"Is Barnard okay?" I changed the subject because we didn't need to talk about how I felt. This wasn't about me.

Hades nodded, his gaze never wavering from me, but I caught a redness evident in his eyes that hadn't been there before, and his normally perfect kempt hair was disheveled, and creases lined his shirt.

This soul had affected him for a reason he didn't want to

discuss. Strange for the Lord of the Dead, who must have been used to encountering thousands if not more souls. "That one was hard for you?" I asked.

Muscles in his cheeks flexed, but he remained silent. There was a lot he wasn't saying, a lot he let slide, so I reached for his hand to show him how much I cared for him.

"I lost a wife and child one long ago." I reached for him but he pulled away. "We must leave. Barnard has gone where he needs to go."

A sickening lurch told me that he might have wished to go on to find his wife and his daughter like Barnard. The room spun, and I had to take a deep breath. I was holding on to Hades' hand too tightly, and after a moment, I let it go.

"We should get on the road then," I said, voice flat.

"Of course." Hades led the way again, but the strength had been zapped from his usually powerful stride.

On the other hand, I breathed easier knowing we were leaving.

Someone coded in a room we passed, and I froze for a moment. Alarms sounded and nurses in scrubs flooded the hallway, moving equipment, shouting numbers that I either recognized or almost did, making me feel as if the ground was simultaneously too far away and far, far too close.

With shaky legs, I managed to lurch away from the room where the nurses and support staff congregated, but not before I got a glimpse of a body on the bed. The man shook violently and tried to shout out before being surrounded by people trying to save his life.

For a second, I was dead certain I was going to hit the floor, curl into a ball, and start bawling. But before I could, Hades' arms were around me, holding me tightly, and all I could smell was the fabric of his suit and the slight hint of his earthy scent. I wanted to be tough, to push away and keep going, but I wasn't that tough, was I?

Clinging to him as if he was the only real thing in the world, I buried my face in the side of his chest, concentrating on nothing but his presence, his arms around me, the way he almost squashed me between his body and the cement wall. His warmth helped chase away the cold until I finally got my breath back.

"What do you want?" he asked, voice low and urgent.

I hung onto that, because it was similar to what he had used on me last night. Everything would be okay if I just listened to him. Everything would be fine. Just fine. "Get me out of here."

He nodded and raised his hand to snap his fingers.

CHAPTER 19

Autumn

I STAGGERED , groping for something to steady my spinning head. Hades found me, bracing me against his body once more. I sucked in gasps of air perfumed with fried foods, machine grease, and sweat. Confused by our location, I looked around wildly, prompting a few startled people to skitter away from me.

Throngs of people wearing smiles. Candle lanterns hung like pink, blue, and green moons in the dark sky as a parade of women in traditional Asian dresses wove large fans in a dance. Men carrying umbrellas with tassels. We were in the middle of a carnival.

"What... the hell?" I mumbled.

Hades stood next to me, as out of place as ever in his black suit, his hair ruffled more than before, a hint of panic in his gaze that I had never seen before.

LADY OF THE UNDERWORLD

"You told me to get you out."

People marched past hoisting a golden paper dragon on tall poles, each motion fluttering the scales. The man holding up the head swooped it in close to Hades, and he brushed it aside.

"I suppose I concentrated on that more than about where *out* meant," he added.

Cute. I liked that he had taken me someplace else. Someplace livelier and without the gloom of the hospital. The explosion of colors, smells, and noises lifted my spirits.

"So where is this?" I gazed around, out of place as we were among the few white people on the street. Everyone else was Asian, dressed in bright colors and intent on having a good time.

"Vietnam, I think," he said after a moment, uncertain. "Festival time, clearly, though I don't know for what. I can send us back."

He raised his hand, but I pulled it down. I still felt nauseas, my stomach churning and head whirling. I wanted to stay and explore. I'd never been out of the country before. The festival was expansive, and the motion made him freeze because he stared at me with his lips slightly parted.

Oh. He's falling for me. Or some part of me. That realization, coming on the heels of everything that had happened earlier, absolutely did not need reflection from me right this moment.

"Do you want to...?" He looked everywhere but me as if lost for words.

"Come on." I dragged us deeper into the street despite the lingering effects of the teleportation. "Doesn't this look like fun?"

"I don't–" he started, but I didn't give him a choice.

He could drag me to a halt, let me go, or follow, yet after

that strange revelation I'd had, I knew exactly which one he would do. I darted into the crowd, and Hades rushed after me. Each step made my teleportation sickness sink to the back of my mind.

Being a florist with a high school education meant I didn't get a lot of opportunities for travel, though I'd always longed to see out-of-the-way places. I had a vacation fund, but it was regularly dismantled for things like emergency health issues and new tires.

I also always worried I would be too nervous or too shy to have a good time, but at the street festival I was surrounded by people who wanted to celebrate, and I could do that.

The rain had recently come to an end, but the humidity lingered and heat blanketed heavily over me. I laughed for what felt like the first time in ages. Vendors along the streets sold charred things on a stick, and I wanted to try all of them.

Hades continued to follow me, his pace slow and cautious, but he kept up and paid for the food, occasionally pulling me back from getting run over by some granny on a scooter.

Everywhere, people were having a good time. I saw everything. Gold stars. Dragon also made in gold. The pretty girls in their traditional dresses and white trousers.

In a moment of pause, I clung to Hades, suddenly afraid of being stuck in Vietnam alone. We stopped every few feet to exclaim over this or that, and every time, he smiled and pulled me closer. I liked being in his arms. *This must be what it feels like to have a boyfriend.* But I still wasn't sure how to classify our relationship. Whether it was just for the time we worked together or for longer. Now, I just had to be content with being with him for as long as it lasted.

I couldn't stop watching him, marveling at the wonder in him as his gaze panned the sky, or the way his body eased through the crowd and the smiles that passed between us. He had gotten me out of that hospital in the best way possible. I couldn't imagine a better place, so full of life, so bright, so cheery. Perfect and gorgeous.

Lights blinked on the Ferris wheel at the end of the street —the tallest structure in the area, calling to us. Hades sighed a when I looked at him with wide eyes.

"I don't know when they last serviced it," he said uncertainly, critically examining the rusted bolts.

No wonder he was so stuffy. He didn't seem to get out much to have fun.

"It'll be fine until it isn't."

He narrowed his eyes but paid for two tickets anyway. "That's not an appropriate way to assess risk."

Despite his apprehension, we got on and the Ferris wheel started its first rotation with two bone-jarring jerks. I feared he might be right and clutched his arm. When we were level with the top of the nearby two-story building, the wheel continued with an impressively slow ascent. Hades' face paled as he looked over the edge. *Oh!* An Underworld god with a fear of heights. The irony!

"Why are you *laughing*?" Hades demanded.

I swallowed my giggles enough to respond. "Why aren't *you*?"

He started to respond but sighed and pulled me close to him instead, throwing one arm over my shoulder.

"Laugh at me again and I may just demand another twenty-four hours," he warned softly, sending a thrill dancing along my spine.

"I'd like that," I whispered into his chest. I felt his smile through the movement of his jaw against my head.

We rose almost to the sky once more, admiring the festival—a long street lit up with lights that ended at the deep darkness of the sea. I sat up higher, staring at the beauty. When Hades took my hand, the gold lantern lights reflected in his dark eyes as he drank it up. His gaze spoke of the same wonder in his heart as mine.

"Hades," I uttered.

Slowly, he turned to me as we hit the apex of the wheel's arc. Leaning in, I kissed him, our hands clasped tightly. Although there was always a hunger waiting in the wings, for the moment, it seemed content to wait. Tonight, we shared the wonder of where we were, the heat, the color, the smells. The sweetness of the moment and dizzying height all came together to make the kiss one that seized my heart and wouldn't let go.

Oh… I'm falling for him, too.

My whole world pivoted in an instant. I'd sworn to myself I'd never love anyone after my dad left and my mother died. It had just been too painful. But I couldn't deny the attraction, and that terrified me. Unable to think clearly in the stifling and humid heat, I dug my fingers into Hades' jacket and broke our kiss.

"What do you want?" he asked as the wheel started its descent. Right then, I could have asked for the world, all of it, and somehow I knew he would kill himself to get it for me.

Answers tumbled through my mind. I wanted him. I needed sleep. I wanted to be home. To hug him and laugh. To kiss him more. For him to take me right there in the gondola. Talk about a pathetic mile-high club, but I'd still count it as one.

The request that came to my lips, however, was different. I also needed flowers, plants, nature, the sounds of crickets, a warm evening breeze on my skin, and the moonlight. "Take me to a garden."

Hades hesitated, something flashing through his eyes that I didn't understand. His lips parted as if he were a man processing what he wanted most in the world. He raised his hand, and I braced myself for more sickness as he snapped his fingers, sending us someplace else.

CHAPTER 20

Autumn

THE QUIET HIT me like a hammer wrapped in velvet. Hades and I stood under a clear night sky studded with stars, the only source of light besides the lantern-like moon. The combination of warm air softer than the heat in Vietnam, the scent of Hyacinth and more bitter scent of dill, and my feet sinking in the soft earth, cleared my mind of the building pressure and the teleportation sickness that had hit with a vengeance.

I almost couldn't remember being shaky and scared at the hospital. That had been someone else. I might not have been entirely sure about who I was now, but that barely mattered to me. I needed to address my feelings for him, but I wasn't sure about how to approach it, having never done it before.

"Thank you," I said, letting him go and glancing around. "Where are we now?"

"Elusis," he said. "North of Athens."

I gave him a playful look. "And where is that? I'm not exactly well traveled."

"Ancient Greece," he replied, studying me and standing as still as the headless statue behind us.

"Back in the home country?" I teased, trying to push away the nerves bunching in my stomach. He smiled and shrugged.

Somewhere in the distance, a lonely dog yipped above the call of an owl. Enjoying the tranquility, I traced the nearby pillar, its broken edges reaching up to the sky. Vines as thick as my wrist had dismantled them year after year. I paced the broken marble walk, guarded on one side by garden plots filled with flowers and greenery. By the look of it, the plants that bloomed weren't what had been planted there previously.

"It's been left to grow wild," I noted more to myself to break the wall of silence that had sprung up between us. "No care. No love."

"Do they need love?" Hades asked me as I stooped down.

"No, only water and sun," I said, picking a small bouquet of white flowers. Tiny blooms we could only use for filler at the shop gave off a thick and heady perfume that intensified after I plucked them.

I held them up for Hades to smell, and he bent his head obediently, his eyes on me.

"They're beautiful, though, aren't they?" I was startled by how wistfully my observation came out.

A strange sense of vertigo overcame me again, as if a memory stored in my subconscious was trying to unearth itself. It was muted, though, by the sweetness of his eyes and the way he reached out to touch my face.

"You're more beautiful than any flower," he said quietly, and I smiled.

"Flatterer," I replied, loving it. "But I'm not a flower. It's not a contest."

"You're the most beautiful thing in the world to me." It should have sounded like a line, but I believed it, and there was no one else in the world for him but me.

"Hey." I felt another pun coming on I couldn't resist. "What did the flower say to his date?"

Hades pressed a firm finger to my lips, but I muttered past it anyway. "I think you're dandy, and I'm not a lion."

He narrowed his eyes and his lips formed a tight line, even as his jaw muscle twitched, and my heart melted and palpitated simultaneously.

Words bubbled from my throat—specifically *those* three words. They hung on my lips, ready to spill out. But then he kissed me, kissed them away, and the words became much less important than what he showed me in a more ancient language. His kiss was filled with love, and underneath that a passion, a need, and an understanding I'd been craving all my life. Along with it, I understood him, too. This was us, and in the end, was all that mattered to me.

Acting on instinct I could barely grasp, I cupped either side of his face. I held him still as I kissed him in return. Soft and biting nips at first, there and gone before he could make them longer until finally, I kissed him deeply, pressing my whole body against his and falling into the wonder of what it all was. It was like falling into the sea, but I knew I wouldn't drown because there would only be him, waiting for me at the bottom, arms open and with a longing in his black eyes.

"Don't," he protested the moment I pulled back.

Before I stepped back, he wrapped one hand around my wrist and stopped me, lifting my chin to make sure that I was looking straight into his face. Desire wrapped with a wild kind of grief stared back at me, his expression both powerful and intense. In that moment my view split. On one hand, I saw the power of something existing for thousands of years, but at the same time, a kind of desperation that could only belong to a man.

"Don't kiss me like that if you don't mean it," he said, his voice hoarse. "If you can't stay."

His words made me picture a velvety white rose opening in my heart. My whole life, the bud had been tightly furled and closed off, beautiful but more for its promise than for itself. His words, his need, acted on me like water and sun, and I opened my other arm toward him. I twisted my arm in his grasp but didn't break our hold. Rather, I wrapped my hand around his wrist so I could drag him closer as I thought how much I would never, ever let him go.

Apparently, it takes less than a week to remember you're in love, and that's strange, isn't it?

Remember was a word ringing in my head, but it was less important than how good it felt to be in his arms.

The world slowly fell away around us, leaving behind a world or ruin over time. A romantic thought. And Hades, with his classical sensibilities, might have liked it, but I was a human and made out of much more mortal stuff.

"Come on." I beckoned by giving his arm a gentle tug. "This way."

I led him through the ruins of what once was a temple. Weren't there thousands of temples across Greece dedicated to the gods who once had been great and were now only footnotes in a historian's papers?

As we walked along the old stones of halls long gone, I imagined how dim it would have been then, with only torches and stone dish lamps to light our way. We ended up in a space enclosed on three sides by stone walls. The ground, a lush bed of grass that was soft, thick, and gorgeous in the center. I lie on my back, sighing as the cool of the earth diffused into my warm skin, literally grounding me. From there, I got an incredible view of the stars, and I wondered where the rest of the gods might have resided.

I held my hand out to Hades, who looked at me with wide eyes, as if I were made of magic.

"Be here with me," I murmured. "Give me what I want."

"Every day of my life," he swore, and I ached with his promise.

He came to lie down with me on the grass, leaning over me on his elbow to kiss me. I kissed him back, but I did it in my own time exactly as I liked, tasting him, getting the measure of him resting against me. The moon had risen over a wall, bathing everything in black and silver shadows. With his lips on mine, he was just as beautiful and mysterious as the moon, but I felt as if I contained mysteries myself—ancient and sweet, that I could choose to reveal to him or not.

"Take off your clothes," I commanded. "I want to see you naked now."

"Imperious." It didn't sound like a reprimand, and a bolt of pure need shot through me.

He rose and started to strip. With every piece of clothing Hades removed, he revealed a body I was growing to love. One that seemed as if it had been shaped exclusively for my pleasure. When he was finally bare, his cock already stood at half-mast. I stood to meet him, welcoming him with another kiss.

I was wearing the green dress he'd provided for me back in the Underworld, but at the moment, I didn't feel much like removing it. It was more important to kiss him and feel him against me. What a wonder it was to know that a man like him, a god like Hades—someone so solitary, so lonely—needed me. Something in us both called to one another.

"Tell me what you want." His voice rumbled through both of us.

Bracing myself against the wall, I stood with my legs slightly spread. Silently, I pointed at the ground in front of me. Last night, he was the one in charge, the one whose command was absolute. He'd pleasured my body to exhaustion, now I made the demands.

His body stiffened and stilled. He took one breath then another before he knelt in front of me. The look he gave me could have put a hole in steel while he lifted the skirt of my dress up to my waist. I thought he would slip my underwear down with the same courtesy, but he twisted his fingers in the band and tore them from my body. I yelped at the drag of the fabric over my hips.

"Another pair you owe me," I reminded him.

"Imperious little thing." He grinned up at me, and I was seeing something in him that he rarely showed, if he ever did at all. "No matter what I'm doing, I'm still me," he said, leaning over to kiss my thigh. "Best you not forget that."

Okay. He still liked an element of being in charge.

"I like that." I tangled my fingers in his hair. I didn't pull him forward, letting him lean in of his own accord and opening me with his thumbs to bare the parts that we both wanted him to touch.

His urgent movements belied the controlled way he moved. The moment he tasted me I groaned, pushed my head back against the wall. He used his mouth and his hands to turn me into a quivering mess as I moaned and whispered his name, lost in the way he touched me. For all he knew, I might have kept him kneeling for fifteen minutes or fifteen years. I didn't care though, so long as he kept on making me feel like this.

Tension built, ready to snap. At some point, the rope would drag me along with it. No other options existed there and then, and I mindlessly held on, knowing the eventual reward for doing so would be all the greater.

I groaned when Hades pushed two fingers inside me, curved just enough to send sparks of pleasure through my body. It was almost overwhelming, but it wasn't enough. My knees buckled, and now he was the only thing holding me up against the wall. I pressed my hips against him, crying out without any concern for who might hear me.

"Oh, please!" I begged when he stopped and pulled back.

I looked down into his eyes but caught my breath. He had transformed into something wild summoned from out of legends, an unearthly being that predated the lies we told each other about love and what it meant. We'd both been distilled into something strange and essential in this place, this garden, and I nodded at him.

"Let me have you," I voiced, but I couldn't tell if he was the one who was being commanded or if I was.

He stood, and with his hands under my thighs, raised me higher against the wall. My legs curled around his hips, and I clung to him. I knew that if I let go, I might fall, but the prospect of being farther from him frightened me more.

Hades leaned in to kiss me, and I marveled at how good I tasted on his mouth as he entered me with one smooth thrust, filling me and making me cry out. *Perfect*. He drove into me with quick snaps of his hips that left me reeling with need and desire.

Soon, I felt too full. As if there was nowhere to go but up. The only thing that mattered in the entire world was the two of us together, and now that we'd found each other, we would never be apart.

Heat built low in my body, like a fire blackening wood, and I tried to fight it. I didn't want this to end so I pulled back from the idea of completion to enjoy the need, the tension so taut between us it thrummed. I reveled in the way he whispered my name, the way he bit down on my earlobe as he drove into me.

The pleasure overcame me, and I no longer had a choice. Stars exploded behind my eyes while my orgasm burst through me like a river forced through some narrow channel. I shouted his name, digging deep scratches into his arms, and one last shuddered plunge told me that he followed a after me.

He held me there, his mouth pressed against my temple, his lips murmuring in a foreign language. The words entranced me, but after a while, a twinge in my legs told me I needed to get down.

I gave him a soft kiss on the cheek, squirming, and though he grumbled, he set me on my feet, allowing my dress to fall and cover me. Except for the way my hair fell around my face in flyaways and how my mouth felt swollen, I imagined I looked fairly innocent of everything we'd been doing.

"You better watch out," I teased him. "If you let me have my own way too often, I might become the one in charge."

He growled at that, pinning me hard against the wall for a final searing kiss.

When he let me go, I discovered the space of grass behind us entirely covered in flowers of all kinds. They were all icy white, some the size of half-dollars, some bigger than my hand. They waved in the faint breeze, and I was terrified.

"What is all this?" I demanded, pushing around him to lean down for a closer look. "This one doesn't grow in the northern hemisphere and this one doesn't grow at all without greenhouse conditions... I don't think you can even get this one in white. What's going on? Did you do this?"

CHAPTER 21

Autumn

I TURNED TO HADES, half-expecting him to say that the flowers were some kind of gift for me. I'd already seen him do things less than a week ago I once thought to be impossible. *He* was impossible. If he would have told me he magicked impossible flowers just to startle me, I would have believed it.

But no. He didn't. His tight face and thinned lips was rife with guilt and panic.

A much, much different answer was coming to the surface, and it caused my throat to tighten, making me feel afraid. It was the exact feeling I'd felt several times already. With the appearance of the flowers, I knew something was wrong even before I asked him.

While I'd been examining the flora, Hades had redressed in his black trousers and white shirt, still half-unbuttoned.

His hair remained rumpled from me putting my fingers through it. If I leaned closer, I'd smell the both of us on him.

He opened my heart in a way I never even dreamed possible. Broken through the barriers I'd put in place to protect my heart from losing someone I loved. Three times, he studied my body like it was his favorite book.

Even now, a trace of need from before swept over me. It would always be like this between us no matter what happened. The thought felt odd in light of what I knew and didn't know—what he hid from me. A blistering betrayal replaced that passing urge, leaving me scorched and bruised like a flower caught in a bushfire.

"You know something," I said into the silence. "You've been hiding it from me."

"No. Not hiding." It sounded like the words were being dragged from him, but I didn't care.

I took a step toward him before I remembered what a silly idea it would be. He was far more powerful than me. Nothing I could do would threaten him, not even a, but I still shook with anger. And I wasn't an angry person.

After my mom died, I could've been a screaming furious wreck lashing out at everything that set me off, whether it was an attempt to comfort me or not. But lashing out was a choice, and it felt strange to me even though it was the only word I could use to describe the rising emotion inside of me. A sense of righteous unfairness.

Behind me, the plants moved as if they had a life of their own, curling and waving, almost snapping with my anger. My feet sank into the earth, connecting to something old, something powerful, a force to be reckoned with.

I stopped just short of Hades. He hadn't moved, watching me with fascination.

"Tell me," I ordered. "I deserve to know, don't I?"

He glanced down at his hands and then buttoned up the rest of his shirt.

"Do you know who Persephone is?"

"The name's familiar." But the moment I heard her name, I knew it belonged to me somehow.

Shaking my head, I staggered back from Hades as if he'd struck me. I stumbled toward the flowers that had sprouted during our lovemaking, stepping into them without flinching. The roses should have torn me up with their thorns but walking through them was as easy as stepping onto a Persian carpet. Stalks and wands twined around my ankles and wrists, tickling and stroking me. Instead of fear, I knew they were only trying to comfort me, to reassure me everything was all right. Without thinking, I reached down to stroke their nodding heads with my fingertips like scratching a cat behind the ears.

I didn't take my gaze off Hades, who stayed still, watching me with those night-dark eyes. A memory resurfaced from our first meeting in the funeral parlor—his repeated questions that carried over into Mama Tickey's.

What are you?

"Tell me," I demanded, my voice choking. "What in the world is happening to me? What am I?"

"Human," he said, and I laughed, not out of humor, but because it was the same answer I'd given him. "I promise you, you're human."

That actually relieved me a little. I nodded but continued to regard him warily. "Are you stalling? I feel like there's a 'but' coming."

A ghost of a smile tilted his lips, prompting me to wonder whether he meant it for me or someone else. "But you have a goddess sleeping inside you."

Tell me the whole story!" At the look in his eyes, I relented. "Please. There's no one else I can ask."

He glanced behind me at the plants and responding to my uneasiness. "Will you come to me? Or allow me to come to you?"

I glance down at the stalks curled around me. Plants didn't feel love like people did, but they understood simpler things like light, water, heat, cold, and the tickle of bees collecting their pollen. Under the brilliant moon, I could have sworn they appeared spontaneously after we had made love. I heard them inside my mind. They considered me their light, their sun, their water. Hesitantly, I reached to touch another.

It's all right. I'm fine. Um... stand down.

I wasn't sure what would happen, but the plants seemed to understand. They uncoiled from me and returned to nodding in the breeze or curling up to sleep. One of the rose stems moved away, and not a scratch on me.

"Come here," I beckoned.

Another man might have been concerned about approaching someone who could control plants, but he never hesitated, crossing to me among the profusion of wild-flowers. Gently, he took my hand.

Despite how tense my body felt, despite everything that had unfolded between us, I relaxed at his touch. At least the part that he called to did. The other part, the one who had sworn off love to protect my heart, remained on guard.

"All right, talk." I desperately wanted answers.

The Lord of the Underworld sighed. He hadn't stalled at all; he merely had no idea how to tackle this subject. Something told me he'd been pondering how to broach the subject for a few days now. I never got the idea he spoke to all that many people in the first place, and he certainly wasn't used to having conversations like this.

Well, neither do I, but I'm doing it anyway.

He'd buried this issue long ago. When the goddess had

left. But now she returned. That must have been why I dreamed of her, why I felt something powerful and ancient inside of me awaken.

"Start at the beginning," I suggested. "Go on until you get through the middle and stop at the end."

A humorless smile stretched across his lips. "I don't know where to start and I'm afraid you aren't going to like what I have to say."

"Fair enough."

He didn't let go of my hand as he started, but he didn't look at me either. His gaze seemed lost in the moon that was beginning to set, causing the long shadows in the garden to extend and darken.

"In today's world," he started. "They only consider the twelve major gods of ancient Greece who ruled over his or her own domains, covering every aspect of the world. It all looks very neat and tidy until you start learning more and realize that there are a great many more gods than that dozen. Humans are not so easily categorized, and gods are no different."

I cocked my head, yearning to know more.

"A select few of those gods sat up in Olympus," he explained. "I did not. I ruled my kingdom in the Underworld."

Under his words I detected a lie or something he wasn't saying. I was determined to dig to the very bottom to find out.

"Persephone." He said the name slowly as if it hurt to speak it. "The daughter of Demeter did not reside in Olympus either. When she was young, they called the goddess Kore, named for her youth and beauty, and when she grew up, she became the wife of Hades." He stopped short.

"Your wife," I repeated bluntly, ignoring the sting that bit me. I'd asked him about a jealous wife when I first met him. Apparently, I should have asked more questions.

"Yes... and no."

An icky heat bubbled at my core. "That's... not very clear."

"No, it's not." His shoulders sagged as he exhaled. "I'm trying to get through the middle, but it's a very long and strange middle."

He looked lost and so helpless I wanted to soothe him, but not until I got my answers.

"So, Persephone and Hades lived together in the Underworld," he continued. "For six months of the year, the springtime goddess dwelled on Earth, making the flowers grow. The other six months she returned to Hades, and winter descended upon the world. That's the start of it, and where it gets more complicated is the inclusion of avatars."

"Avatars?" I narrowed my eyes at him.

"Yes." He stared long and hard, examining me again like he often did. "Gods can't work their will on Earth. Eons ago, they were banned by Zeus because Ares destroyed a long-lost planet in this solar system."

A bolt of recognition shot through me at that mention.

"Ever since, the gods had to choose a human, an avatar, to work their will in the world," he said. "These people contain aspects of the god, the fury of Ares or the wit of Hermes, or the strategy of Athena for example. They are, themselves, part god and part mortal."

I glanced at the sea of flowers swimming around us. "And... that's what I am?"

Hades shifted, looking uneasy. "In a way. Persephone... did something that no god had ever done before by sealing herself away, her essence passing unnoticed from mortal to mortal who should have become her avatar. Over the centuries, she grew weary of the way things were and how they were done. She wanted to rest, to go fallow for a time. And so, she went."

I swallowed, barely able to keep up with the reality of what he told me. It was too much to believe, too much to bear, and it strained the limits of my own mind even though his story registered in me.

I lifted my chin higher. "How long has it been since she's gone fallow?"

"She's been gone from the world for almost six hundred years," he filled in with a strangely dark, calm voice, but beneath it dwelled a distant longing.

My stomach sank with dread. Hades still loved her. Then what did that mean for me? That I was just someone to keep him company since his wife had left? No. No. No!

When he finally turned to me, his expression shone with need barely restrained by self-control, which said it all. Without that self-control, he'd have me in his arms and devour me, but just as part of me was willing and even eager, another half rose in protest at the same time. It reminded me I didn't really know him. Didn't understand this twisted and complicated relationship or how exactly I fit into it. All I knew was I was not going to let some faulty six-hundred-year relationship tell me what to do.

"Autumn… you know what's in you, don't you?" His words were careful, gentle, but layered with steel, told me he wasn't going to let me deny what was happening.

"I–I've had dreams," I admitted, trying to piece everything together after shock had smashed everything to bits. "Walking in a garden. Things like that. And strange ones. Places I've never been before, things that feel real, too real."

I started to tell him about the rest—the strange edges of the dreams where things went from gardens to something darker, a wintery night that never ended, but then another thought occurred to me.

"So... you're an avatar?" I asked. "I mean, I've never heard of anyone just walking around calling themselves Ares or Athena."

"It is different for every god and avatar," he explained. "Some relationships are fraught, and some are more congenial. Some are antagonistic, while others are tenuous. Your relationship with Persephone can take many forms."

"My relationship with–?"

"She's waking up," he said, sparking a terror within me as heavy as a weight being dropped on my shoulders.

"No," I protested, taking a few steps back from him. "No! That's not... that's not me. I don't want that."

He frowned. "It's within in you. She's a part of you."

From his look, I could tell he wanted to say more, but the plants woke up at my fear and cut him off. They wound around his legs and arms, bringing him to a halt. He released a harsh breath. A dark trickle of blood flowed down his arm where the rose thorns had sliced him.

"Don't say that!" I cried. "I don't want that!"

Hades, still and trapped by the flowers, lifted his eyebrows, helplessness, and I wanted to weep.

"You are still you," he promised, his tone low and urgent. "I swear this to you. Your own spirit will always be a factor. You will not be overwhelmed and made into something else nor will everything that you are be cleared away to make room for something alien. That won't happen."

"How do you know?" I demanded. "You just told me that everyone is different. What if I'm one of the ones who have that happen? This is my life, my body! I'm not going to give it away just because some goddess woke up from a six-hundred-year nap!"

"You won't because I know you," he assured quietly. "You'll still be yourself. It is just that sometimes you will be yourself and a little more."

Hades gestured at the plants around him as well as he could. He probably could have broken away if he tried, but then he would have torn them, and the roses in turn would rip his arm to shreds if he did.

"Your defenders here. You couldn't do that before, could you?"

"No."

"And yet you did it without thought. It is just another part of you, something that's been dormant in you for some time. It's all right, Autumn. I'm here for you. I won't let you go through this alone."

I swallowed, took a deep breath, and forced my breathing back to an even pattern. The flowers, this time responding to my calm, let go of him and relaxed back into a strange grove of beautiful blooms. He stepped toward me, wrapping me in his arms. I let him as I pressed my forehead against his chest until another thought occurred to me.

"And–" I swallowed the words clogging my throat. "This is why you're with me?"

"No." He denied it so quickly I knew he must have expected the question. Well, fine. Everyone was allowed to ponder, but I also needed the truth. I didn't want him pursuing something with me only to dump me once the goddess returned.

"You're Hades," I reminded him. "And you and Persephone were married."

He was frozen so long I looked up at him. I might have expected him to be indignant or nervous, or even angry or upset. Instead, a strange emotional vagueness settled across his features, and it startled me, almost as if he were trying to grasp at something he had forgotten. As I studied him, he shook it off, offering me a slight smile.

"Hades relationship with her was a long time ago," he said with a thin smile and I wondered why he chose to refer to himself in the first person. "She chose to leave. We're different people now. You and I get to determine what we mean to each other. No one else."

"What if she returns?"

"She won't. It ended a long time ago."

It was the right thing to say. I let go of a deep breath. God, I needed to hear how we weren't just puppets for some greater shadows behind us. I hated the thought of being something other than myself, or that the powerful feelings I'd discovered for Hades were based on something from beyond my control.

"I don't know if I can think about this anymore right now," I admitted. "That doesn't mean I get to stop thinking about it, I know, just... this is a lot."

Hades nodded, dropping a surprisingly quick and gentle kiss on the crown of my head. "I understand. Let me know if your dreams become disturbing to you, or if you have any questions. I can give you answers, or I can find you people who will."

I nodded and then mustered a slight grin from the sunny part of myself I'd lost for a moment. "Thanks. And hey, was that our first fight?"

He frowned at me. "I don't think so. Learning about who you are and needing time to deal with it doesn't really turn into a fight."

"Whatever." I nudged him in the side. "But if we had a fight, that means we can have loud, messy make-up sex." I wagged my eyebrows at him.

He offered me his crooked smile again, the one that made him so human to me and told me how underneath all the god stuff was someone who could fall in love. "Appealing. I'll take it under advisement."

Well, I hoped he took it under *serious* advisement because later I wanted to do what we'd done again and again. I craved the feel of him on top of me so I could forget all about this god and avatar business for the moment.

He glanced around. The garden had darkened from the moon's descent, and a chill hung in the air not there before.

"Would you have any objections to leaving now?" he asked.

"Actually, no, but… could we go to my home?"

"Of course."

And he made it so.

CHAPTER 22

Autumn

I KNEW I'd made a stupid mistake when we appeared in the hallway outside my studio apartment. Besides the fact I swayed on my feet and felt ill, I'd forgotten about the ugly brown water stain on the wall that stood out like a sore thumb. Or the skunky scent of my neighbor's weed that clouded the hallway. Someone three doors down abused my ears with Lou Bega.

Mortified, I winced and closed my eyes for a second. "Um, maybe this isn't such a good idea. We should go back to your palace."

I thought Hades would agree and snap those sexy fingers of his to transport us to his palace, but instead he placed a hand on my door.

"No, I'd love to see your place. Unless you're not comfortable with me here?"

Junipers!

"You live in a magical palace," I said. "I live in a five-hundred-dollar studio directly above the dumpster. I guess I'm concerned you aren't going to be too comfortable."

He was a god, after all, surrounded daily by marble, fluffy pillows, the finest silks, and everything inlaid with gold and jewels. Whereas my apartment was barely larger than a shoebox.

"Let me decide." His voice held that edge of command I liked, and I relaxed as he magicked my purse from somewhere.

Hades didn't do things for my benefit. I couldn't force him to do anything he didn't want to do. Everything he did was because he wanted to, including being with me, I reminded myself. That provided some comfort.

I sighed and unlocked the deadbolt. My apartment gave off the slightly musty smell from being unoccupied for a few days. Quickly, I went to my kitchen bench and lit a pineapple and coconut scented candle to replace the odor.

Hades looked around with a curious expression, his wide-eyed gaze absorbing everything, his mouth slightly agape, and I saw my place for the first time through his eyes. Thank God I had cleaned it before I left. But then again, it didn't take that long to clean such a small space. He smiled and pointed at the clutter of green plants on just about every surface.

I clutched one hand with my other. A tattered brocade comforter that I found at a yard sale covered the bed, along with a pile of mismatched pillows stacked something like a couch. Beside my bed rested a small bookshelf. In front of that, a rug that someone else had thrown out covered the stained floor. That was pretty much all my furniture because I didn't have the space, so I used my bed as a sofa.

"Look, I know it's not much, but–" I started.

"Shush." Hades tilted his head to inspect posters, plants,

and every pillow around the room. In my apartment, he looked more like a person than some all-powerful god, and I couldn't take my eyes off how gorgeous he was moving through my space in the faint dawn light.

My place was cozy for one person. With two, it verged on crowded, but it didn't feel that way to me. Having him in my space felt strangely right. Everything I had accumulated might not add up to a lot, but it was mine, and the shame and nervousness I initially felt vanished as I sat back on the bed to watch him.

"I like it," he finally said, and I laughed at the faint note of surprise in his voice.

"I hope so," I replied, relief streaming through me. "I like it too. I know it's not a palace, but it's mine."

Hades stroked one of my many potted plants, and I pulled out a special pun just for him.

"Did you hear about the lazy flower?"

"Not again. You torture me with these."

"I know." I smiled. "He got a kick in the bud!" I patted the side of the bed. "Come here."

Just a few days with him had changed me enough to where the dawn now indicated I should be sleepy instead of awake. It occurred to me it would be a pain getting back on a regular sleep schedule for when I returned to work at Pearl's shop… no… my shop now.

He stood at the side of my bed for a few seconds, but with a soft laugh I pulled him in.

"When this is all over," he said with a sudden seriousness, "when we have collected all of the errant dead, we should discuss what will come next for us."

"Wow," I teased, using humor to diffuse a tense question. "We're already getting that serious."

He teasingly bit me on the neck for that.

"Because I'm Persephone?" I had to know. Things in that regard were still fuzzy. And I felt like he had more to tell me.

"Because you are you, with all that entails." He reached up to lay a gentle hand on my head, smoothing back my hair, causing me to lean against him with a blissful sigh. "She is a part of you. She always has been. You cannot deny it, you know. I think that if you look deep within yourself, you won't even want to."

He was right, but I wasn't ready to admit it yet.

"I think I'm going to need some time on that one, boss," I deflected quietly, fingering the button of his suit.

Although he smiled, I wondered if it contained some strange, twisted ancient grief he didn't want to tell me about. If it did, I decided it would come out sooner or later. He'd lived far longer than I had. I could deal with a few skeletons in the closet, at least for a while. It wasn't like my life didn't have them. Just so long as said skeletons didn't return to make trouble down the track.

I started to speak, but a long yawn cut me off. When it finished, I asked, "Can we sleep here tonight? Tomorrow night we can take a turn at your palace of wonders."

"You want to be home. Of course, but on one condition." *Oh, God, not another deal.* Just what did he want to bargain for this time?

"What's that?" I asked, raising an eyebrow.

He ran a finger along my collarbone, sending a zing of delight through my chest. "That we get out of our clothes and get under the covers."

I laughed at his slightly disapproving tone. "How dare we wear clothes!"

I kissed him on the nose.

"I suppose I can handle that. But no funny business. I don't want to give my neighbor a heart attack."

He quirked his brow in a way that conveyed how he was

considering punishing me for daring to raise that topic. Well, that had been my aim at least.

I flicked my fingers at him as if I ordered a servant to do my bidding. "You may undress me now."

Now, it was Hades' turn to snort. "Imperious little thing. I fear I've created a monster."

"Is that going to be a problem?"

"When the monster is as beautiful and sweet as you? Not at all."

Charmer.

Just as long as he kept up those sweet words, we were all good.

Slowly, and without ever taking his eyes off me, he stripped to the skin.

"Yeah!" I clapped. "Do a little dance."

I wasn't sure if he would humor me, but wouldn't it be fun for strict and rigid Hades if he did? *Please, please, please!*

To my surprise, he shimmied his hips slightly as he hung his clothes up on a hook by the door, then twirled in his underpants as he crossed back to the bed.

"Yeah!" I clapped again, encouraging him to loosen up more even though I liked him the way he was.

He crawled from the end of the bed all the way to me. With his typical fierceness, he stripped me out of my own clothing, this time taking care not to damage the green dress he had given me. I purred when he pressed stray kisses on my shoulder or on my waist.

Soon enough, we were naked and under the covers as he requested, and I sighed with delight. Enjoying the warmth and hardness of his body, I snuggled under his arm, resting my head on his chest. Tonight, we were content to just lie in each other's arms.

Even though we had lain together before, this felt new. My body still glowed with the warmth of everything we had done together in the garden, but a strange normalcy came over me as we fell into a deep sleep together. *This is what I was missing.* It felt beyond good to have his nude body cuddled up beside me, his breath in my ear.

I feel safe...

By now, my eyes felt as if they were weighted down with sandbags. I closed them, wondering what in the world my life might look like next week considering everything that had happened in this one as I slipped into another strange dream.

***

I LOVED PARTIES, and this one was just as amazing. Under an open night sky, the air was so warm it whispered of the very beginning of summer when the heat switched on, but the humidity hadn't set in yet. In my hand I held a flask of something sweet and fizzy. People kept offering me fruits and meats, but I didn't care for any of it because I was waiting for someone.

We were all in an open field dotted with bonfires, and I knew the guest I waited for would come to celebrate with me, to be a part of the warmth that I'd brought to the land.

From where I sat by the largest fire, I saw people kissing each other, sharing sweets and drinks, and dragging each other into the dark with shy giggles and loud laughs. My chest fluttered with the love all around us.

I strained my eyes against the darkness, hoping for a glimpse of the person I sought even if I couldn't exactly say who it was until I saw him. But then I spotted him across the fire, and he looked the way he did at his home underground, far away and distant—a pale god with the stars in his eyes.

LADY OF THE UNDERWORLD

Hades was and wasn't a part of my world, and as he turned to leave, I knew I couldn't allow it.

I got up from my golden throne and followed him, laughing, because wasn't that part of the fun? Plenty of our guests chased each other between the glows of fire, so many of whom caught their loved ones in their arms, and I couldn't see why I should be any different.

His path led me around and around the flames, the flutter of his robes always beyond my grasp. I called to him, but he wouldn't turn even when I ran as fast as I could to catch up.

Next time, I'll make him take a turn at chasing me. Let's see how he likes it then.

The fun ebbed out of my pursuit. My feet hurt, my lungs were on fire, and smoke wafted all around us, concealing the white of his robe, the flash of his face as he turned his head to look at me. Still, he didn't slow, and my happiness soon turned into something darker and angrier.

"Stop! You have to stop!" I called out after him.

He didn't, and the chase began in earnest. Our guests cleared away. The fires reduced to embers. The ground beneath my bare feet turned rocky and hurt my soft skin, but that was less important than catching him. At this point, I wanted an explanation more than I wanted a kiss, and that was saying something.

My breath came hard and sharp. I was a goddess and thus never intended to be a runner. If I didn't reach out and catch him now, I'd never be able to catch up with him. Drawing on one last burst of speed, I lunged and finally managed to snatch a handful of his robe. He stopped, but still, he didn't turn.

"What's the matter?" I asked. "Why did you run away from me?"

At last, he twisted to face me, but something changed in his face. While it still contained his usual beauty and power, it was more human and strained with fear. It felt utterly wrong. Hades couldn't be afraid, could he?

"Who wouldn't run from you?" He gestured to the world around us.

The scenery changed. Snow dusted the logs and rocks rings around the fires, and the flames had all died. Thick flakes covering the plain burned and stung my feet. That would have been bad enough, but when I spotted shapes underneath the snow, I gasped and recoiled. The dancers who had been having such a good time between the bonfires were laid down as if to sleep, but they had let the snow cover them up. My mind told me if they rested there too long in the cold, they would die. I tried to run to the one closest to me, ready to shake the woman and demand she wake up, but Hades snared my wrist in an iron grip.

"We have to go," he said, his voice remote. "We have to go home."

I woke up with a startling cry, sitting up in my bed, stirring Hades next to me. He opened his eyes, but before I could do more than catch my breath, he pulled me into his arms, stroking my hair.

"Did you dream again?" he asked.

"I… I did." Already it faded like a distant memory, but I could remember parts of it. Something had upset me. I'd needed to find Hades, but I couldn't? Summer had turned to winter. I didn't understand.

He kissed the top of my head. "Would you like to tell me about it? Sometimes that helps."

I shook my head. "No. I will if I remember."

"Of course." He looked at the clock and winced. An adorable human gesture. "We should get up and get on the road. The next one we have to collect is more distant."

Ah, yes. The mission. Better not leave the dead roaming the world.

"At least I'm doing this with all my own clothes this time," I joked, hopping out of bed. "Dibs on first shower. And before you offer to come with me, no."

He was behind me in an instant, and I spun, pressing a finger to his chest.

"My shower is tiny and unpredictable, and I can't dodge the spray when it scalds me if you're in there with me."

Hades smiled, taking my hand and pulling me back for a kiss. It almost turned into more than a kiss with the way his tongue explored my mouth—so warm, so sensual, so inviting. My blood surged south. Arousal hit with the speed of a freight train.

I giggled, using all my willpower to step away. "Save it." I waved a finger at him. "You were the one who said we had things to do, and you're the reason I can't just keep sleeping, so I'm going to shower."

He scowled at me. I shrugged and left him on the bed.

Under the spray of the shower, heat streamed across my skin. It allowed me to remember more of my dream. Judging by the throne I'd sat on I ruled the place. My guests, the dancers, and those who had come to celebrate with me were now dead, and I got the sense they were dead because of me. I shivered, shaking my head. My dream didn't feel right, and I wondered all over again whether I would get used to all of this weird stuff.

"Hey, Persephone," I murmured softly, unsure she would hear me. "Think you can take it easier on me with all of this dream stuff? If not for my sake, then for his? All of these creepy visions are probably freaking him out."

I blinked as I realized I received an answer. Not words, but a sensation that felt like a tender new leaf unfurling—something new coming into being. It hadn't come from my mind, but it resonated from inside me, and the reality of what Hades had unloaded on me sunk in a bit more. The goddess and I were parts of each other.

I trembled even more, because this was all insane and not my cup of tea. I shook my head, rinsing off quickly, and stepped out of the shower.

"Your turn," I said distractedly to a naked and waiting Hades, but almost shyly accepted a kiss as he passed me to go into the stall.

The heat from his lips reminded me that no matter how crazy things got, he was always there. He wouldn't let me fall any more than he had let me fall in the quarry. Everything was going to be fine. Or so I thought.

CHAPTER 23

Autumn

His car was waiting for us by the curb, and its presence made me uneasy.

"Does the world just shape itself around you?" I asked as we got into the vehicle, still not clear on the limits of his power.

He spared me an amused glance as he steered the car out onto the road.

"Would you rather teleport to the hospital to collect it?" I shook my head at his suggestion, remembering how woozy it left me. "Shall we take a taxi next time?"

"Well, no." *Damn*. He had me there.

We drove through the darkness, and as he'd said, the hours rolled over from the long drive across the state. I slept for some of it, while the rest of the time, I stared out the window or studied him out of the corner of my eye.

"You're looking at me," he remarked without turning his head.

I smiled at the teasing note in his voice. Wow. Serious and stern old Hades had loosened up, making me wonder about how relaxed he'd become around me.

"Why shouldn't I?" I traced his cheek. "You're handsome. But no, I was looking at your arm."

"Oh?" He glanced at the dark cotton of his suit.

"I remembered that Ms. Mae scraped you up something fierce when you tangled with her."

"Thank you for bringing up the fight I lost with a deceased old woman."

I chuckled at the wry note in his voice. "That's not what I'm talking about. She scraped you up pretty well, but you healed completely. Is that one of the privileges of being a god?"

He hesitated. "It's one of the powers of the Underworld. It's something that can heal despite originating in a place where the dead linger. It can also be unreliable and strange, but yes, it keeps me from harm. It'll keep you from harm as well when you come into your full power."

"When Persephone awakens, you mean?"

"Yes."

I gulped, inexplicably panicked.

Hades seemed to sense this and set his hand on my wrist. "She's gentle. Wonderful. She won't harm you."

"Is it going to be weird, having me and your ex here at the same time?" I asked.

He smiled at me despite the sassy tone I took with him. I warmed. Sometimes he had such a stiff upper lip I had no idea how we could get along, and then, to my surprise, he would smile or say something amusing and I knew exactly why we did.

"It's not like that," he said. "I promise you. You are a part of her. She is a part of you."

"Do… do you think she likes me?" I asked, afraid of how ridiculous I sounded; but I couldn't stop myself.

"I know she will," he promised. "She wouldn't have chosen you as one of her avatars if she hadn't liked you. I believe she'll adore you."

"I want to know more about the other avatars," I told him. "What they make of all this god business. If there are people like me, well, I should get to know them, right?"

I wasn't sure why Hades' smile looked guarded.

"You can," he said. "Though maybe when the restless dead are called to order. I would not like to leave them too much longer given how long some have already waited."

That I could understand.

We rode in silence for another few hours until Hades pulled up to a convenience store. If I were honest, this whole trip had been full of creepy locations, and I guess I'd been expecting something similar, but this was just your average stop on the freeway. Brightly lit and slightly rundown, with a sign promising us as many cheese sticks as we could eat. A diner was connected to the right side of the gas station. It was the kind of place where customers could reliably get eggs, bacon, and toast, all swimming in your choice of grease. My type of place!

"Really?" I asked. "This place?"

Hades ducked his head to examine the sign on the diner. "Yes. There's someone around here, but it feels strange."

I bit my lip as he turned to face me.

"Do you want to try?" he asked.

"Try the cheese sticks? Sure, I'm hungry."

"No. To find the soul."

I waved my hands. "No. Maybe next time?"

While I might have had a talent for convincing the souls

to go to the Underworld, sensing one out was too much for me. Persephone was the Goddess of Springtime. She may have lived in the Underworld for six months out of the year, but it wasn't like she was part of it. Anyway, the goddess part of the adventure was still giving me problems, so I thought that the last thing I should do was try to force it.

He nodded, and together we headed into the convenience store. The only person in the shop half of the structure was a young clerk leaning her elbow on the counter, resting her chin on her palm, doing her level best to stay awake. She gave us the kind of bleary greeting I remembered well from being a shift worker, the one that started with a widening of the eyes. The only thing she cared about was whether we were going to shoplift, and we weren't.

We checked the bathrooms for the soul but found nothing so we moved onto the diner. The combination of food scenting the air and soft babble from four customers in the booths livened the place. A single waitress was working a crossword at the counter while the cook manning the grill in the back looked like he was taking a nap standing up. I had a lot of affection for places where I could get a meal for under five bucks. Quiet. Homey. Semi-good food. Enough for me.

"Eating in or taking away?" the waitress asked as she bound up to me, looking glad to see another customer. Her nametag read "Laura," and she handed me a menu.

"Eating in," I answered, flipping through.

"Take any table you want." She left.

Hades wandered through the diner area while I perused the menu, his attention focused on sensing the lost soul. Once he located it, and I did my thing, I figured our meal would be ready, so I waved the waitress back over to place an order.

"What'll you have?" she asked.

"Some hot tea to share and two bacon and egg rolls," I

told her. "We're just going to wander around and stretch our legs for a while. We've been on the road for hours now."

"Driving late's a chore," she agreed, and went to get our drinks.

As Hades scoured every corner and each booth, I stifled a smile at how out of place he appeared.

The people in the booths were my kind of people. Everyday Joes who worked all year and never made quite enough for rent, bills, and food. He walked through places like, well, some god of wealth, and he must have been visible to the customers this time because his actions elicited irritation from the faces of those awake enough to muster it. They might not know why they disliked and distrusted him, but they did.

You know, if I'm staying with you, we are definitely going to work on your people skills. You really don't need to wear a fancy suit everywhere.

It wasn't like his suit was hard on the eyes, and if he wanted to keep wearing it, fine by me. But he did look conspicuous, especially in a place like this. He needed to fit in better if we were to continue this line of work.

While he further scoped out the place, I lounged at the counter until the waitress brought me two teas and a glass of orange juice. Icy cold and fresh-squeezed. I blinked. Hades had put more money than I knew what to do with into my bank account, but I was still mostly used to ordering water or tea wherever I went.

"I didn't order that," I said dumbly.

She winked at me. "The last of the jug. On the house."

"Thanks," I replied with a grin, taking it gratefully. While it might have been frigid outside, drinking orange juice was like drinking sunshine. It soothed me in a way, in that I was just beginning to understand, but it might have something to do with the presence of the goddess inside of me.

"Your man's a bit of a strange one, isn't he?" She wiped idly at the spotless bar top next to me.

"He is." I glanced at him, admiring how good-looking he was, how the dark suit fit him so well. "But he's a good one, too."

"Are you sure about that, my lady?" She kept buffing diligently. "Are you absolutely sure?"

At her words, the hairs on the back of my neck stood up, and I turned to look at Laura. Her hand still moved in a pointless circle on the counter, but her eyes were fixed on me. Her increasingly edgy and jittery movements made me suspicious.

"Who are you?" I forced myself to ask, even as my skin broke out in goosebumps.

"I used to be Delly." She leaned in, whispering, "I found a good place with Laura here. Please, my lady, just leave. Take the dark man away. I'm happy here."

I examined her more closely. It took a few moments for what she said to register. Delly had somehow inhabited Laura's body, but that meant she was wearing poor Laura like some kind of ill-fitting suit. My stomach clenched. I was standing face to face with a real-life demon. A bit of sour resentment curled in my gut.

I crossed my arms. "And what does Laura have to say about that?"

"Laura doesn't say much," Delly answered with an absent-minded shrug. "She never did. She wasn't using this life. I will. I'll do such good with it."

I took a deep breath, because this wasn't much weirder than all the rest of the things that had happened to me lately. Sure, why wouldn't dead people hide inside the bodies of truck stop waitresses all the time?

"That's not the way it works, Delly." I fixed my eyes on her, not sure whether to call Hades over or not. "There are rules for this kind of thing. You had your time, and now it's up."

"It's not fair." She reared back and pouted, and the truth of that statement struck me. I remember saying that over and over again when my mother had died. But there'd been absolutely nothing I could do about it, nothing at all.

"It's not, hon," I countered. "But it's time to go. Give Laura back her life."

The waitress, or rather, the thing that had possessed the waitress's body, gave me a pouty-lipped stubborn look. I wondered if it was possible that the spirit inside her was a teenager.

Delly tucked the rag into the pocket of her apron. "No. My lady, we have missed you, but I'm not going with him."

I pressed my fingers to my temples. "No, you've mistaken me for... Look! Delly. Please. I'm so sorry for what happened to you, but you don't want that to happen to Laura, do you? It's not right, and it's not fair. Please. You need to come with us."

Delly shook her head, her lips and cheeks twitching like she might cry.

The cook behind the counter peeked through the service window, squinting at us. He wouldn't be much use to her when he was maybe seventeen at most.

"You all right, Laura?" he asked.

"I'm fine. Don't worry about it," Delly said in a voice that sounded a little more normal.

We both waited until he went back into the kitchen to turn to each other.

"Laura has a life," I pressed as gently as I could. "She has friends. They don't belong to you and you know it."

Delly wavered for an instant. It might take time, but I had all the time in the world right now to persuade her. We could sit and talk all night if that was what it took. I'd tell her whatever it was she needed to hear to get her to let go of Laura and come with us.

But then Hades walked to the counter beside me. "There's no one here but–" He took a closer look at Laura and paled, then reddened.

I knew him well enough to have a vague idea of what was coming, so I laid a hand on his arm. "Hades, please…"

His lips peeled back into a snarl. "You stole her life! How dare you? You're dead. Your time is over. This is–"

Although Delly shook like a leaf, her hand was steady enough to reach under the counter and pull out a hidden shotgun. She lifted it and pointed it straight at his chest.

I blanched. It wasn't a good stunt to pull against the Lord of the Dead.

He didn't flinch, but the rest of the restaurant broke out into horrified shouts. There were hardly enough people in the little place to cause pandemonium, but pandemonium happened. A stampede for the exit started and someone pulled the fire alarm on the way out. All through it, Hades stared at Delly without blinking.

"This is not right," he said adamantly, his voice as hard as stone. "You shouldn't have done this."

Delly glared at him. In moments of rage, she and Laura seemed to meld together, Laura's movements more fluid and graceful despite Delly borrowing her body.

"You can't make me go back!" she snapped, her finger hovering over the trigger. "Not to your land. It's cold and lonely! I didn't have my chance! It's not fair."

"You escaped?" Hades shook with anger.

Delly clutched the shotgun tighter.

"None of it is fair," Hades growled. "Nevertheless, it's the way things are. You cannot expect the rules to bend and break for you. This is pointless. You're only delaying the inevitable."

I expected her to keep arguing with him, but instead, she turned her beseeching eyes to me, the gun drifting off target for a moment. "Great lady, Goddess of the Winter. Please! Your husband knows no mercy, but you must have some."

"Whoa. Whoa, no, not me. I'm not–" I glanced at Hades as a look of abject misery and sorrow swept across in his face. Quickly, I realized beyond a shadow of a doubt that he was still keeping something from me. I didn't know what it was, but it was big.

My stomach lurched, and that made what happened next even more confusing in my mind. I couldn't say what transpired first.

Either Delly took advantage of my confusion to help herself or Hades decided that talking things out in a diner wasn't his style. I didn't know who did what or acted, but suddenly Delly swung her shotgun toward Hades as he reached for her, and a blaring thought echoed through my head: *FIX THIS!*

In times of trouble, I could never sit still. It wasn't my nature. And now, I reached for Delly, lunging over the counter. Knocking my orange juice over, I tackled her low around the hips. I was doing my best imitation of a linebacker. All those days watching high school boys play football must have stuck. The glass struck the ground before we did, shattering and flinging the juice in spatters and puddles. Laura's body hit the ground as Delly let out a surprised squawk, and the gun went off like a cannon next to my ear. The sound was so deafening I thought I must have been hit. But then a shower of plaster came raining down, covering us all in white dust.

Delly started to cry and thrash, trying to get the gun back under control, but her limited abilities were coming to an end. Her hands twitched, and the harder she cried the less motor skills she seemed to wield. Before she managed to get the gun level again, Hades grabbed it by the barrel as if planning on pulling it right out of her hands.

"I'm stronger than I look," Delly panted, and a mad grin arched her features as Hades froze.

In that moment, with Hades at point-blank range and her finger on the trigger, there was only one possible outcome. God or not, it could seriously injure him. Aunt Mae had only scratched him and made him bleed. So had the rose thorns.

I couldn't stand to see him bleed. Nor could I stand to see him die, and that was why with a sharp cry, I summoned my powers. When I latched onto an invisible force, I curled my fingers and pulled, resulting in a scream.

I hadn't heard another gunshot or a mortal cry from Hades. Sweat broke out on my brow as I gritted my teeth. I did what I was made to do, what came naturally. With an almost audible pop, a teenage girl, translucent pale, and shorter than me and with tears in her eyes, stood nearby.

"No!" Delly wept. "It's not fair. I only got to live for seventeen years! I want to get married, have kids, a white picket fence."

"I'm sorry," Hades said as though he'd found some compassion for her in spite of previously having had a gun pointed at him. Maybe I was making a difference after all.

"I don't want to go!" she wailed.

"You don't have a choice," he reprimanded quietly. "But come, I'll go part of the way with you."

Reluctantly, she took his hand—because what else was she going to do? As they stepped away, I realized Laura was still laying prone on the ground.

I expected that after we got Delly out, Laura would be fine. She would sit up and go on with her life and everything would be what it needed to be. Instead, she lay shaking on the ground, her eyes closed, her skin pale.

"No," I whispered. "No, no, no…"

I slid down by her side, putting my hands on her chest, pumping it, giving her chest compressions the way I'd been taught in first aid class.

I did this, I thought with a dark certainty. *This is because I reached for her because I couldn't... Just like I killed the dancers in my dream.*

Hades tried to pull me away. "Come on. We need to leave now."

"No! We can't! *I* did this to her, didn't I? When I pulled Delly out..."

He hesitated, and I went back to working on Laura. I could taste my own tears at the corners of my mouth, and I thought of my mother. I couldn't save her either.

"There is much we don't know," he explained, but I knew he was only trying to comfort me without lying to me outright.

"Fix her," I demanded, turning to him. "You said you were able to heal with the magic of the Underworld. Heal her! I did this to her. Please. Please!"

The look Hades gave terrified me. Calm, cold, and nothing human about it. "We can't interfere here. She is not bound for my world."

"So, you're just going to leave her?!" I demanded to know. "She hasn't done anything wrong! It's my fault."

"And you cannot do anything about it."

"And you won't!" I shot back. "How can you say that? Fix her!"

Hades shook his head. "There's nothing we can do."

I swear I nearly took a swing at him. We'd started this adventure with him getting decked by a dead man, and it now looked like we might finish it with him getting punched in the face by a florist.

Instead of giving into my frustrations, I chose Laura.

"Wake up, Laura." I resumed the chest compressions,

losing myself in the passing haze even after she went still and two men in uniform dragged me away. "No. I have to save her."

"Leave it to the paramedics," one of the men said, keeping a strong grip on my arms.

It was only then I glanced around with tears staining my face, realizing cops had swarmed the place and Hades was nowhere to be seen.

CHAPTER 24

Hades

"Let me go!" The guilty soul fought against my iron grip. She dug her feet into the ground on the banks of the River Styx.

I squeezed my fingers around her arm, holding her tighter. She whimpered.

"Please, dark man!" The wild movement of her gaze darted around the judgment hall, to the three judges seated at their throne, the line of souls awaiting their future in the afterlife, and Cerberus growling at her from the edge of the marble floor.

"You agreed to come with me," I clenched her tighter and dragged her to the front of the queue. She deserved a harsh punishment for stealing the entire life of an innocent. A forbidden and traitorous act. "There is no turning back now."

"My lord," Minos said with a nod. "Welcome back."

The other judges, Rhadamanthys and Aiakos, crossed

their scepters over their chests and nodded their greetings along with Minos.

Before I could respond, the wretched soul yanked against my grip. "Take me back, dark man. I don't belong here. I don't want to go!"

Such a young and foolish soul. So unaware of the world and the way it worked. Her fate was sealed.

Anger flashed through me, my pulse spiking into dangerous territory. If I didn't get a hold of myselfI stopped the thought.

Her eyes widened, and she went limp in my grasp.

"Do you know what you did?" I shook her. The judges gasped. The souls backed away from the queue. Cerberus growled at them. "You stole a life that wasn't yours to take. You had no right. You make a mockery of my realm and of me!"

She shook her head. "Laura wasn't using her life. She wasted it working at the diner. I took her to college, and we were graduating!"

"How dare you." My voice rumbled like thunder. The floors shook with my rage. I leaned over her, my shadow swallowing her. Her pupils expanded, making her eyes almost entirely black. Her mouth opened ready to scream.

In all the merged years shared by this God and me, we had never encountered such a soul that had used another's body to forcefully insert themselves in place of another to extend their own life before.

Delly bent her head as if she feared I might strike her. I let her go. My hand flinched as I panted for air. What was I doing?

"Come with me," I murmured, holding my hands tight at my sides. "Or I will make you."

This time she submitted and followed me without protest.

"My lord." Rhadamanthys' voice chased after me. "Where are you going?"

"To see to it that this soul has a thousand years to consider her crime!" I shouted, heading for my chariot. The girl stumbled to keep up.

The judges materialized in front of me, causing me to break my stride.

"My lord," Aiakos started, "It is our duty to judge her."

"This girl possessed the body of another," I snarled. "And when she was removed from her body, she pulled out the other soul, killing the host. How would you punish her for her crime?"

The judges looked at each other, their mouths moving, but no words came out, formulating a punishment befitting the soul's deeds. After a few moments, they turned back to me.

"Delly Fitzmyers," Aiakos declared. "You stole your parent's vehicle, drove it without permission, crashed it, and killed both yourself and your passenger. For that you are guilty of taking more than one soul."

She tugged at my grasp.

I clenched her arm and drew her closer.

Rhadamanthys lifted both the scroll of light and his scepter. Light streamed from the scepter, hitting the words formed on the document.

"One hundred years is fitting for her crime, my lord." Minos lifted his scepter, ready to tap it on the ground and signify the conclusion of their judgment. "Deliver her to Tartarus."

"No," I interrupted. "That punishment is too short. She deserves a thousand years minimum. Enough time to consider her actions and repent."

"But that is against the rules, my lord," Minos argued.

"This is my decision," I countered.

"My lord," Aiakos challenged. "Your decision does not enter the process. It will disrupt the realm."

I groaned. Was I not Lord of the Underworld? Could I not make the rules? Gods broke rules all the time. Surely, I could, especially when it came down to judging this soul. Delly deserved to be thrown into the pits of hell for her crime. A millennia ago, I had appointed these judges, awarded them the honor of weighing souls of their good and bad deeds. Nothing could stop me. I was master of this realm.

"I don't care." The halls shook as my rage exploded with my words. "I am Lord of the Underworld, not you! This realm is my responsibility!"

Rhadamanthys nearly dropped the scroll of light.

Aiakos' jaw fell open in outraged silence.

Minos' grip on his scepter slackened.

I had offended them and insulted their authority. An offence not to be taken lightly. For a moment, I feared their resignation. But I would face those consequences and consult with the Council of the Demigods.

I stilled my pulse and calmed my breath.

"I must depart to deliver her to Tartarus. When I return from conducting my business in the Land of the Living, we will convene."

I shoved the soul forward, decision made. My judges would see her punishment was recorded on the scroll and she'd be delivered to Tartarus as I decreed. Chains of light clamped around her wrists and ankles, preventing her from fleeing.

The judges retreated without the usual courteous bow and mention of my title.

I'd insulted them. My stomach twisted with dread. I already had enough to mend, especially with my realm freezing over, souls not showing up, and some recently escaping. Now this, too.

I seized the soul by the upper arm and dragged her down the hall.

Pain stabbed me in the heart. I had left Autumn alone to deal with the aftermath of Laura's death. Something I hadn't intended. I didn't trust this wretched soul would make her journey to the afterlife. That's why I left. To personally deliver her and ensure her punishment in the fiery depths of the underworld, where escape wasn't possible. The safety of my realm depended on it. I had to prevent the underworld from descending into further chaos. Before any more souls escaped. Before winter consumed my realm and turned it to ice.

We reached my chariot, and I whistled. Immediately my four dark horses appeared chained to the golden cart. I gestured for the soul to get on. She obeyed.

"Hold onto the guild." I pointed to the lip at the front of the chariot. She gripped it, her face morphing with down-turned lips and eyes. Absolute misery.

The horses whinnied as she climbed aboard the chariot. Her fingers traced the jewels encrusted in patterns along the top.

I wasn't above pity. She'd experienced such a short life. Her soul longed for more. To live out the rest of her life until death. To finish high school, study medicine, get married and have a family. But that wasn't her fate. The act of possessing another body was a crime that made my blood boil.

But I was a fair and just God. Calm, composed, and stoic. Today, I led with a temper tantrum. And not the first time, either. My grip on morality was slipping from my fingers. What was becoming of me?

"My lord," a voice interrupted our departure from the room.

I turned to see Melody hovering in the entrance.

"What is it?" I asked her, climbing into the chariot and grabbing the reigns.

"General Thaddeus has requested an urgent audience with you." Melody's wary eyes flickered between me and the wretched soul cowering beside me.

I did not have time to visit The Crag. Autumn awaited me above. I had to get back to her. Protect her. Comfort her. Pulling the soul from Laura's body had horrified her and filled her with such guilt. She mustn't be alone at a time like this.

"Master," Melody said softer this time. She leaned against a pillar in the room. "Where is the mistress?"

"She is not the mistress!" My voice came as a roar I hadn't intended. Autumn was an avatar, not the goddess.

Melody shrank away. She nodded then retreated, having delivered the message, and probably fearing a further outburst.

Shame flooded through me, and my shoulders drooped. She didn't deserved to be spoken to that way. I wasn't a tyrant like my brother. It was because of my reputation for fairness he spread such lies about me, made me something to fear. I wouldn't embody these lies now.

"Hold on," I told the wretched soul.

She clutched the edge of my chariot for dear life as the horse took off, gliding across the lands. In a matter of minutes, we arrived at Purgatory. The wails of souls echoed from inside the burning chasm. This was what a soul like Delly deserved for what she'd done to poor Laura.

Alucious, my general, greeted me. "My lord. A personal visit to deliver a soul?"

I did not entertain his inquiry. "A thousand years. Summon me when she repents."

My general nodded and took hold of the wretched soul. "Yes, my lord."

"Please, dark man, no!" Her cries echoed in my ears as she was carted away.

I didn't have time to linger and retreated to my chariot, making a quick stop at The Crag on the way back. My horses protested with snorts and whinnies as I pulled them onto the rocky platform.

"Thaddeus!" I shouted.

He appeared, drifting out from the rock, solidifying in front of me. "Thank you for coming, my lord." He bowed his head.

"What is it?" I asked, desperate to get back to the Land of the Living. "I have business. I don't have much time."

My general nodded. "Sorry to disturb you, but I bring word from the hellhounds."

My body unwound from the tension I had been holding. Some good news, at last. Right now, I needed this. Something to soothe my frayed nerves. Calm my simmering temper.

"What did they find?" I asked, my forehead tight. I wanted to get back to Autumn before she could worry about my absence.

"They found two of the souls," Thaddeus stated. "One is in Las Vegas, the other in California."

"Excellent work," I replied. "Don't let them out of the hounds' sights. I'll retrieve them immediately."

CHAPTER 25

Autumn

"It was just an unfortunate accident," the police office droned, but I wasn't entirely listening.

Even though Laura had died, the cook hadn't seen anything, and everyone else in the diner had fled. The customers who'd seen what happened had a different idea of what went down. Some of them said there had been another man there. Others said there'd been no such person.

I didn't know where Hades had gone. Every other time we'd persuaded a soul to go, he'd touch them, and teleport the soul. This time he'd gone along and left me there to deal with the fallout, to be taken to the station for questioning.

When they asked what had happened, my response was to wrap my arms around the blanket they'd provided around my shoulders. I could barely mumble out an, "I don't know."

After some time, I was able to tell them Laura had aimed a gun at me and fired. I didn't know why she did it. She was acting crazy, and I fought her to get the gun. I ended my story with, "She collapsed and there was nothing else I could do."

All I wanted was a cup of tea to soothe my shock. The humming fluorescent lights of the police station put me on edge. Everything that happened tonight was too much to take in. I stared at the floor in front of me, counting the specks in the linoleum tiles to pass time until dawn.

After everything that went down, I would probably never sleep again. When I closed my eyes, the shot rang out, and I saw Laura's face in the moment I dragged Delly from her body. I felt what Laura had felt as I tried desperately to save her.

What in the world was I?

Hades had called Persephone Goddess of the Springtime, and maybe there were similarities between us. All my life, I'd loved flowers and plants. In winter, I felt so tired and dull. The stunt with the plants in Elusisthat was indicative of some spring goddess stuff. If that was all it was, I'd be fine.

But, there was more. Because of course there was. I could see dead people.

I thought of my dream, the one where I'd dug through the earth and finally had come up with not a mask, but a skull. Even in a place as well-lit and heavily populated as the police station, the memory still made me shudder.

Maybe it was my subconscious trying to warn me about what was within me. Some kind of message from the goddess herself. The very one beginning to stir inside me. A terrifying prospect. What would I be when she finally woke up? Would I have to go live underground with Hades? The thought had a certain draw to it, but it was impossible after everything that happened tonight.

My chest stung. He'd left me to face the authorities by

myself. Coward. On top of that, he'd kept the extent of my powers—the death goddess side—a secret.

"You're free to go," the desk sergeant finally told me.

I stared at his dull brown eyes that matched his dull brown hair and his duller brown uniform before his words registered.

In a haze, I stood, gathered my shit, and walked out of the police station into the grey haze between day and night. The sun remained below the horizon, but night hadn't given way yet. I stood on the curb looking at the small town I had been brought to. Across the street there was a diner—not like I'd go to one of those again anytime soon—a book store that hadn't opened yet and the post office. Nothing about those buildings told me where I was. I pulled up my phone. According to the search engine, there was a train station a few blocks east. I had plenty of cash in the bank and a debit card in my pocket to catch a ride back to my apartment.

I could do whatever I wanted with the money I had. The thought made me sick. How could I touch it after what had happened? I could just let it sit forever. Not touch a cent. The thought was all I had to stave off the bile rising in the back of my throat. After everything that had occurred to put that money in front of me. After a woman had died at my hand.

Hades appeared, a few blocks later. His car pulled next to the curb ahead of where I was walking. He climbed out and walked back to me, looking utterly perfect in his suit, not a hair out of place.

I'd spent three hours giving my statement and been ordered to stay in town, but I wasn't planning to follow that particular order. I probably looked like I hadn't showered in a month or even had ever made the acquaintance of a hairbrush. And he looked like a model.

He strode toward me, stopping in front of me. His arms were rigid by his sides, as if he was at a loss as to what to do.

"Where have you been?" I snapped. "How could you leave me like that?"

"I had to take Delly to the Underworld," he said.

"You never took them before," I countered. "You sent them there and stayed here. Why leave me?"

"Because..." His voice wavered as if he didn't know how to explain himself. "Autumn, we have a lot to talk about." Yes, we did but it didn't matter anymore.

I walked around him. No need to talk to him. He lied. He left. He failed me. What else was there to say? "Tell you what. You talk to somebody who cares what you have to say, okay? But leave me alone."

"Autumn, please." He took my arm, using his grip to force me back to him.

It was the wrong gesture at exactly the wrong time. Suddenly, everything that I'd been holding in came out. I spun around to face him.

"You're a liar!"

He stared at me. "There was no way for me to tell you—"

"Really? You told me plenty of other things. Told me about your precious Persephone. Told me about your rose garden."

A cold fog clouded his eyes. Their depth and expression disappeared. He didn't resemble the man who smiled so sweetly at me or one who kissed me until my hair curled and my eyes rolled back. No. A remote and strange expression took hold of him. Like some alien thing detached from humanity, something that simply did its duty and at the end of the day, genuinely didn't care if the mere mortals in its life lived or died.

"Don't talk to me like that," he started, but I cut him off. I stepped closer to him, and a flitter of surprise passed across his clouded eyes.

"No!" I snapped. "Given what I know about all this? I'm

actually one of the people in the world who can. I may not be a god in my own right, but I have one sleeping inside me. One you didn't even see fit to tell me about until we were in Greece."

"There are reasons–"

"No! No there aren't. Hades, we *slept* together. I don't know where you come from, but that means something to me."

"Maybe that doesn't mean anything to you, but it does to me."

"But it doesn't, not anymore," I argued, causing hurt and outrage to stretch over his expression.

He reached to cup my cheeks, examining me as if I had the answers written on the colored parts of my eyes.

"Of course, it does! How could you think that?" he replied with uncertainty.

"Stop," I growled, and he stepped away from me.

Hades looked at a complete loss, stuffing his hands in his pockets, his head bent. I held up my hand.

"You didn't care about Laura dying," I argued. "Didn't want to help her or me. What about striking a deal?"

"There is a limit to what I can do," he said, then sighed. "Your powers are yours to explore."

I didn't believe him anymore. His credibility went out the window when he decided to hide things from me for so long. He was too chickenshit to tell me about my true nature until it had expressed itself. He knew of the goddess' potential for destruction and even feared it, had tried to run from it in my dreams. Why hadn't he warned me about what I could do?

"I've fulfilled my end of the bargain as far as I'm concerned," I said. "If there are more dead people to be found, deduct it from my pay. As of right now, I'm out. I can't work with you. I can't have you hiding things from me. Important things about who I am."

"You can't leave me," he repeated.

I stared at him. "Of course, I can," I said matter-of-factly. "What year are you living in?"

Before I could move, Laura appeared beside me, walking dazed, glancing at her hands, at Hades and I. She asked me why I was with the man who had not saved her. Poor thing. I didn't know where to send her. Hades had said she belonged to another afterlife and refused to take her.

"I'm leaving," I said, not wanting to stick around any longer. "I'm going to get on a train. I'm going to figure things out. You're not a part of this, and I hope I never see you again."

He flinched.

"I don't know what I can do against a god," I added softly. "All I know is if you cared at all for me, if you ever actually meant even a tenth of what you said, you'll leave me alone."

In response, he swept me into his arms and kissed me hard on the lips. For a moment, just a moment, everything was all right. I was safe with him. We were together. All the pleasure and sweetness threatened to overwhelm me, convince me to change my mind, but before I could do something like forgive him, I remembered what had happened just a few hours earlier. I remembered how he'd abandoned me, left me, and given up on Laura.

The kiss made my insides churn, so I pushed him away. And it ripped my heart in half, but it had to be done. I wobbled, shocked I was somehow still standing.

"No." I managed to push back the tears and raise my voice. "No! Don't touch me like that. It's *over.*"

I turned and walked away, the train station sign on my left. It took everything I had to not look back. Somehow, I managed. I tried to remind myself of all those platitudes of comfort, things you needed to hear when your life breaks apart in some kind of final and awful way. When you leave someone who might have been the love of your life.

Laura walked beside me. She was dead, and I'd killed her, then Hades refused to save her soul. As we walked together, she faded away. I smiled, hoping she ended up where she needed to go.

I arrived at the train station and bought a ticket for the train traveling back home that departed in ten minutes. In the end, I couldn't hold back the tears. I sniffled and hid my face.

In the train car, I sat with my head tilted against the headrest so I could stare out the window and watch the sky outside lighten and soften as a batch of autumn rains began to fall.

Deep inside me, something stirred. The word *soon* rose to the forefront of my mind.

Please, please, no more.

***

Six Months Later

I ENDED up in Las Vegas. Not exactly by choice, but since I was hiding from the God of the Underworld, I didn't mind it. A friend from the community garden that I volunteered at had agreed to sublet my apartment. I even offered it rent-free for six months, if she agreed to look after my plants. Looking back, I must have been scary when I told her how to care for them and emphasized how important they were to me. Her eyes had grown to the size of saucers, and she'd nodded while telling me she would remember my instructions.

LADY OF THE UNDERWORLD

The desert seemed like a strange place for the avatar of a springtime goddess to end up, but it suited me. Sure, it was hot as hell and dry, but there was plenty of plant life if you knew where to look, and I knew where to look. Plus, the local nursery was happy to find someone with actual experience.

As for the goddess inside me, she seemed to have gone quiet for the moment. Sometimes, when I was grafting a lemon tree or taking care of fresh new bulbs, I'd feel some foreign part of me stretching or yawning, getting ready to awaken. Thinking of her was always risky, as it brought up memories of Hades, and I couldn't go there.

At night, I put off going to bed to avoid dreaming of him. The frightening nightmares of skulls and dirt were bad enough, but the new ones were interspersed with visions of him—each one telling me how he needed my help.

He would call for me, but I could never quite hear him. The silence between us was the worst. There was a place in the world where he was meant to be and it wasn't here.

Sometimes, when I was sitting up late at night in a new apartment that felt bizarrely like the one I'd left behind, I wondered what would happen if I tried calling to him, if I tried praying. But I couldn't. I just couldn't.

Every time I closed my eyes, I thought about the woman in the diner. Her death. The more I thought about it, the more I realized how much Hades withheld from me about my powers and how I could hurt people. It made me furious, but also left me blanketed in a sorrow so deep I didn't even know what to do with it.

I wanted to tell myself it was normal to feel like this way after my first real breakup, but there hadn't been anything normal about my life since I'd met Hades in the funeral parlor.

I went to sleep wanting him. I woke up crying because

there was something in me that missed him so much my entire being ached.

Rinse, repeat. My life became an endless cycle of torture...

Until one day in June. I left my shift early and returned home to find a man waiting for me on my doorstep. Tall and thin, but well-muscled, he was pale enough I hoped he'd remembered some sunscreen. His cheekbones were so sharp, they could have cut butter.

Unlike me, he hadn't broken out in a visible sweat despite the oppressive Vegas heat. Not many people lounged on doorsteps in my neighborhood when the temperature scaled the thermometer. Especially not anyone in designer clothes or playing on a phone that cost eight hundred dollars.

When I paused in the open hallway, he looked up, pocketed his phone, and smiled. It was a smile that inspired trust, even though it held an edge of mischief. I found myself smiling in return.

"Autumn Rankin?" he said, his green eyes sparkling.

Okay. Who the hell was this? I took a careful step backward.

"Hey, hey, don't be scared," he assured me, holding out a hand and inching toward me like a man trying to coax a scared dog. "I'm like you. An avatar. My name is Mads."

I straightened. Hades had never told me how to get in contact with the other avatars. I'd wanted to reach out to find out more about myself and them, but it wasn't like there was a Facebook group titled Godly Avatars. Still, Mads had found me without any avatar directory. I wanted to know how.

"Yeah, tell me exactly why that shouldn't scare me," I replied.

Mads gave me a sympathetic look as he shoved his hands into his pockets. He didn't scream 'someone dangerous,' but

I'd gotten a more cautious in the months since my Hades interaction.

"Hades said you would be nervous," Mads said. "Probably an understatement."

Hearing his name sent a thrill down my spine, along with a feeling of grief so great my legs wobbled, and I crashed into the wall.

Mads rushed to steady me. "He really did a number on you, huh?"

"What do you know about it?" I asked, not sure how much I liked the idea of him knowing so much about me or my personal life.

"Nothing." Mads offered me a small smile and shook his head. "That's not why I came."

"Why *did* you come?" I crossed my arms.

"You're not the only avatar, you know."

"You're the first I've met…"

He cocked an eyebrow, but before I could question him, he nodded. "I'm the avatar of Hermes. You know, thieves, messengers, commerce, your all-purpose trickster god and jack of all trades. I have a proposal for you."

"Go on," I said cautiously.

"How would you feel about meeting the family?" His smile turned into a wicked grin. "I mean, we don't really get along. Ares is a hot head. Hera's a real bitch. Zeus is a manipulative jerk. Basically, we're human manifestations of our gods. But, boy, is it fun to mess with them."

I laughed. "You make it sound so inviting."

He leaned against a doorframe as I stood.

"They'll want to meet you, sooner or later."

I bit my lip, considering the offer. Maybe the avatars could give me more insight on what I was and who I had residing inside me. Help me learn more about my powers. Or more importantly, teach me to control the whole pluck-a-soul-out-of-someone's-body gig. I never wanted to do that ever again.

"All right, Mads," I accepted. "Let's go.

The End of Book 1

*Loved Lady of the Underworld? **Why not leave me a review and let me know. Or purchase Lord of the Underworld, the next exciting chapter.***

ABOUT THE AUTHOR

Never say never. That's Skyler's attitude, and she fills her heroines and heroes with that same philosophy. Skyler is an Aussie who loves traveling and her goal is to one day visit every country in the world. When she's not writing, she's snuggling with a good book and her furbabies. At heart she's a gaming nerd, Pilates and martial arts enthusiast.

Become a darkling and join my **readers group** Skyler's Den of Darkness for exclusive content, latest news, and giveaways.

Sign up to my **newsletter** here skylerandra.com/index.php/subscribe/

Are you curious to read the other novels by Skyler?
   Operation Cupid completed series
   Battlefield Love
   Quicksilver Love
   Awakened Love
   Stupid Cupid - a Valentine's short story

Operation Hades
   Lady of the Underworld
   Lord of the Underworld

Guild of Shadows series
Darkfire
Wildfire
Crossfire
Hearthfire - available by signing up to my newsletter http://eepurl.com/dCOqkb
Hellfire

Guild of Guardians - a Guild of Shadows spin off
Witch Hunt - novella available in the Tales Out of School box set (all free!).
Hindsight's a Witch
Resting Witch Face (novella available in the Wicked Souls collection).

Fire & Shadow Series - sexy angels!
Fall From Grace
Fall From Darkness

Winter Queen (part of the Haven Realm Universe)
Heart of Frost - a Snow Queen retelling

Dark Reflections series (part of the Haven Realm Universe)
Born into Darkness - a Snow White retelling

Haven Realm series
Charmed- an Aladdin retelling
Claimed- a Little Mermaid retelling

Printed in Great Britain
by Amazon